Deep Deception

James North

CROOKED CAT

Discover us online:
www.crookedcatpublishing.com

Join us on facebook:
www.facebook.com/crookedcatpublishing

Tweet a photo of yourself holding
this book to **@crookedcatbooks**
and something nice will happen.

To Mom and Dad… Thanks.

The Author

James North is a former U.S. Navy intelligence officer, consultant to the U.S. Government, political analyst, and university lecturer. He currently lives in Europe and is contemplating owning a four-legged, furry friend for the first time in decades.

Acknowledgements

I wish to thank Alex, Anne, Carmen, Floyd, Hillary, Joseph, Julie, Linda, Michelle, Moiya, Sarah, Sue, Tammy, Taylor, and Tony who, much to my surprise, seemed to find great pleasure in reading and commenting on the manuscript during various iterations. I would also like to acknowledge Jane Leigh-Morgan, Lorna Read, and Maureen Vincent-Northam for their sharp eyes and editorial quip. Finally, I wish to acknowledge and say a big thanks to Stephanie and Laurence Patterson at Crooked Cat for supporting the project.

Deep Deception

A Vanguard Novel

Prologue

The four women sat at a table, far in the back of the Xin Cuisine Chinese Restaurant in Kuala Lumpur's Golden Triangle, reflecting on their first day together in Malaysia. Kristie Bremmer, Amanda Costanti, Patty Maynard, and Beth O'Connell had not been together since they graduated from university five years earlier. Oddly and somewhat paradoxically, it had taken something phenomenal to bring them all together again. Two of the world's most hotly debated issues, global warming and climate change, had reemerged and were again politically charged, except this time the furor was greater and all four of them had been pulled into the fray.

When they left university, all of them, except Beth O'Connell, who went on to do a Ph.D. in environmental science, had taken staff jobs with their legislative representatives. Patty, the Canadian among them, took a position with her Member of Parliament. After a few years, however, she and Amanda moved on to jobs at the United Nations (UN). She and Amanda were very much alike. Both were intelligent and shy. They also resembled each other. They were both tall and slender with dark hair, which they often wore in similar styles. Some people thought they were sisters, even twins.

3

Unlike Patty and Amanda, however, Kristie Bremmer became jaded by the hypocrisy of politics and traded in the corridors of power in Washington, D.C., for a full-time place at graduate school. It therefore came as no surprise to the others when they learned that she had been spending all of her spare time working with the global environmental movement. For Kristie Bremmer, seeing and hearing François Dupré, the young, charismatic organizer of the next three days of demonstrations, was just as exciting as seeing her old friends again.

It was well past 10:30 p.m. when the four women polished off their fifth bottle of Sauvignon Blanc. Shortly afterwards, Patty, Beth, and Kristie rose clumsily to their feet and shuffled toward the front door of the restaurant, while Amanda stood in front of the waiter, swaying as she rummaged through her purse for a credit card to pay the bill.

Once outside the air conditioned confines of the restaurant Amanda's head spun; she stopped to steady herself. Her eyes scanned Jalan Sultan Ismail in both directions before she spotted her three friends. They were rubber-legged, warbling as they started across the road toward a taxi stand on the other side—arms locked together, trying to steady each other. But as they stepped off the curb, the engine of a darkened windowed, silver Toyota sedan, near the corner of Jalan Ampang and Jalan Sultan Ismail, sprang to life. The car took off slowly and made a left turn onto Jalan Sultan Ismail. As the three women approached the middle of the road, the driver accelerated, threw the car's headlights on at high beam and began to swerve, first left, then right.

The three women were half-way across the road when Amanda saw the car bearing down on them. Beth O'Connell, Kristie Bremmer, and Patty Maynard were stretched across the road, locked together like a daisy chain. They swayed to and fro and tugged at each others' arms, trying to gather momentum, but their efforts were futile. A split-second later one of Patty's shoes came off and she broke loose from them, stumbled and fell.

Amanda looked on horrified as her friend struggled to her feet in the path of the speeding car. Her adrenalin surged and she dashed toward Patty, but as the distance between her and her friend closed, the car straightened up and the driver drew a bead on the woman. Patty Maynard had just gotten on her feet and was stumbling forward, arms outstretched, shoe in hand, when the car struck her. It ploughed into her and her slender body flew into the air, flipped several times then slammed onto the road.

Seconds later, only the car's tail lights were visible as it turned off Jalan Sultan Ismail and headed south.

PART I

Chapter One

Brooklyn, New York
Present Day

Caroline Dupré sat bolt-upright in bed. It was only 6:30 a.m. Her already shortened and restless night had been interrupted by a premonition that seemed more like a bad dream. She was tired and feeling a deeper level of loneliness and worry than she had ever felt. The night had been a long, stressful one. She had stayed awake until the early hours, waiting for a call that never came. She and François had had an agreement. He had arranged to call her at 1:00 a.m. eastern standard time and she had promised to be awake when he called. But when one o'clock came and went and there was no call, she grew anxious. She had waited another hour and a half before calling him at his hotel in Kuala Lumpur. She had even turned off the television so she could hear the phone when it rang.

Having waited until 3:30 a.m., she put through a second call to the Concorde Hotel, left another message then waited until 4:00 a.m., but still no call came. It was the first time he had missed an arranged call since their marriage.

Now fully awake, she felt physically drained. She was sure that something had gone wrong, but didn't know what to do. She climbed out of bed, slipped on her bath robe over the T-shirt and a pair of his boxer shorts and went to the front door to collect the newspaper. On her way to the door, the phone rang. She was relieved and excited, but also angry. *You've finally decided to ring!* Unable to wait to take the call in the family room where she could see the caller on a video-phone, she answered through an interactive intercom in the hallway. Before the caller could utter a word, she fired off a barrage of questions.

"Do you know what time it is?" she said angrily. "Where are you? Why didn't you call? I've been worried sick about you!"

"*Chérie? C'est Papa!*" the voice said at the other end of the line.

"Papa? Is that you?" she asked, tellingly disappointed.

"*Oui! C'est moi, chérie.* Have you been watching the news?"

"No, I haven't," she replied after moving into the family room and seeing Henri Gagnon on the monitor. "Why? Is there something wrong?"

"Yes, I'm afraid there is," he said. "There was some trouble yesterday in Kuala Lumpur."

"What kind of trouble?" she asked. "Is François alright?"

"*Non, ma chérie.* I'm afraid he is not."

"Has he been hurt?"

Henri Gagnon paused then said slowly and calmly, "François was killed yesterday. I am so sorry, *ma chérie.*"

Caroline's legs weakened and she sank into a nearby chair. For several minutes there was only silence then he heard sobbing. He waited helplessly as the sobs grew louder. He had never seen her in such a state.

"Where are you, *ma chérie?*" he asked finally. Are you alright?"

"Yes!" she said, her voice trembling. "How did it happen? Where did it happen?"

Henri Gagnon felt the small lump that had developed in his throat swell. He hadn't had a disturbing feeling like this since the day the American Red Cross called to tell him that his wife had been killed in a plane crash in northern Italy. This time it was his daughter's grief and he couldn't figure out how to share her pain or the burden of it. But he knew that if he was in her place, he would want to know everything.

"*Ma chérie*, I only learned of it this morning and didn't quite know what to do. It hadn't been confirmed, so I didn't want to call you in the middle of the night to tell you something that would have upset you which may not have been true. I guess I panicked. I froze and instead did nothing. Please forgive me. I thought that by morning it would be confirmed and I could call you. I'm so sorry that you had to learn about this horrible thing later than you should have."

"Thank you," she said, still sobbing. "I'm not angry with you, Papa, but you should've called me right away."

"You're right. I should have rung sooner and my failure to do so weighs heavily on me."

"Tell me what happened, Papa. Please... I need to know," she pleaded.

Henri Gagnon took a deep breath. "Reports here this morning say there was a walkout by the American, Australian, and Canadian delegates at the Climate Change Conference, which caused fury among the protestors. Somewhere in the midst of all the anger and chaos, some protestors threw Molotov cocktails which set several security personnel on fire. The security forces responded with tear gas, water cannons, and rubber bullets, but that didn't stop the protestors. They threw more homemade bombs, so more security personnel were brought in to clear the crowd from the area. The hard-liners or radicals refused to leave, so they fired some kind of new ammunition. Those fired on apparently thought their comrades were being killed and became even more violent."

Describing the events was painful, but Henri Gagnon continued. "The hard-liners isolated some of the security personnel, stripped them of their weapons and shields then set about stomping and kicking them. The situation deteriorated so fast that some security forces personnel started using live ammunition. François and his two friends were among some

108 people killed. The latest report said another 219 were wounded, some of which may also die."

"How did he die, Papa?" Caroline again pleaded. "Did he suffer?"

"Alain Belland, a good friend and the former editor of *Le Monde,* said he was shot twice and that either of the shots would have been instantly fatal."

Henri Gagnon didn't have the heart to tell his daughter that the wound to her husband's head was so destructive that it made identifying him difficult.

"Why didn't the people at the hotel tell me when I rang this morning?" she asked angrily.

"*Ma chérie,* they probably didn't know. They may have known about the riot, but they couldn't have known who or how many people had been injured or killed."

Henri Gagnon sighed heavily. "I'm so sorry, my love. I only wish that I could say or do something to make it better."

"I know you do, but you can't!" she snapped.

There was a long pause. He didn't know what to say to fill the void of silence.

"I'm sorry I snapped at you," she offered humbly. "You've always been there for me, and I know you always will be."

"Of course I will," he said. "If you need me, I'm only a telephone call away," he added reassuringly. "I presume François' mother and father will want him brought home to France."

"I'm certain they will," she said. "I know that's what he would've wanted. I should go now, Papa," she added, "I have a lot to do. I don't know how to begin to tell Nicolas what happened. He's going to be devastated."

"You must be gentle with him, but you must tell him the truth," said Henri Gagnon.

"Thank you, Papa," she said, still distraught. "I love you very much."

"And I love you very, very much too," he said.

As soon as the call ended, Caroline went straight into the kitchen. She stood in front of the sink and began to hyperventilate. She tried to make a cup of tea but her hands shook uncontrollably. Overcome by nervousness, frustration, and anger she dropped the cup on the floor. It shattered and she let out a muted scream and shrank to the floor.

Chapter Two

Crouched on the floor with her back pressed against the sink, memories from the distant past flooded Caroline's head. They were an eclectic set of thoughts and images, some foreboding—revelations of an emerging pattern of tragic and untimely deaths of people she loved. First, there was the death of her mother in a plane crash when she was a child, now her husband. Before the call from her father, she had begun to believe that when François returned from Kuala Lumpur she would have him all to herself. She would no longer have to compete with the rest of the world for his time and attention. Now it seemed as if anyone she dared to love would be tragically taken away from her. *Who would be next?*

Caroline sat grieving. Her mind raced back through time. Two memories, both vivid and profound, seemed to take over. The first was the story her father had told her when she was five years old—the story of how he and her mother had met and fallen in love. He, a wealthy businessman, had met U.S. Air Force pilot Pamela Gordon. The attraction had been instant and mutual. She could hear his voice mimicking Pamela telling him that she wouldn't be another one of his sexual conquests. He confessed that it had taken him nearly a year to convince her that his feelings were genuine and a further six months and countless proposals before she agreed to marry him. The second and perhaps the clearest memory was of the day her mother was killed—a day tragically similar to this one. Henri Gagnon had held her and looked lovingly into her eyes before telling her that

14

her mother's C-141 transport aircraft had crashed into the side of a mountain. The tragic event had occurred just one day before their fifth wedding anniversary.

Although Caroline was just over four years old, she could see how devastated her father was by the loss of the woman he called his soul mate. Even after her death he remained devoted to her. He never remarried and was determined for her to get to know her mother's family. For that, she remained grateful. The times she spent with her mother's family and relatives were special, not just because they were joyous, but because they gave her a chance to learn more about the woman she had known only a short time.

Growing up with her father in Paris had not been difficult; she could not have hoped for a better relationship with him. He was supportive, caring, and sensitive and always put her first. He had told her on many occasions that he wanted her to be well-rounded—to succeed, not only in her own life choices, but to contribute to society by helping others fulfill their potential. He encouraged her to participate in and experience life, instead of simply passing through it, to make a difference. He believed it was important for her to participate in and appreciate competitive sports, as part of a team and as an individual.

As a young woman she excelled as an equestrian, became an outstanding field hockey player, and an expert rifle and target pistol marksman. But of all the sports she participated in, rifle and target pistol shooting were her favorites. She loved them mainly because he had taught her to shoot and was her coach.

She recalled meeting and falling in love with François when she was just fifteen years old. They had met when they entered Lycée Henri IV and had remained together until it was time to leave for university. But instead of going off to university, she elected to go to the U.S. to spend time with her American relatives. Soon after she turned eighteen, she returned to France to live with her father and to continue her education at the Haute École Commerciale in Paris. During her absence

François had secured a place at Sciences Politique in Strasbourg. Unlike her, however, his entry into the prestigious Lycée Henri IV and the Haute École Commerciale didn't happen because of a privileged background and private schools. He was the son of a fisherman who had grown up in a small seaside village in Brittany. Hard work was a way of life; he had been diligent in his studies. She had heard him say many times that working on the sea with his father was the source of his determination and discipline—the same determination and discipline that secured him scholarships at Lycée Henri IV and Sciences Politique.

Like her father and mother, the attraction between her and François was immediate. She had spotted him when he was working at an environmental awareness booth. He was handing out pamphlets. Because it was International Earth Day, she had wanted to make an impression. There had been lots of discussion about climate change in the news and she knew that there had been drastic changes in global climate conditions, but she had never taken any real interest in the campaign.

"I've never seen you before at any of our meetings," he had said when she approached his booth. "If I had, I would have remembered you and I'd know your name," he added flippantly.

She had thought for several seconds before firing back. "OK Einstein... You really are a genius if you can remember every person, by name, who attends your meetings. It sounds like a pretty clever trick! How did you learn to do it? Did you practice memorizing telephone directories or do you have a photographic memory?"

The retort had given her a winning feeling, right up until the moment he exposed her superficial intentions and embarrassed her. She remembered how angry she had felt when she snatched the pamphlets from him and ran off. "You will read them, won't you?" he yelled as she stormed off.

Despite the delight he seemed to take in embarrassing her, he had later admitted that he had fallen in love with her the first time their eyes met. But because of his tactlessness during their first encounter, he thought he had destroyed any chance of her ever speaking to him again. But as luck would have it, two weeks later he had seen her in the library, asked her to have coffee with him, and she had accepted.

Their second encounter marked the beginning of an endless love.

Chapter Three

It was the sound of Nicolas' voice that brought her back from her journey into the past. He was standing in the kitchen door, leaning against it, watching her with growing concern. The nine-year-old was not fully awake, but he could tell she was in distress. He knew something must be terribly wrong. She was sitting on the floor with her back against the sink, knees drawn up to her chest, arms folded around them, with a blank stare in her eyes. It was not until he called to her a third time that she realized he was there.

"*Maman!*" said Nicolas. "Were you talking to someone? I thought I heard you crying. What's wrong? Why were you crying?"

She looked at him and tears began to flow. She knew that she had to be strong for him, but his probing questions opened up feelings of helplessness. Arms outstretched, her eyes red, she beckoned him to her. He rushed over and knelt in front of her and she threw her arms around him. "Just let me hold you for a moment," she said. There was nervousness in her voice.

"Has something happened to Papa?" he asked. "Has he been in an accident?"

She pulled him away so she could see his face. Once again, she fought to hold back the tears. "Yes," she said, her voice trembling.

"Is he dead?" Nicolas asked hesitantly.

"Yes, he is," she said softly, pulling him close to her again and holding him until their tears stopped flowing.

As the day wore on Caroline listened to news reports about the incident. Some of them gave eyewitness accounts of the carnage and commentators had begun describing the demonstration as '…an event which from the onset had the makings of a violent uprising.'

In the mid-afternoon the American Embassy's Consular Office in Kuala Lumpur called to arrange transportation for François' body. Caroline rang François' parents and explained the arrangements to them. She was worried about Nicolas-Émile and Adèle Dupré because they were elderly and François was their only child—a miracle baby born to Adèle Dupré when she was in her mid-forties—a child she miraculously fell pregnant with after the doctors told her she could never have children.

They all agreed that the funeral should be held quickly—not later than two days after the body arrived—and cremation done immediately afterwards. Because of François' love of the sea, his ashes would be scattered on the sea, just off the coast of his home village, Croisic. Returning to the sea was a wish he had expressed on numerous occasions to Caroline and his parents.

Chapter Four

Kuala Lumpur, Malaysia
UN Conference on Climate Change
Four Days Earlier

Malaysia's hot, humid air struck François Dupré, Dieter Metzger, and Jonathan Barber like a warm, wet blanket when they emerged from the Concorde Hotel. After leaving the hotel, they walked briskly and silently toward the Putra World Trade Center, site of the three-day Climate Change Conference. Some forty-eight hours earlier, a police barricade had gone up around the Center's main building and bomb sniffer dogs had completed two sweeps of the building, inside and out. The ramp on the east side of the building had also been closed to pedestrian traffic, and regular and paramilitary police, outfitted with shields, batons, teargas, rubber bullets, a new kind of immobilization ammunition, and water cannons, were positioned on all sides. A special security force contingent had maintained a vigilant eye on the area, stopping and questioning anyone who looked suspicious or who might have ventured into the area by mistake.

Malaysia's Interior Minister had taken every precaution to ensure that the conference would take place in a secure environment. In fact, he had declared a few days earlier that the 171 international delegates would not be threatened, nor would the conference be disrupted by violence. He promised that if any violence occurred, his security forces would deal with it swiftly.

As the men strode toward the Putra Trade Center, François' heavily French-accented voice broke the silence. "Nothing will go wrong!" he said buoyantly. "We're well-organized and we're gonna carry this out as planned."

At thirty-seven years old, François Dupré looked a great deal younger, almost boyish. He was tall, dark, and slim with dark hair and deep blue eyes—the latter owing to his Celtic ancestry. He didn't look the part of a hardened political activist, but he had been a student and practitioner of mass protest for more than two decades. He had been a long-time supporter of Greenpeace and Friends of the Earth, but after working his way up as far as he could go inside both organizations he left them behind to do things his way. Less than two years after leaving Friends of the Earth, he founded, almost single-handedly, the organization Total Exposure of All Resource Squandering, or TEARS. Despite TEARS' short existence, it already boasted a presence in more than fifty countries.

Before the Kuala Lumpur Conference, its protests had been much smaller and often served as the core for gatherings targeting conventions, summits, and conferences on greenhouse gases and ocean levels. Today in Kuala Lumpur, however, François Dupré was about to launch the biggest protest he had ever organized—one that would consist of some 150,000 TEARS members and another 50,000 protestors from other organizations.

"This isn't the 2000 World Trade Organization Summit in Seattle," François piped suddenly and admonishingly as he looked at his two colleagues. "We're not some unorganized, ill-disciplined mob looking to grab headlines by causing a disturbance. We're here to expose the hypocrisy of a handful of countries and their self-serving politicians who continue to conspire with large industries to pollute the earth and deplete its resources. Millions of people are depending on us to put a

21

stop to these things and we can't... no, we *won't* fail them! They want justice and that's what we're gonna give 'em!"

As the three men neared the Trade Center, silence fell over them again; François began to run through his opening remarks in his head. He was passionate about the need to resolve the most pressing environmental issues; if anyone could get the support of the masses, he could. He had the ability to excite and motivate people without turning them into 'tree huggers'— get them to take action and get involved.

As they drew closer to the Mall area, Jonathan could see that François was in a meditative state. He had seen the look many times. He was psyching himself up. And as he saw François emerge from his place of deep concentration Jonathan asked teasingly, "You wanna turn back?"

"Not a chance in hell!" François replied. "This is much too big! In fact, it's probably bigger than you realize."

Dieter was listening intently. He was German through and through—a pragmatist who liked everything in its place and no surprises. François' comment had disturbed him. "Damn it, man!" he barked, leaning his stocky frame toward François, his blue-gray eyes widening behind the tuft of long, blonde hair that swung down over his face. "What do you mean, bigger than we realize? There aren't supposed to be any surprises! No secrets... remember?"

"Just relax!" François said playfully. "Just chill for a minute, will you?"

"Relax? Chill?" said Dieter. "Why should I? You said you'd told us everything! Is there something you haven't told us? Is there?"

"Yes," said François. "There is something I haven't told you. I'll fill you in on the last day of the conference," he added, pausing and looking pensively. "You're gonna have to trust me on this one," he declared. "Now is not the time."

He could see that he had failed to convince Dieter to be patient. But he knew that certain things needed to be verified.

He had to be right about his suspicions.

"Look, guys!" François said, "In all the time we've known each other, have I ever lied to you or misled you?"

"No, you haven't!" said Dieter. "But that's not the point! You said…"

But before Dieter could finish Jonathan cut in. "The point is, Dieter, if he says we should wait then we'll wait!"

"Thanks," said François. "I'm not holding out on you guys. I just need to make sense of it all myself. And when I do, I promise I'll fill you in."

Chapter Five

Television, radio, and print media from around the world were on hand for the conference. Media interest in climate change conferences was suddenly higher than it had ever been. Some observers speculated that the large number of protestors and rumors that violence was almost certain to break out were driving up media interest. There was, however, also a modicum of interest in finding out whether or not the large number of protestors would influence the delegates' decisions.

François, Dieter, and Jonathan made their way through the sea of protestors to the stage. As François moved up the steps, the crowd began chanting his name. Once on the stage he waited for the noise to die down. When it did, the public address system crackled to life.

"Friends and colleagues..." François began. "Today we are about to make history! Correction... We have already made history just by being here in such great numbers! But more important than our presence is *why* we are here. We are here to unleash the energy of human spirit—an energy like no other on earth. Why you ask... because it is what is needed to head off disaster—disaster caused by man's reckless behavior. For more than a third of a century, we have known that global warming has been occurring at a rate much faster than scientists earlier predicted. In 2001, the United Nations' own International Panel on Climate Change warned that global temperatures would rise by 5.8 degrees Celsius by the end of the twenty-first century. To show how inaccurate and conservative their prediction was, that figure had to be doubled a short time later. So you see, despite its best efforts, the UN Panel was wrong! And in view of recent weather patterns and major changes in temperatures, the scientific community now estimates that the global temperature could rise by nearly 12 degrees Celsius in our lifetime. Yes, 12 degrees!"

He was interrupted by a loud hum from the crowd. When the hum subsided, he continued. "Did you know that early in this millennium, scientists provided evidence to governments which showed that the average temperature in Alaska was rising almost ten times faster than the world average?"

An angry protestor shouted. "Why didn't they tell us this? The lying dogs!"

"That's a good question," said François. "But all of this and more will be revealed in the next few days. You see... more than thirty years ago, scientists warned that if global warming continued, large-scale crop failure would lead to the loss of a quarter of the world's food production capacity, mostly in the poorest countries. Even back then it was known that human pollution, especially the burning of fossil fuels, was contributing to rising temperatures. Today, there is greater evidence of this. But some politicians in the richest countries, backed by powerful business interests, have armed themselves with evidence from sophisticated, well-funded research to refute these findings. At the onset of the millennium, the United Kingdom collected evidence which showed that it had experienced five of its warmest years in a ten year period. They were the warmest years experienced in more than three centuries. During the same period, climate observers at a well known research institute in the United Kingdom also predicted a rise of between 12 and 67 centimeters, or 4.7 to 26.4 inches in global sea levels, caused by increases in rainfall and melting polar ice. This warning wasn't heeded."

He paused once more then continued. "Unfortunately, this grim prognosis is supported by the reality that technology that could have, and still can reduce greenhouse gas emissions, is being resisted. And that resistance is greatest from the petroleum industry. During the energy crisis of the 1970s, which only a few of us were around for, I hasten to add, the oil industry showed just how powerful it was. It successfully prevented the development and mass production of a prototype engine that delivered cleaner exhaust emissions and more fuel efficient performance. Why? I'll tell you why... because it was easy to do and financially it wasn't in their best interest. All it took was for one of them to buy the patent from the inventor and shelve the design. We haven't done much to change the situation since then!"

The hum of the crowd rose again; when it subsided, he continued his exposé. But as he spoke, an ominous-looking security officer and several heavily armed security personnel fixed their gaze on him.

Turning and pointing to the Trade Center, he warned, "Even as I speak, the delegates from 171 countries have begun to gather in this place to convince the hold-outs that responsibility and a pro-active position on this matter is our only hope. It's our job to let those resisting know that we will no longer leave this matter to them to resolve. That's why we are here, and this is what we will do!"

The words caused a roar from the crowd. He tried to shout above it, but waited for it to subside. "Because... because... we are the last line of defense between the powerful, greedy, and wealthy few who squander what belongs to all of us, we say to them, no more! Enough is enough!"

The roar from the crowd swelled again; when it stopped, he resumed. "My friends... during the next few days, you'll learn of the cunning of greedy politicians and industrialists that will leave us without hope. But before we completely abandon trust in all politicians, we must allow the representatives assembled here to confer and debate, even if we believe that many of them have lost the will to fight for us." Pointing again to the Trade

Center, he shouted, "And if they fail, and we know they will, we will gain strength!"

François turned away from the microphone and made his way off the stage.

"That was one hell of an opening!" Jonathon shouted, grinning.

"Absolutely incredible," said Dieter. "Did you see the way the crowd was tuned in?" he added, turning to Jonathan.

"Awesome!" said Jonathan. "They were mesmerized!"

"How do you top that?" asked Dieter.

François spun on his heel. He was face-to-face with both of them, wearing one of his impish grins. "The best is yet to come!"

Chapter Six

It was just after 9:00 a.m. and over two-thirds of the delegates had already arrived for the start of the conference. As the last representatives clambered from their armored limousines, sedans, and sports utility vehicles, they were confronted with disdainful messages emblazoned on placards: *It's Time to Stop Selling off What Is Not Yours*; *You Must Pay for Your Greed!*; *No More Lies, No More Banditry!*; *Locusts of the Earth!*; *Exterminators of the Human Race!*

Separated from the demonstrators by a barricade and dozens of armed security personnel, the delegates rushed from their vehicles into the Trade Center. None of them looked in the direction of the protestors. Meanwhile, on the stage, an impressive lineup of speakers and entertainers stood ready to reinforce François' message and entertain the crowd.

After leaving the stage François, Dieter, and Jonathan waded through the sea of protestors and made their way to the area where the media was set up. As they approached the media area, television cameramen and reporters rushed toward them shouting questions.

"As much as I look forward to talking to you, if all of you bombard me with questions at the same time I won't be able to hear anyone and none of you will get your story," said François. "So, if you don't mind, I'll take your questions one at a time?"

His sporting attitude, despite the sarcasm, brought laughter from the group.

"Unfortunately, I can only give you a few minutes," he said. "And while I value any and all opportunities to speak to the press and work with it to find the truth, I need to be available to the people who have come to gather here. So, who will go first? Perhaps my friend from CNN will lead off?" he said, pointing to a young female reporter.

"Me?" the woman asked, seemingly caught by surprise.

"Ellen, are you no longer with CNN?" he asked jokingly.

The young reporter quickly recovered and pitched her first question.

"Mr. Dupré…" she began. "Please permit me, if you will, to paraphrase something you said in your opening remarks. You said that you are going to reveal a cunning plan by greedy, corrupt politicians and industrialists to continue to exploit the earth's resources for wealth and power, despite overwhelming evidence that the earth is in serious ecological trouble. Can you tell us what this plan is, who is behind it, how you will expose it, and what evidence you have?"

"Those are all good questions, Ellen," François replied. "But, I also stated in my opening remarks that I am not yet prepared to make those revelations. We want to see how far this conference goes toward achieving what needs to be achieved without making such a revelation. We intend to give the governments gathered here a chance to resolve these problems through negotiations and diplomacy. Otherwise, it will make getting their cooperation and support on these and other environmental issues all the more difficult in the future."

Before he could finish, the CNN reporter fired another question, pre-empting her competitors.

"Are you then saying that there's some kind of plot, a conspiracy of some kind, that's being hatched by someone or a group of some sort? If this is true, who is it, or who are they, and what are they doing, exactly?"

"Hold on a minute, Ellen!" François shouted. "You're taking this a few steps too far! I'm not saying that there's a conspiracy.

It's just that we all know that businesses are in business to make money, politicians want to stay in office, and the rest of us simply want all of them to do what's right for us and the environment. This means identifying problems, applying pressure in the right places to correct them, and holding those who refuse to be accountable responsible for their actions. Putting it more succinctly, we expect any and all violators and abusers of the trust we place in them to be punished, when it is deemed appropriate and necessary. Next question please! Ellen, I'm sorry but we're gonna have to give someone else a chance!" he admonished.

A reporter from the *Singapore Straits Times* chimed in.

"Mr. Dupré. Do you and the members of TEARS hold any hope at all that this conference will change the attitudes of the Americans, Australians, Japanese and Canadians, the so-called hold-outs?"

"Yes, we do," he replied. "But, as I said earlier, if the required adjustments are not made and if it appears that they cannot be made, us ordinary citizens are prepared to apply greater pressure. But first we must see what progress is made here."

After François answered the question from the *Singapore Straits Times* reporter, he raised his hands and declared, "I'm sorry, ladies and gentlemen. I've run out of time. I must go back and take my place with my compatriots."

Speeches and testimonials continued throughout the day and musicians and singers took to the stage between the testimonials to entertain and keep the crowd's morale high under the sweltering sun and repressive humidity. When all the speakers had finished and departed, musicians and singers took to the stage again and played and sang for thousands of protestors who remained near the Center.

Chapter Seven

Little India,
Kuala Lumpur

At exactly 6:00 p.m., with a satchel containing his freshly laundered shirt and pressed uniform slung over his shoulder, Deepak Kerejaan left his family's apartment above the shops and stalls on Jalan Tunku Abdul Rahman in Kuala Lumpur's Little India, just as he had done six days a week for nearly two years. Each day on his way to work he stopped for a brief visit with the elderly Hindu woman who lived a few doors down from his family. Since starting work as a bellhop at the Concorde Hotel, stopping at the woman's house had become a ritual; each time he called in she received him with great excitement.

Like Deepak Kerejaan's family, the elderly woman was a Tamil Hindu. She had been kind to him and his family when they arrived in the city; had it not been for her help, they may not have survived. Checking on her each day was his way of showing his family's gratitude.

Deepak Kerejaan had taken the job as a bellhop at the Concorde Hotel to support his family. He had worked mainly on the night shift, 8:00 p.m. to 8:00 a.m., in order to free up his days so he could learn to speak Bahasa Malaysia and attend culinary school.

He, his mother, and two younger brothers had moved to

Kuala Lumpur from southern India after his father died. After moving to Kuala Lumpur, he dreamed of becoming a chef in one of the city's popular restaurants or in one of its major hotel kitchens. He knew that if he succeeded as a chef, he could make a better life for his mother and his two brothers, both of whom were too young to work.

Exactly one hour after entering the woman's apartment, the young Tamil Hindu man left to catch the commuter train into the city. As he left Jalan Tunku Abdul Rahman and turned onto Jalan Masjid, a man, a stranger, stepped from a side street in front of him and started walking toward him. The man looked out of place. His sophisticated attire was not commonly seen in the working class area. Nevertheless, he seemed comfortable in his surroundings, as evidenced by his whistling and confident stride. When he closed to within a few feet of the young immigrant bellhop, he nodded politely and smiled, and the young man smiled back at him. But the well-dressed stranger's smile was only a distraction for what was about to happen. A split second later, the young Hindu felt a large hand clasp over his forehead from behind. The unseen attacker wrenched his neck violently to one side; then it snapped. The young man felt a sharp pain run from the base of his skull to his shoulders then down the full length of his body. His vision became impaired and he could feel himself losing consciousness.

In a matter of few seconds Deepak Kerejaan's body went limp. His unseen assailant held onto his upper body and the stranger who had distracted him grabbed him by his feet. Together they hauled him over to a side alley, lifted the satchel from his shoulder and propped his lifeless body up in a doorway. After stashing the young man's body the two men left the alley, turned back and walked briskly toward a car that had been waiting for them at the end of Jalan Masjid.

Chapter Eight

It was just after 7:00 p.m. when François Dupré, Dieter Metzger, and Jonathan Barber left the Putra Trade Center for the Concorde Hotel. They had had a long day and were exhausted. The streets near the Trade Center were closed to regular traffic which left them with the choice of a ten minute walk to Jalan Raja Laut to get a taxi or a forty-five minute trek to the hotel. With their clothes clinging to them like wetsuits on scuba divers, the choice of a taxi was an easy one.

"I can hardly wait to get out of these wet clothes, step into a hot shower, and have a long, cold rinse," said François as they clambered into the taxi. "And when I'm all cool and clean, I'm gonna call my wife and my son and let them know how much I miss them and what a success today has been!"

"Don't you think we should wait until we see what comes out of the conference today before we start sayin' we're successful?" asked Jonathan, who was using his discarded outer shirt to wipe away the sweat cascading from under his dreadlocks down his neck and onto his dark brown, hairless chest.

"No, I don't," François returned. "If the gathering of nearly a quarter of a million people without incident and serving notice to politicians and industrialists aren't milestones and successes, what are they? I say they are!" he added forcefully. "And that's something worth sharing with two important people in my life."

As the taxi pulled away from the stand and headed toward the hotel, François thought about what he had just said to Jonathan. The words reminded him of a serious mistake he had made earlier in his life—a mistake that nearly cost him the woman he loved and eventually married.

As soon as he had laid eyes on Caroline Gagnon he knew that he was in love with her and wanted to be with her. The image of her shapely, well-toned body, accentuated by her marble-smooth *café au lait* skin and her long, wavy, brown hair and soft brown eyes, had been etched in his mind.

He and Caroline had spent nearly three years together in Paris before she headed off to New York for graduate school. When she left, he was determined to keep her in his life. But despite his desire to be near her, fate dealt him a different hand. Near the end of her studies she had become pregnant and his crusade to save the planet was beginning to work against them. He had become increasingly absorbed with building and expanding TEARS' support base; it wasn't long before he was torn between his feelings for her and his work—a dilemma in which Caroline found herself competing for time with him. Before long, the time they spent together grew shorter and his visits less frequent.

Over the next year they grew farther apart, then one day during a trip to South America, it dawned on him that he couldn't go through life without her. It was this sense of unfulfilled destiny that prompted him to call her; it was during that call that he learned that he had a son, whom she had named Nicolas-Émile, after his grandfather.

Chapter Nine

When the taxi dropped them off at the Concorde Hotel, François, Dieter, and Jonathan headed straight for their rooms. Physically exhausted, they decided while on the elevator to skip dinner together and have room service. François' room was on the sixth floor, one floor above Jonathan and Dieter's. When the elevator stopped on their floor, he reminded them to be on time for breakfast. When the elevator reached his floor, François stepped off and walked briskly toward his room, which was near the end of the corridor.

As he walked along the long corridor, he heard what sounded like muffled screams ahead of him and he quickened his steps. As he moved toward his room the sounds grew louder. They seemed to be coming from the housekeeping supply room, just off to his right. When he reached the door he stopped and called out. "Are you alright in there?"

The noise stopped. Then after a beat, he heard a muffled scream. He reached for the door knob, but before he could turn it the door flew open and a man in a bellhop uniform sprang toward him, slammed a forearm into his chest, and fled. Caught by surprise, François was sent flying backward and landed against the wall. The unexpected blow winded him, but he recovered quickly.

He pulled himself up and turned just in time to catch a glimpse of the back of his attacker crashing through the door that led to the emergency stairwell. After the bellhop fled, François looked inside the small, dimly lit room and saw a young woman, dressed in a housekeeper's uniform, slumped on the floor, crying.

"Are you alright?" he asked. "Did he hurt you?"

"No, not really," said the woman, confused and still frightened.

"What did he do to you?"

"I'm not sure," she said, "but I think he was trying to rob me."

"Rob you?" said François. "Did he take anything?"

"I'm not sure," the woman replied. "When I came in, he came up behind me and grabbed me, and started going through my pockets. Then he snatched my handbag."

"Do you know this man?"

"No, I don't. I've never seen him before."

"But he was wearing a bellhop's uniform! Surely you must have seen him before?" François pressed.

"No! Never! I am always here when the bellhops arrive for the evening shift, so I know all of them. This one I have never seen before. He must be new."

"Are you sure?" François asked, looking more concerned. "Will you be alright?"

"Yes. I am fine. I cannot thank you enough," the woman replied, seemingly calming down. "What about you?" she asked. "Are you OK?"

"I'm fine," said François. "Just a bit out of breath, that's all. You know you should report this to the hotel manager. Whoever this creep is, he should be fired and arrested."

"Yes, I will tell the manager and the security officer immediately. Thank you again for helping me."

"I'm glad I was there to help," François replied. "If the manager or security officer needs to speak to me, my name is François Dupré."

Chapter Ten

François thought the incident with the hotel maid strange, but concluded in the end that it was probably the work of a thief hoping to get his hands on the maid's pass key. He was fairly confident that once the incident was reported to the hotel manager and the security officer, it would be dealt with.

When he reached his room and entered it, he noticed a red light flashing on his bedside video-phone. There was a message for him. He went straight over and pressed the message button on the device. He keyed in his PIN code and Caroline's face appeared on the screen.

"Hello, my love! It's 9:00 p.m. here and I would love to have spoken directly to you but you are many time zones away and I know by now you are in the thick of the excitement," she said. "I miss you very much. As you can see, Nicolas is here with me and we both want to tell you how proud we are of you and that we want you to win this battle and come home. We also thought you'd be happy to know that the television networks ran a story on you and TEARS and are calling the protest your 'crusade in Malaysia.'"

She grinned, ear-to-ear, and continued. "You'll also be pleased to know that after the stories ran, the networks said their switchboards and websites were inundated with calls and messages from people wanting to know more about you and TEARS. You're a hit!" she added, giggling. "We both thought you'd like to know that your support base is growing."

He could hear his son, Nicolas, badgering her to speak to

him; after a while she conceded. "Nicolas wants to say hello to you," she said.

"Hello, Papa!" the boy said, before his image appeared on the screen. "I miss you! When will you be home? When you come home, can we go to the park for a bike ride?"

"I'm sure he'll take you cycling, but you should talk to him about it when he gets home," Caroline said in the background. "So, say goodnight. It's getting close to your bedtime."

"Goodnight, Papa. I love you," Nicolas said, disappointed.

Forgetting momentarily that he was listening to a recorded message, François replied. "I miss you too, my precious."

Chapter Eleven

The next morning François lay still in the darkness of his hotel room, staring at the ceiling, before turning on the light. The quietness of the early morning was broken only by the noise of air rushing from the air conditioning vents. After a while, he sat up, and swung his feet over the side of the bed.

As he made his way to the bathroom, he paused, took the remote control and turned on the television. He flipped through the channels until he found CNN. From the bathroom, he could listen to the news to find out if anything worth knowing about the conference had happened during the evening. Within minutes, the CNN newsreader turned to the conference. He was not surprised to hear it described as 'an all-out effort to apply pressure on the United States, Australia, Canada, and Japan to take a more proactive stance on reducing greenhouse emissions, which are said to be speeding up global warming.'

The newsreader went on to describe the first day of the politically-charged event as peaceful. He finished by declaring that, '...there were no significant developments from the first day of discussions.'

After showering, François got dressed and made his way downstairs. Walking toward the elevator he felt confident that there was a higher purpose worth pursuing—a purpose higher than he had ever felt. When he stepped off the elevator, there were only a few guests milling about in the lobby. As the doors started to close behind him, a courier from a florist shop, carrying a large flower arrangement, rushed past him to catch the doors before they closed.

A few minutes later Dieter stepped off one of the other elevators and made his way over. "Did you sleep well last night?" Dieter asked.

"Like a baby!" François replied, smiling. "And you?"

"I was asleep before my head hit the pillow," said Dieter.

"Same here!" Jonathan added, popping up behind Dieter.

"Good then!" said François. "Let's get some breakfast and do what we came here to do!"

Chapter Twelve

When François, Jonathan, and Dieter arrived at the Putra Trade Center it was just after 8:00 a.m. The sun was well into the sky and the heat from it had already blanketed the city. Today, however, the muggy, dense air, which visitors frequently bemoaned, was of no concern to them because their thoughts were focused on the day's events.

Only a few thousand of the souls that had filled the assembly area the day before were on hand. With only a sparsely populated square, the unusually large, orange garbage bins and dumpsters that dotted the pavement were immediately noticeable and seemed to have sprouted from the pavement. Situated between them were dozens of mobile vendor carts, manned by eager traders. They were the lucky ones. They had been fortunate enough to secure a license to work the area. Being in the midst of hundreds of thousands of people in need of food and refreshment was a lucrative opportunity; the vendors were confident they would sell every item they could lay their hands on.

Looking across the near-empty square, Jonathan reminded François and Dieter, "There's still a ways to go."

"We'll get there!" Dieter replied.

"Dieter is right," François added confidently. "We'll get there!"

Chapter Thirteen

The speed at which the assembly area filled up was almost miraculous. François, Dieter, and Jonathan looked on as protestors converged on the area from nearly every direction. The Mall area and beyond to the northeast of the Trade Center was still cordoned off, but when opened, it filled up in less than fifteen minutes. Much of the media, sound crews and technicians had readied themselves before the crowd began to arrive. A trio of acoustic guitar-playing musicians took to the stage moments after they arrived and began playing a medley of Bob Dylan songs. As the crowd swelled, the musicians switched to the song, *The Times They Are a Changin'*, repeating the chorus over and over.

As François, Dieter, and Jonathan ascended the stairs to the stage, the trio's lead singer stopped singing and began highlighting big accomplishments in François' résumé. The build-up culminated in an introduction suited to a rock star. As François moved toward the microphone, the crowd cheered. Some whistled while others chanted his name.

François knew that the second day of the protest had to be equal to, if not more intense in its focus than, the first. The atmosphere, now charged with growing excitement, gave him the feeling that there was no cause for concern. He was ready for the day's activities and he would do his part.

It took nearly twenty minutes for the buzz from the crowd and the flow of people into the square to begin to die down. Looking out over the square, he could see skimpily-clad bodies massed at close quarters—some sitting on rolled-up or open sleeping bags and others on backpacks, all with their gaze directed toward him.

"Good morning!" he shouted into the microphone. "Did everyone have a good evening in Kuala Lumpur?"

The crowd responded with whistles and a roar. He continued, "Well, here we are... Day two and there's been no progress to speak of between the delegates. And what makes matters worse is that this morning we learned that there are already stories from inside the conference that there is still strong resistance to renewing the Kyoto agreement. We've also learned that some delegates have threatened to walk out if their interests and those of their benefactors can't be protected."

He paused, then after a moment continued. "If this happens, you know what we have to do, don't you?"

"Yes, we do!" the crowd roared.

"We're gonna have to take it to the next level!" he shouted.

The declaration drew applause and yells. He waited for the noise to die down. "We've got a full lineup today. Among our guests are several distinguished individuals, who will share with you some astounding information about what climate change has been doing for the last seventy-five years or so. Because they have so much to tell us, we should get started."

Another roar and whistles went up from the crowd. "So... without further delay, I would like to introduce to you a well respected marine biologist, researcher and faculty member at the University of San Diego, my friend Dr. Michael Lansing."

It was nearly 9:15 a.m. when Dr. Lansing took to the microphone. Dr. Lansing immediately launched into a diatribe on rising ocean levels. As he began, François, Dieter, and Jonathan made their way off the stage and headed for the row of mobile vending carts they had observed earlier on the west side of the Conference Center. They walked briskly. They were on a mission. They were on their way to a hastily arranged meeting with Kristie Bremmer, a TEARS member with

43

connections to one of the staff assistants of the American delegate. The woman had sent François a text message before he went onstage telling him about the planned walkout and asked him to meet her. Her message also said that she had more information about what several of the delegates were planning and what had happened in a secret closed door session that took place after the conference adjourned.

François had met Kristie Bremmer only once—during a trip to TEARS' Seattle office. But he knew from her message that she had just become an invaluable link to a conference 'insider.'

Chapter Fourteen

As they walked down the line of vendors, they saw a dark-haired woman in her mid-to-late twenties, dressed in shorts, hiking boots, and a sleeveless white top, sitting on a chair looking toward them. Clutching a cell phone in her right hand, she had a look of confidence on her face—a look which suggested that, in the scheme of things, she had just learned something monumental.

As they approached the woman she started to rise to her feet, but François quickly instructed her to stay seated. François, Dieter, and Jonathan took the three remaining chairs around the small table and François introduced everyone.

"Jonathan, Dieter... this is Kristie Bremmer. She's one of our part-timers. She's a dedicated supporter with our Seattle office. She was also a college friend of Amanda Costanti, one of the U.S. staffers with Ambassador Hollingsworth's delegation."

Jonathan and Dieter greeted the woman without shaking hands.

"So, what have you got for us, Kristie?" asked François.

Barely containing her enthusiasm, the woman began her report. "I received confirmation earlier this morning that Ambassador Hollingsworth is leading the charge to get the other hold-out nations to walk out of the conference just before the delegates break for lunch tomorrow."

"They're gonna walk out that early on the last day of the conference?" François barked.

"Yes!" said Kristie Bremmer. "But the word is that the

Japanese aren't going along with the plan. They say they'll stay and sign. Their justification, real or imagined, is that they're already experiencing the devastating effects of global warming. In fact, because of the 2011 earthquake, and tsunami that caused the Fukushima nuclear power plant disaster, they're convinced that the effects of global warming are happening much sooner and are much more severe in Japan than they were a few years earlier."

"What about the Aussies and the Canadians?" asked Jonathan.

"They plan to follow Hollingsworth's lead," the woman replied. "It was all a ruse from the beginning. The hold-outs, possibly with the exception of Japan, never intended to consider, let alone renew, the Kyoto Protocol. They don't care about greenhouse gasses, sea levels, deforestation or anything. None of it!" she added angrily.

"Now we know for sure!" said Dieter.

"So what do we do?" asked Jonathan.

"We do what we planned to do!" François fired back. "We kick it up to the next level."

François thanked Kristie for sharing what she had learned and told her that he was sorry about the loss of her friend, Patty Maynard.

Kristie Bremmer stared at him momentarily, silently locking eyes with him; then a tortured look swept over her face. "The police said Patty's death was a hit-and-run accident, but it wasn't," she said abruptly. "The only accident was the mistake her killer made," she declared.

"What do you mean mistake?" asked Dieter.

"A screw up," said the woman. "I believe that my friend Amanda Costanti, Ambassador Hollingsworth's assistant, was the real target. She knows too much," the woman added. "If you were involved in what's happening here and what's possibly been happening for years, wouldn't the leaking of information, like the kind I just gave you, make you more than just a bit uncomfortable? Of course it would," she said, answering her own question. "The bastards who killed Patty Maynard can see that Amanda is alive, which means they screwed up!"

A silence fell over the small table. Several minutes passed before Kristie Bremmer rose from her seat. For François, the woman's comments had caused serious concern; during the brief bout of silence he began to feel ill at ease, uncomfortable —the kind of feeling one gets when being watched by someone with ominous intentions. His feelings were justified. He had been under surveillance since the day he arrived in Kuala Lumpur. His every move had been scrutinized; the whole time while he, Dieter, Jonathan, and Kristie Bremmer sat and talked, the eyes of a tall American-Asian-looking man, dressed in a khaki safari suit, were fixed firmly upon them. Another man, not far from the tall man, disguised as a media communications technician, carried a small parabolic dish antenna which was aimed at their table. The antenna had picked up every word François, his associates, and the Bremmer woman had spoken and stored it on a digital recording device.

Sensing the presence of observers but not knowing who they were or where they might be, François told Kristie to return to the assembly area. He had hoped that contact with her in the crowded space would have enabled them to meet unnoticed, but he had been wrong.

After hearing what Kristie Bremmer had said, he knew that he now had to tell Dieter and Jonathan what he had promised to share with them later. He looked at both of them in silence for a moment. The time had come.

"Do you remember yesterday morning, when I told you that there was something important that I had learned and would only tell you about it when I had confirmation of my suspicions?" François asked.

"Yes. How could I forget," said Dieter.

"Well… at the time I thought it could wait, but after hearing what Kristie just said I think it's time to fill you in." He sighed.

"What I'm about to tell you may sound unusual, even a bit bizarre, but I'm convinced now that it shows just how important and sensitive the issues for this conference are for some very powerful people."

"Alright… You've got our attention!" said Dieter.

François paused. "About a month ago, a man I have never seen before came up to me in Central Park and asked me if I knew right from wrong, and if I believed that the truth could set you free. At first I was startled. He was dirty, his clothes were tattered, and his question, to say the least, was weird. I thought he was a bum or some guy down on his luck, or possibly a nut case. Then I noticed something rather odd about him."

"What do you mean odd?" asked Jonathan.

"OK… not odd, maybe unusual. He had an intelligent look about him, particularly in his eyes."

"An intelligent bum? Now I've heard it all," Jonathan scoffed.

"Yes, an intelligent bum," François returned. "His eyes suggested a high level of alertness."

"He was probably on speed or something," Jonathan quipped.

"Joke if you must," said François, "but there was intelligence in this man's eyes, not the sadness you'd expect to see in the eyes of a bum or a crazy man. Anyway… he asked me the same question again. So I said yes. Then I asked him his name, but he said it wasn't important. He said that the only thing that was important was that he knew mine. And when I insisted on knowing his, he told me to shut up and listen. As you can imagine… it pissed me off. He had become aggressive, which was starting to make me feel uncomfortable, yet at the same time, I felt that he had something important to say. So I stood there… wide-eyed, almost paralyzed."

François paused for a moment to get Jonathan and Dieter's reaction.

"Is that it?" Dieter asked, impatiently.

François resumed. "No, it isn't!" he snapped. "He told me

that a few months earlier he had been working for a private foundation that was involved in research on climate change and its relationship to fossil fuel use. They were also looking at the latest estimates provided by governments on fossil fuel reserves, specifically oil and shale gas deposits."

François paused briefly once more and continued. "He didn't know exactly who paid his salary or provided the bulk of the funding for the research, but he said he suspected that everything was being bankrolled by some oil tycoon somewhere in the northeastern U.S. At that point, I began to believe that this man was in some kind of trouble and was on the run. He genuinely seemed to fear for his life and wanted to tell someone he thought might do something about what was happening."

Jonathan cut in again. "His fear may have been real, at least to him. After all, wouldn't he be afraid of something if he was a paranoid schizophrenic?"

"That wasn't the case!" François snapped once more. "He was far too lucid, too alert, and too intelligent. He didn't ramble or repeat himself like the schizophrenics we see almost every day on the streets of New York. It was clear that this man was in full control of his faculties. So I asked him again to tell me his name so I could verify his story, but he insisted, this time more angrily, that his name wasn't important and that it wouldn't matter because before long his body would be found somewhere in a gutter or an alley and he'd wind up in a morgue with a 'John Doe' tag affixed to one of his big toes."

François' face registered deep concern as he described the encounter. "This stranger told me that the information this private group discovered showed conclusively that petroleum reserves are at least forty percent lower than the latest estimates provided by governments, and that conclusions about the increase in global temperatures and other destructive climate changes identified decades ago are right. He said the group he worked with consisted of twenty of the brightest scientific minds in their fields and had all the financial and materiel support it needed for research. He said that after collecting and analyzing several centuries' worth of data, the group concluded that the earth is dying, and that humans are without a doubt hastening its death."

He paused once more then went on. "What makes matters worse, he said, was that given the current pattern of fossil fuel usage and the release of other destructive pollutants into the atmosphere, global warming will increase exponentially and much faster than the scientific community and governments realize. I was shocked because of the sense of urgency and eloquence he delivered the message with. But that wasn't all. The next thing he told me made the hairs on the back of my neck stand up. He said the group estimated that within thirty to forty years, devastating rain, hurricanes, monsoons, inland flooding, rising sea levels, and tsunamis would wipe out millions of unsuspecting people and destroy crops worldwide. There would also be an exponential increase in deadly diseases like skin cancer and respiratory ailments, brought on by further deterioration of the earth's ozone layer and the increasing number of carcinogens being released into the air."

"It all sounds too elaborate and too sophisticated," said Dieter. "Surely you didn't believe any of this? Did he offer to show you any of these findings?"

"No, but I believe him," said François. "Look! I can't lay it all out for you here and now, but he told me there are some rich and powerful people who've made sure that they won't suffer the fate that awaits the rest of us in the few decades ahead." He looked at Dieter and Jonathan. "You see… It's clear now."

"What's clear?" Jonathan asked, still puzzled.

"The reason why they're going to scuttle the conference!" said François. "It's all part of the plan."

François was about to continue when he noticed that several security personnel had arrived and were only a few yards away from where they were sitting. The people tailing him were no longer passive like they had been on the previous day or the day when they arrived in Kuala Lumpur. They were bolder, no longer trying to conceal their presence. It was obvious they were looking for someone; François surmised that the person they were looking for could only be him. He was soon proven right. When they spotted him, the tall, authoritative-looking American-Asian man spoke into his radio, presumably to give instructions for the men nearby to keep an eye on him. François knew that it was time to end the conversation.

"I'll fill you in on the rest back at the hotel this evening," he said abruptly. "It looks like we've attracted some unwanted attention."

As they rose from their seats and started walking back toward the Trade Center, one of the vendors took a radio from his cart. "They have left my sector and are en route to your location."

Chapter Fifteen

It was almost noon in Kuala Lumpur; the sun was directly overhead. The air was filled with music and the heaving crowd gathered near the Trade Center was still active. The number of placards raised in the air had quadrupled from the day before. But by now, many who carried them were using them to shelter from the sun's burning rays. A tarp had been drawn over much of the stage and some of the demonstrators were filtering in and out of the area for a reprieve, or to look for food and refreshments.

As the three TEARS leaders ascended the stairs and took their place on the stage, applause erupted from the crowd. When the excitement died down, they listened as the experts gave testimonials and speeches and the performers sang songs of encouragement. The second day of activities had gone much the same as they had gone on the first day. But as time passed, it was clear that many of the delegates would be staying well beyond the 6:00 p.m. departure they had made on the first day.

News filtering from inside the conference suggested that a sizeable number of the representatives were locked in heated debate over the conclusions of the latest report on global warming prepared by the UN International Panel on Climate Change. Opponents of the report were said to be taking the position that weather patterns during the last four to five decades were cyclical, occurring every three to four hundred years, instead of the unique meteorological and environmental phenomena the Panel had described.

At 8:00 p.m., the debate was still raging and by 10:00 p.m. intransigence had prevailed. Recognizing the deadlock, the delegates called an end to the day. When news of the stalemate reached the demonstrators, many of whom had lingered late into the evening, they lofted their placards in the air and began shouting and singing protest songs.

Minutes later, the delegates poured out of the Center and climbed into their armored limousines and sports utility vehicles. As they sped away, François took center stage and warned the crowd once again that the conference was likely to fail.

Chapter Sixteen

A half hour before the conference broke up, the bellhop who had attacked the chambermaid the day before entered the Concorde Hotel through the service entrance. He was confident that the police wouldn't connect the death of the young Hindu immigrant whose uniform he was wearing to his presence at the hotel for several days. His first attempt to get a pass key to the rooms had ended in failure, but this time he was in no doubt that he would succeed. Today the woman he had attacked was working overtime. She wouldn't finish work until 10:00 p.m.

After entering the hotel, he stealthily made his way to the sixth floor and took a position in the stairwell to wait for his prey to enter the supply room where she usually changed out of her uniform. He waited quietly and patiently; when the woman appeared and opened the door to the supply room, he sprang from the stairwell and pounced on her at lightning speed. He pushed her into the small room and wrapped a garrote around her neck. The woman was taken by complete surprise, but she was surprisingly strong. She fought hard. She thrashed about wildly, arms flailing, knocking supplies off nearly every shelf before her brightly painted red fingernails began clawing at the thin wire biting into her neck. The struggle was useless. She couldn't get her fingers underneath the fine strand of metal.

Her assailant pulled harder as she struggled. A beat later he had severed her external carotid artery and crushed her larynx. When the struggling stopped, he released her and she fell to the floor in a limp heap amid the trolleys and cleaning supplies. He searched her pockets and smiled. He had found her pass key.

Having gotten what he had come for, he slipped from the supply room, returned to the emergency stairwell, and waited for François Dupré, Dieter Metzger, and Jonathan Barber to arrive.

Chapter Seventeen

It was well after 10:30 p.m. when François, Jonathan, and Dieter arrived at the Concorde Hotel. Having spent nearly fourteen hours in the sweltering heat and humidity they were tired, but also worried about the turn the day's events had taken. There were good reasons for concern. Based on what Kristie Bremmer had told them and because there was already a deadlock in the negotiations, it was clear that whoever was pulling the strings was beginning to have things go their way.

They took the keys to their rooms and headed off to take showers, agreeing to meet a half hour later in François' room. To save time, they would have dinner sent there.

When François entered his room, the 'message waiting' light was flashing on his video-phone. He rushed over to retrieve it. As expected, it was Caroline. He smiled when the message file opened and her image and voice projected from the machine. A message from her and the sight of her face were just what he needed.

"Hello, my love," she said. "You've been away from me for nearly a week now and I can't begin to tell you how much I miss you! I've been thinking of you all day," she added, smiling. "Thanks for the beautiful message you left the other day. It made me feel warm all over. I hope this message does the same for you. This morning's news reports said that leaks from inside the Center suggest that the hard-line delegates may be planning to scuttle the conference by pulling out early. There was also a report which said that TEARS is planning to expose important information that links certain business interests to the derailing of the conference. But the officials interviewed in Washington, Ottawa, and Canberra said the story was a rumor started by the opposition, and left-wing, tree-hugging zealots, to discredit the delegates and their country's policy on climate change. Please be careful," she said, pausing, as if waiting for a reply. "Remember, I love you very, very much. Sweet dreams."

After listening to the message François was on his way to the bathroom when the video-phone rang. He thought it might be Caroline, so he rushed back and answered it straight away. But when the screen opened, it was blank. The line remained silent for several seconds. He was about to hang up when a man with an Asian accent cut in.

"Dupré!"

"Who is this?" François demanded.

"Shut the fuck up and listen!" the caller growled. "You clearly don't know who you are dealing with!"

"Who is this? What do you want?" François asked again.

Obviously irritated, the caller began shouting. "Listen, you little ass-wipe! Why don't you behave like a good little boy, pick up your marbles and go home while you still can? You are meddling in things that are far too big for you. Do you understand? As the Americans say, 'you're skating on thin ice.' So here's my recommendation... Leave Malaysia and go home! Go home now!"

After the warning, the line went silent then went dead. François reached over to turn off the unit, but his hand shook so violently that he had to steady it on the top of the bedside table to press the off button. He had received hundreds of harassing and threatening calls in the past, but none as ominous as this one. He was gripped by fear, almost paralyzed.

He sat on the side of the bed for nearly ten minutes after the call ended. He was mortified. A sudden, sharp, and very loud rap on his room door and he jumped to his feet. He was afraid, unsure about what to do.

"Who is it?" he asked nervously.

"It's us!" said Dieter. "You wanna open the door?"

Still shaken from the call, he walked over and let them in. As soon as Dieter and Jonathan saw the look on his face, Jonathan asked. "What's wrong? You look as if you've seen a ghost!"

"Worse than that," said François. "I just had a threatening call and I feel like someone just walked over my grave."

"What do you mean?" Dieter asked.

"I just had a death threat…"

"Death threat? What kind of death threat?"

"The kind where someone tells you they're gonna turn your lights out if you don't stop doing whatever it is you're doing! What other kind is there?" François shouted irritably. "It's obvious… it's all coming together now!"

"What are you talking about? What's coming together?" Jonathan asked.

"Sit down!" said François. "You'll understand when I tell you the rest of the story I started earlier today. I'm sure you'll see that there's a connection."

François moved over to the couch, took a seat on it, and began.

"Remember the stranger I told you I met in Central Park? The one who came up to me and told me about the research he was involved in at some high-powered laboratory?"

"Yeah," Jonathan replied. "The nut case!"

"He was no nut case!" François retorted. "Anyway, as I was about to tell you earlier, this man told me that he and the other scientists he worked with never really knew the real source of their funding. He didn't explain how or why, he just said that he suspected that big oil industry money was backing the research and there were no plans to make the findings available to the public. Since my encounter with this guy, I've been thinking… Why would anyone spend so much money searching for information as important as this and not share it with governments, the public, and the rest of the oil industry?"

"Well…" said Dieter. "Why wouldn't they?"

"It's obvious!" said François. "If governments, not to mention the public, found out about it, there probably would be a moratorium on the use of fossil fuel and a rush to find cleaner and more environmentally friendly alternatives."

"But wouldn't it be difficult to keep all of this information a secret?" asked Jonathan. "I mean… look at the number of scientists involved and who knows how many other people! And wouldn't whoever is doing this need special permission to conduct research in some of the most important, restricted areas? What about the governments themselves? Wouldn't some governments, or at least some of their officials, have to be aware of what they were doing? They'd have to be part of it."

"You're probably right," said François. "But I believe what the stranger told me that day was just the tip of the iceberg. I still haven't figured out exactly what he meant when he said the rich and powerful people behind the research have made sure they won't suffer the same fate that awaits the rest of us."

A look of deep disbelief swept over Jonathan's face. "You don't know this guy from Adam!" he said. "How do you know he was telling the truth? He could've been some lunatic—a madman who escaped from Bellevue or some other place for crackpots."

Without speaking, François leaned forward and picked up the small toiletry bag from the coffee table in front of them and emptied out its contents. He then lifted a flap folded down over the bottom of the bag and removed two memory sticks.

"Look!" he said. "I didn't want to pull the two of you into this until I was certain it had to be done. The stranger in the park gave me these to back up his story. He agreed to meet me again after I had examined their contents, but I never saw or heard from him again."

For the first time since he began to explain the strange encounter, he looked deeply worried. "I reviewed as much as I could of what was on these, and from what I can tell, they contain mostly data sets. Scores of them! More than 60 gigabytes worth! Test results and data on ocean levels and conditions, air quality, fresh water, the polar ice caps, and ground water, from a number of locations around the world. There's also geological survey data on oil reserves and natural gas. The plan was to go public with this stuff. You know… hand it over to the media if the conference fails. And if I'm correct, the media will round up the top independent scientists and tell us what this business is all about. I think breaking this as news would help identify who's pulling the strings of the hold-outs at this conference."

Showing growing concern, Jonathan interrupted. "Don't tell me you've been carrying these damn things around with you? You have… haven't you?" he said, answering his own question. "How long? Two, three, four weeks?"

"These are not the only copies!" François said. "Look, guys! Now that we know that the U.S., Australian, and Canadian delegates plan to scuttle the conference, we can hand these over to one of the major networks. Maybe CNN or the BBC, right after the delegates quit the conference. When CNN or the BBC gets this data, they'll assemble the experts to examine it and have a special report prepared by the time the evening news airs in the States."

"I hope you know what the hell you're doing!" said Jonathan.

"Trust me! I do," said François. "We've got 'em, whoever they are, by the balls and we're not gonna let go!"

Before François could add another self-congratulatory word, the hotel's fire alarm sounded and an emergency announcement came over the public address system instructing all guests and employees to evacuate the building and assemble on the west side of the hotel near the Hard Rock Café.

Chapter Eighteen

When the alarm sounded, Dieter and Jonathan rushed back to their rooms and collected their backpacks containing all of their valuables. Afterwards, they returned to François' room and the three of them headed downstairs together. François took the memory sticks with him.

As they moved along the crowded corridor toward the emergency exit, François spotted what looked like the bellhop who had attacked the housekeeper. It seemed odd that the man was wearing an earpiece and walking hurriedly away from the nearest emergency exit. He tried to turn to see where the man was going, but the congestion and steady flow of guests made stopping or even turning around impossible.

By the time all the guests and staff arrived in the assembly area near the Hard Rock Café, it was 11:30 p.m. Flashing lights and sirens from fire engines and emergency vehicles pierced the night air. François, Jonathan, and Dieter waited with the other guests near the street. As they stood waiting, François noticed a florist's delivery van parked across the street. It belonged to the same florist as the one he had seen outside the hotel when they had left that morning.

For a moment he thought there might be something to it, but then decided that the vehicle probably belonged to the florist shop in the hotel. He had failed to connect the van to the delivery man he had seen that morning at the elevator and was unaware that the hotel's florist shop did not open until 9:00 a.m. If he had not been so dismissive of these things, he would have been more suspicious of the man who entered the elevator that morning carrying flowers—the man who had been let into his room by hotel staff under pretense of an urgent delivery—the same man who had planted a listening device under the coffee table in his room before declaring that he had mistakenly asked for the wrong room.

Chapter Nineteen

Thirty minutes after all the guests arrived downstairs, the night manager came out and informed them that it was safe to go back inside. He apologized for the inconvenience and explained that someone had accidentally or perhaps even deliberately set off the alarm and that fire safety procedures required that everyone be evacuated.

While waiting outside the hotel they decided it would be better if they all stayed in one room, and agreed it would be Jonathan's. Even though they were hungry, they chose to skip dinner. François never mentioned the florist van or the bellhop to Jonathan or Dieter. He didn't want them to think that in addition to believing in lunatics, he was also becoming paranoid. But telling them about his suspicions probably wouldn't have made any difference, because the two men inside the florist van, perched on seats in front of a console, arrayed with electronic eavesdropping and tracking equipment and wearing headphones, had already heard and recorded what they needed from the listening device in his room.

When they entered Jonathan's room, François was still nervous. It had been a long, agonizing day for all of them, and François was more frightened than he had ever been. Trying not to show his fear, he turned to his friends and said, "I think we've had enough excitement for one day. We've got a big day ahead of us tomorrow and we need to be sharp and focused for it. We should get some sleep."

Chapter Twenty

The next morning the three men were still groggy and tired. They had slept in their clothes, and without showers. François managed to make his way to the bathroom first and when he emerged, he announced that he was going to his room for a shower and a shave. "Jesus... I look like hell!" he said, as he passed in front of a large dressing mirror.

Dieter laughed. "You always do!"

Trying to put on a good face, François slid his feet into his sandals. "We've gotta get going." He grabbed his backpack and instructed the others: "Shower, get dressed and I'll meet you downstairs at seven sharp."

When François opened the door to his room, his heart began to pound. He couldn't believe his eyes. His room had been ransacked. "Dammit!" he shouted, as he took in the chaos around him. The mattress had been removed from the bed and flipped against the wall and the sofa and chair had been overturned and their cushions slashed. Drawers from the dresser and bedside tables had been removed and their contents strewn all over the floor. The closet doors were gaping and all its contents, including his clothes, were in a pile on the floor. After surveying the mess, he went into the bathroom and found the contents of his shaving kit spread all over the countertop and in the sink.

After recovering from the shock, he punched in Jonathan's room number on the video-phone.

"Yeah," Jonathan answered, still groggy.

"Jonathan?" he said. "Somebody tossed my fuckin' room!"

"François? Is that you?" Jonathan shouted.

"No! It's Mother Teresa! Of course it's me!"

A few minutes later Jonathan was standing in the doorway to his room. "Shit!" he shouted. "Do you think they were looking for the memory sticks?"

"You bet your ass they were!" François said furiously.

"How did they know about 'em?" Jonathan asked.

"I'm not sure, but I've got a pretty damn good idea."

François' French accent got stronger as he grew angrier. "We only talked about the memory sticks in this room, which means someone must have been listening. *Maybe the bastards are still listening...* Help me collect my things, will you?" he said. "And stick those damned drawers back where they came from!" he shouted angrily.

"Shouldn't we tell hotel security about this?" Jonathan asked nervously.

"Why? What good do you think it would do?"

"Sorry... You're right," said Jonathan.

Neither of them bothered to call Dieter. Instead, they hastily rearranged the furniture and threw François' clothes onto the bed.

"You'd better get showered and dressed," he told Jonathan. "I'll be alright. No one would dare come back this early."

When Jonathan left, he put the chain lock on the door and turned the deadbolt for good measure. He then grabbed the backpack containing the memory sticks and took it into the bathroom where he could keep an eye on it. After showering, he figured it would be safer to round up Jonathan and Dieter and go downstairs with them to breakfast, rather than go on his own and wait for them. He went first to Jonathan's room and then the two of them went to Dieter's. When they arrived at Dieter's room and knocked, the door swung open quickly, as if he had been behind it, waiting for them.

It was just after 7:00 a.m. when the three men sat down to breakfast. For the first few minutes, they sat in silence, mulling over everything that had happened.

"What's wrong?" Dieter asked. "Why the long faces?"

Jonathan looked at François as if asking permission to answer. "Someone tossed his room."

"When?" Dieter barked.

Jonathan shot an annoyed look at Dieter and Dieter realized that he was drawing unwanted attention to the three of them, so he lowered his voice.

"When did it happen?" he asked again, this time almost whispering.

"Last night?" said Jonathan.

"Do you think they were looking for the memory sticks?" Dieter asked.

"Of course they were!" François cut in. "But they didn't find them. They were with me."

Dieter sighed. "Thank God!"

"They didn't stop us!" François said angrily. "They wanted 'em, but they didn't get 'em. Enough questions!" he snapped. "Order your breakfast and let's eat and get the hell out of here."

Chapter Twenty-One

After the threatening phone call and the ransacking of François' room, all three of them were worried and frightened and visibly agitated. Instead of walking to the Trade Center, as they had done on the first morning, they decided to take a taxi. They left the breakfast room and passed through the hotel lobby where at least a half a dozen policemen were rushing around. The police had arrived while they were having breakfast. One of the men, who looked as if he was a detective, was in civilian clothes. He was clearly in charge. He was talking to the night manager and occasionally directing the uniformed officers who were ushering employees in and out of the hotel's business center, where they were almost certainly being questioned. The police seemed to be interviewing the entire night staff, which probably meant that they had been called in to investigate the fire alarm, François guessed.

As they passed through the lobby, the plain clothes detective turned away from the night manager and looked in their direction. For a brief moment, he made direct eye contact with François. After meeting the man's gaze, it occurred to François that the man might want to talk to him. *He might have made a connection between the fire alarm and my room break-in, or maybe someone told him about the incident involving the bellhop and the chambermaid on the sixth floor the day before. Maybe he knew everything and he wanted me to know that he knew who I was.* François couldn't let himself dwell on the matter, so he dismissed all of these notions as the manifestation of fear and a nascent but growing paranoia. After all, he hadn't told anyone about the break-in. And even though the young woman knew his name, she probably hadn't mentioned him when she reported the attack to hotel security.

Outside the hotel they climbed into a taxi. As it pulled away and headed toward the Putra Trade Center, François' thoughts drifted back to Caroline's last message—a message he had wanted to see and hear again but never got the chance. After a few minutes the voice of the taxi driver interrupted his thoughts.

"This is as far as I can go," the man declared in broken English. "All the roads near the Center are closed. Only official traffic can enter," he added politely, eyes darting back and forth between the three of them, as if trying to predict who would pay the fare. His eyes finally fell on François. "That will be ten ringgits, please."

François paid the fare and they clambered out of the car. As they began walking the remaining three blocks to the assembly area, the unexplained events of the last two evenings started to pervade his head again. He still couldn't understand why the bellhop who attacked the woman and him the night before had returned to his floor during the evacuation. He knew that something about the man wasn't right, but he couldn't put his finger on it. *There had to be a connection between the man and the fire alarm.*

After the threatening phone call, the mystery surrounding the bellhop was the second most perplexing thing on his mind. But he decided not to let those concerns become a distraction, so he again put all thoughts about the incident aside and began to focus on the immediate and most important task in front of him—figuring out how to take the protest forward when the delegates walked out, without inciting violence. He even managed to push the death threat to the back of his mind and, for the time being, he was comforted by the thought that the presence of dozens of television cameras and news reporters would prevent an attack on him.

The thoughts of what lay ahead caused a sudden rush of adrenalin which seemed to help his worries and fears disappear. His confidence was returning. He was sure that when he turned the information on the memory sticks over to the media, the irreversible wheels of change would be set in motion. Today he needed help from the press more than ever; he concluded that because he had managed to avoid giving them an interview the evening before, they would be anxious to talk to him this morning. They, too, had learned about the impending walk-outs and had focused their efforts on getting the facts from the delegates themselves. But, as expected, the delegates denied any involvement or knowledge of a plot to derail the conference.

He was relieved that the media had turned its focus on the 'back story.' After all, what could he have said to them about the walk-outs without compromising his informants? *I'm holding two memory sticks loaded with incriminating data that's gonna blow the lid off a well-conceived conspiracy, but I can't give the information to you right now.* He knew that in order for the information to have maximum effect, it would have to be handed over to the press after the walk-outs.

Chapter Twenty-Two

When François, Jonathan, and Dieter reached the Center, a steady stream of protestors was entering the assembly area. They could see from the number of people already in place that many of them had been there for hours. The crowd knew that the delegates would begin arriving soon and they wanted to be there to confront them when they showed up. Crews from the major international news networks were also poised and waiting, which explained why they hadn't been outside the hotel when François, Jonathan, and Dieter had left.

Vans and trucks, bristling with antennae and satellite dishes, had been allowed to remain overnight near the Trade Center. Most of the local and international press had also had mobile crews working. The mobile crews had pounded the streets hard the night before, looking for interviews to fill spots in scheduled broadcasts and to uncover breaking stories whenever possible. But despite their efforts, they had failed to find enough well-placed sources to turn the rumors about a walk-out into a headline.

It was nearing 8:00 a.m. when François, Dieter, and Jonathan moved into the assembly area. Once inside the area, they made a beeline for the stage. But before they could reach it they were ambushed by reporters and cameramen.

"Mr. Dupré! We've heard that you were attacked two nights ago in your hotel!" shouted a BBC reporter. "Is that true? If so, why?" he added quickly to make sure he got both of his questions in.

"I wasn't attacked!" François replied. "The notion is absurd!"

The reporters' shouts grew louder. After a beat, a reporter from the *New York Times* yelled, "It's been said Mr. Dupré that the fire alarm at the Concorde late last evening was set off to draw you and your colleagues out into the open for an attack. Are you dismissing this too? Who do you think was behind that plot, Mr. Dupré?"

"Look!" François said. "I don't know who your sources are, but it seems to me that if 'they', whoever they may be, wanted me out in the open they need not go to such extremes. I've been in the open for the last couple of days."

The *New York Times* reporter fired another question. "It was also said, Mr. Dupré, that your room was ransacked during the hotel evacuation. Would you care to comment on that? What were the perpetrators looking for? Did they find it?"

"You have your stories all wrong!" François replied sharply. "It looks as if someone is playing games with you, sending you around on a wild goose chase! That's all, ladies and gentlemen!" he announced abruptly. "I have to go!"

As they turned to walk away, Ellen, the young CNN reporter, shouted, "One more question, Mr. Dupré! Just one more question! A quick one…"

Looking back over his shoulder François called back, "Ellen, none of your questions are ever quick!"

With his back still turned to the reporters, he raised his hand to signal that he had nothing more to say. But he had taken only a few steps when the CNN reporter shouted again, "Mr. Dupré! Some people believe that some of the demonstrators are planning to start violence here today! Do you know anything about this? Is there a radical faction or element within TEARS that might take such action?"

François grimaced. He spun on his heel and glared at the young reporter. "No one in my organization would dare engage in such activity!" he retorted. "We have always worked to stay within the confines of the law. And, with the exception of forming human chains and sit-ins in non-violent protests, we have always operated within the framework of the laws applicable to wherever we may be." He took a deep breath. "Acceptance of our policy of non-violence is a prerequisite for joining our organization. It's not an option!"

The CNN reporter continued. "But there are well over two hundred thousand people involved in these protests. Are you saying that they're all loyal and will follow the letter of the law?"

François replied reluctantly. "That's not what I said. What I said and meant is that most of the people you see here arrived several days before the conference started and we haven't had any problems. Now and then there's been a case where too much drink and unbridled energy caused scrapes with locals and a few minor infractions of the law landed people in trouble. Overall, however, it's been pretty civilized. Don't you think? Once again," he added, "you've been misled by your sources."

François turned and walked away. "Good day, ladies and gentlemen!"

The three men climbed the steps to the stage and moved to the back of it until the musicians entertaining the crowd finished playing. By now, the assembly area was awash with protestors.

After a few minutes the entertainment started to wind down. One of the vocalists turned to François and nodded and he moved forward. It was his cue. "Ladies and gentlemen," the singer said, "I give you the man of the hour!"

François came to the front of the stage amid screams, whistles, yells, and applause. He stood silently, arms raised above his head for several minutes until the clamors died down; then he began.

"Thank you all for being here to answer the call to duty!" he shouted. "Today is the last day of this very important conference and our last day here, and we have to show the world that we are determined to win. We must make sure that justice is done. And the only way to do this is to return stewardship of our planet to the people. Ordinary people… people like you and me."

He paused briefly then continued. "We know that on a few occasions these conferences have made strides in improving the way humans manage and live in harmony with the environment, but they have become increasingly weaker on the tough and important issues. In fact, the last two summits in Copenhagen and Durban accomplished very little. This tells us that some governments are incapable or unwilling to act with the expediency needed to address the problems that must be solved. Our opponents would like the world to believe that our warnings are no more than noise from alarmists and fanatics. Well, over the past two days, you've heard what the experts had to say about that. Many of those who spoke to you and the others who will speak to you today were threatened with removal from their jobs if they didn't remain silent about what they knew. It's because of this campaign to silence dissenting voices that we cannot allow ours to be silenced."

A deafening roar erupted from the crowd; when it died down François called Dieter and Jonathan to join him center stage. They moved forward and took positions to his left and right side and he introduced them to the crowd, referring to them as close friends, colleagues, and part of the bulwark of TEARS.

Dieter and Jonathan waved to the crowd amidst thunderous applause. Dieter shot a quick look at Jonathan. Neither of them had expected what was happening. "This is great!" Jonathan said. "I love it! I fuckin' love it!"

When the applause subsided, François said, "I want to thank all of you for what you have done, are doing, and are going to do. But for here and now, I want us to get on with business. And to do that, "I would like to introduce you to the first speaker of the day. He's an important speaker," he added, "as are all the others. But this speaker, however, has unimpeachable qualifications. He has gravitas—years of experience as a civil servant and practitioner. He's the former director of the National Oceanic and Atmospheric Administration's National Climatic Data Center. He is now a senior researcher at the Hawthorne Centre for Climate Prediction and Research in the United Kingdom. As you may have heard, he ran afoul of the establishment because he is one of that rare breed who refuses to toe the line. For that reason he walked away from NOAA. Friends and colleagues, I give you Dr. Michael Westbrook. He's primed and ready to go!"

Dr. Westbrook moved swiftly to the microphone and began explaining the public statement that had led to his resignation then gave the facts and figures used to justify his statement and why he left NOAA. Dr. Westbrook's speech lasted just over an hour. And when the crowd's reaction to it had died down, musicians again took control of the stage.

When the musicians came on, François, Dieter, and Jonathan left the stage to mingle in the crowd. But as they moved into the crowd, Jonathan noticed that they had come under the gaze of the tall American-Asian looking man they had seen when they were with Kristie Bremmer.

"Don't look now," said Jonathan. "But I think old 'eagle eyes' is watching us again."

François turned his head slowly and looked to the southwest corner of the assembly area. Standing on top of a platform erected on scaffolding, he saw the tall man. Just like on the previous day, he was clad in a khaki safari suit and wearing dark sunglasses. He and about a dozen other security personnel had taken positions on the high platform which had apparently been set up during the night. But this time, instead of speaking into a hand-held radio, he was speaking into a small, military-style, tactical headset with a boom microphone.

After seeing the man, François looked toward the opposite side of the square. There, he saw more security personnel, all with their eyes trained on them. To his surprise, the police detective from the Concorde Hotel lobby was now among them. They seemed to be tracking his movement. Seeing what was happening, he turned to Jonathan and Dieter. "It's not just the tall guy who's interested in us, there are quite a few others. Possibly dozens… Even the detective I saw at the hotel this morning is with them." *What's he doing here?*

"What's with the special attention?" Dieter asked.

"I don't know, but I can promise you this… they're not looking at us because they like the handiwork of our tailors," said Jonathan.

"Real cute!" said Dieter.

"Look! We're in the midst of thousands of people. It would be foolish of them to try something here," François offered.

"What did you do with the package?" asked Jonathan nervously.

François patted his stomach. "They're in a very safe place!"

He had removed the two memory sticks from his backpack and put them in a money belt around his waist.

The three men waded into the crowd and were quickly set upon by a swarm of TEARS supporters. Staying true to form, François worked his way through the crowd, shaking hands and answering questions. But as he moved about the crowd, his eyes scanned the boundaries of the area, looking for signs of what the omnipresent security forces might be doing.

Chapter Twenty-Three

François had been mingling with the crowd for nearly an hour when the attention of the security men and the protestors shifted to the Conference Center. Seconds later, thousands of protestors surged toward the barrier in front of the Center to see what was happening. The front doors had opened, but no one had emerged. The media, which had been allowed to enter the area to cover a progress report from a spokesperson, also seemed agitated. Reporters and photographers were still jockeying for a prime position behind the rope separating them from the front steps of the Trade Center.

After a few minutes, there was movement near the entrance of the Center. Then without warning the Canadian delegate, Ambassador Philippe Le Muir, emerged. The crowd became frenzied. Ambassador Le Muir was followed closely by one of his aides. He paused briefly on the steps then a few seconds later, he stepped from underneath the portico toward a cluster of microphones at the bottom of the steps. As he strode forward, he took a folded piece of paper from the inside pocket of his jacket. He was clearly about to deliver a prepared statement. But before he could begin to speak, several questions were shouted from the crowd of reporters.

"May I have your attention for a moment, ladies and gentlemen," Ambassador Le Muir said. "I have a statement I would like to make, but I'm afraid I won't be taking any questions afterwards. But before I begin, I would first like to express my deepest sympathy and regret to the family and friends of Miss Patricia Maynard. Miss Maynard, affectionately known by her family and friends as Patty, was a member of my staff. I believe that by now, most of you are aware that she was the victim of a tragic accident three days ago. Miss Maynard worked on my staff for almost two years, and I can tell you without reservation that she was a highly professional, yet very personable young lady. She enjoyed her work immensely and had a real zest for life. She always wore a smile and gave everything her very best. Her death is a profound loss to her family, friends, colleagues, and all those whose lives she touched. For me, she is and always will be deeply missed. My heart and my condolences go out to her family, relatives, and the friends and colleagues she left behind. And if you will permit me to add one more thing, I would like to say that no matter how tragic her death seems, those of us who knew Patty, knows she is with God."

Turning to his prepared statement, Ambassador Le Muir declared, "It appears that today I am twice the bearer of somber news, for it is with deep regret that I must also inform you that the Canadian government has not found it possible to come to terms with status quo demands on many of the key issues on the agenda for this conference. In particular, Canada cannot and indeed will not accept or adopt any policy on fossil fuel pollution established by proponents of the rapid reduction approach. The Canadian government believes that such an approach is not in Canada's best interest, as it would cause grave damage to our economy and threaten the livelihood of hundreds of thousands of Canadians through the loss of jobs. We believe and contend that a more subtle and incremental approach should be adopted. We had hoped that the supporters of the rapid reduction approach had come to this conference ready to strike a compromise. Instead, their unwillingness to alter their position in the slightest has resulted in a deadlock— one which my government feels cannot be breached at this time. Accordingly, the Canadian government believes it necessary to withdraw from these discussions until such time as those unwilling to compromise signal their readiness to negotiate in earnest. Ladies and gentlemen, this concludes my statement. Thank you."

Within minutes of Ambassador Le Muir's departure, the American delegate, Ambassador Robert Hollingsworth, emerged. He too was accompanied by one of his aides, Amanda Costanti. Ambassador Hollingsworth made his way to the microphone and also delivered a prepared statement, not very different from the one delivered by the Canadian Ambassador, except he was more specific in identifying the point of contention for U.S. rejection of the rapid reduction approach.

"A major sticking point for the U.S. in the proposed policy on greenhouse gas emission," said Ambassador Hollingsworth "is the failure of the proponents of the rapid reduction approach to factor-in the net effect of reforestation efforts into their analysis and projections. Without consideration and inclusion of this important data, the U.S. can only view the figures supporting current projections with utmost skepticism."

Chapter Twenty-Four

With the exception of the order of the walk-out, Kristie Bremmer had been right. The American Ambassador was closely followed by the Australian Ambassador. And despite Australia's precarious situation of having a severely depleted area of ozone hovering above its land mass, Ambassador Joseph Dougan maintained his conviction by not compromising on his country's rejection of the rapid reduction approach to fossil fuel pollution. This part of his argument seemed to mirror those presented by Canada and the United States. And like the two ambassadors who preceded him, his statement was short and concise. Where Japan was concerned, Kristie Bremmer was right again. The Japanese Ambassador had somehow managed to break rank and yield to the mounting ecological problems his country was experiencing.

While the Canadian delegate was speaking, François had managed to make his way to the side of the assembly area nearest the Trade Center. He knew the time had come for him to make his move. As soon as the Australian Ambassador finished his statement and he was certain that the Japanese Ambassador was not going to appear, he began shouting toward the press. However, the media mob had by now begun to focus its attention on the protest assembly area, where many demonstrators were growing angrier and more agitated by the minute.

François knew he had to make his way back to the stage and the microphones and it had to be done quickly. Just as he began to push his way through the crowd, some of the protestors began shouting at the three departing delegates. "You're a fuckin' bunch of sell-outs! How could we have expected you to do what's right when you're lining your pockets with blood money! You have no honor! You have no shame!"

François pushed his way through the masses. The demonstrators around him tried to help him clear a path. Suddenly, there was a loud explosion... then another, and another. He looked around and saw black smoke and orange flames rising from the perimeter of the security forces area nearest the Trade Center. He looked back toward the opposite side of the area and saw two Molotov cocktails rising from the crowd, sailing overhead like rounds fired from a piece of artillery. The two homemade bombs landed in the same area as the previous three. Several security personnel and demonstrators had gasoline splashed on their clothes and two security personnel and a demonstrator were set on fire.

François couldn't believe his eyes. Anticipating retaliation from the security forces, demonstrators nearest the perimeter area started running in the opposite direction, but security personnel reacted quickly. Backed up by armored vehicles, water cannons, and personnel wearing full riot gear, hundreds of police and paramilitary personnel appeared out of nowhere and fired volleys of tear gas into the middle of the demonstrators. But some demonstrators picked up the canisters and hurled them back in the direction from which they had come.

Two water cannons, one on the Trade Center side of the assembly area and another on the opposite side, began sweeping the area with powerful jets. Some demonstrators were knocked down and trampled by others. The situation worsened when security forces opened fire with rubber bullets and a new type of projectile that immobilized its target. Several demonstrators were knocked down by rubber bullets and the new rounds. Some were rendered unconscious. Security personnel soon began to fire indiscriminately. Screams and cries rose from the square as people ducked, ran for cover, or tried to pull a wounded friend or fellow demonstrator to safety.

Despite the chaos, Jonathan and Dieter found their way to François, who was tucked up behind several large backpacks for cover.

"You alright?" asked Dieter. "What the hell happened?"

"I don't know!" said François, "but I've gotta stop it. I have to get to the public address system."

"Are you crazy?" said Dieter.

"It's the only way to stop this!" François replied. "I'm gonna need your help though," he added. "I need a distraction."

"You've got it!" said Jonathan. "We'll draw their fire. You just get there!" he added. "Dieter, you go left and I'll go right!"

The two men dashed off in opposite directions and were singled out almost immediately by the tall, authoritative-looking, American-Asian man. A moment later, they were set upon by a hail of rubber bullets, but they were prepared. They had both taken abandoned backpacks with them and were using them as shields.

As soon as security personnel's attention was focused on Dieter and Jonathan, François made his move. He grabbed an abandoned backpack to protect the vital areas of his body and zigzagged as he ran toward the stage. He was less than seventy-five feet from the stage when he was hit in his left shoulder. It felt as if he had been struck with a club. The blow pushed his upper body forward and he began to fall. As he fell, time seemed to slow. He was struck again by the same sensation in the upper part of his left leg. A split second later, he felt warm liquid running down his back, like wax from a burning candle. Then he felt a sharp ache in his thigh. Instinctively, he grabbed the area where the pain was radiating from only to feel a warm, sticky wetness. He withdrew his hand and looked down at it. It was covered with blood. Someone had turned on him with live ammunition.

His left leg buckled and he went down, face-first, but he was in sufficient control to cushion his fall with the backpack. Time continued to slow. After falling, he had lain there for only a few minutes, but it had seemed like hours. Blood was spurting from the wound in his thigh. The bullet had hit the artery.

Having seen François fall, Jonathan and Dieter changed directions and ran toward him. Less than twenty feet away from him, Dieter was struck in the back twice and once in the leg; he began what felt like an exaggerated, slow fall. As he went down, a fourth bullet struck him below his right ear. He was dead before he hit the ground.

The indiscriminate shooting didn't stop. Thousands of people were still in the area, scurrying in every direction, seeking safety. As they moved about frantically, security personnel opened fire on them and they fell by the dozen. Jonathan didn't see what had happened to Dieter. He had his eyes fixed on the spot where François lay.

Only feet away from where François lay, he was hit in the ankle by a bullet that ricocheted off the pavement, but he ignored the pain and kept moving. A few more steps and a bullet struck him in his upper left arm, but again his determination kept him on his feet. When he reached François his legs gave out. He was now near his friend who was semi-conscious and lying in a pool of blood. Jonathan turned on his side and dragged himself over to François. He gathered his friend's body between his legs and applied pressure to the wound on his leg with the palm of his hand. François was losing conscious. His head flopped to one side, as if it were attached to a rag doll.

Weakened and barely conscious, François muttered, "Get out of here while you still have a chance. Go now! You have to tell the world what happened here."

"I won't leave you!" Jonathan replied.

"It's no use! I'm dying! Save yourself!"

François was fading rapidly. Images and thoughts of Caroline and Nicolas swirled in his head and slipped away. He couldn't feel any of the pain he had felt earlier.

Jonathan let out a cry for help, but it went unnoticed. By now the scampering of frantic protestors was dying down and the large crowd had thinned out. It didn't take long for the tall American-Asian-looking man to spot them.

"There!" he shouted, pointing. "Over there!"

The marksman nearest him swung the barrel of his Heckler and Koch sniper rifle in the direction of François and Jonathan, but was unable to fire because people were still passing intermittently in front of his targets.

The tall American-Asian man grew impatient with the marksman's hesitation. "What are you waiting for, you fool?" he shouted. "Shoot! Damn you! Shoot now!"

At the first clear line of sight, the marksman squeezed the trigger. His bullet struck François in the back of the head near the base of his skull and his head exploded right before Jonathan's eyes. He then trained his weapon on Jonathan and fired, leaving the two men in a heap.

The American-Asian man and several security personnel rushed down from the scaffolding to where the two men lay. When they reached the two bodies, the tall man squatted over François, opened his blood-soaked shirt and removed the money belt from around his waist. Afterwards, he instructed the security men with him to separate the three men's bodies and place them in different locations around the protest area so that the shootings would look like random kills.

PART II

Chapter Twenty-Five

Croisic, France
The Atlantic Coast
Present Day

Thousands of people turned up in the small fishing village of Croisic to pay their respect and say farewell to François Dupré. The village's tiny church was only large enough to accommodate his family and close friends. Nevertheless, thousands of mournful visitors spilled into the center of the village and lined its narrow cobblestone streets. Caroline's grandparents, Arthur and Lucy Gordon, were there too. They had flown in from Virginia and her father, Henri, had come up from Paris. The service was short and the eulogy somber. François' parents, Nicolas-Émile and Adèle Dupré, had declared the day a homecoming for their son.

In the early afternoon, two days after the service, Caroline, Nicolas, and François' parents collected the urn containing François' ashes and returned to the village. They were met there by the village priest, Henri Gagnon, and the Gordons. Everyone boarded Nicolas-Émile Dupré's fishing boat, *La Provenance*, and sailed to a place about five miles off the coast of Croisic where Nicolas-Émile and Adèle Dupré, Caroline, and Nicolas took turns scattering the ashes on the sea. When they returned to the village, Caroline told Nicolas-Émile and Adèle that she and Nicolas would spend a few more days with them in Croisic before going to Paris to visit her father.

The next day, Caroline dropped her father at the train station and saw her grandparents off at the airport. She promised Arthur and Lucy Gordon that she would visit them as soon as she was stronger. Three days later she and Nicolas left Croisic for Paris. Already, her grief was being displaced by steely determination—the desire to find out what really happened in Kuala Lumpur was lodged deeply in her mind.

Chapter Twenty-Six

Paris, France

Caroline and Nicolas arrived at her father's apartment in Neuilly on Saturday, just before noon. The building where Henri Gagnon's apartment was located, and where she had grown up, was an example of stunning seventeenth century architecture. Henri Gagnon's apartment occupied the entire fifth floor of the exclusive five-story building. It had five spacious bedrooms, each with its own small balcony, a large dining room, a spacious living room, a roomy study, and a generous family room.

When they arrived, her father and his housekeeper and cook, Muriel, greeted them with sympathy in their eyes. They exchanged hugs and kisses and Muriel led Caroline to her old bedroom and put Nicolas in the spare room next to her.

For the first few days, Caroline kept her mind occupied by taking Nicolas around the city, going on walks and seeing things they had not seen during previous visits. The weather in Paris was warm, and they took advantage of it. They took boat trips on the Seine and visited the Louvre, the Orsay, and l'Orangerie. They also visited a few of Nicolas' favorites—the Eiffel Tower and Notre Dame. They browsed scores of shops, including the first of the famous Shakespeare and Company bookstores on the Left Bank. For the first time, she spoke only French to him.

On their second day in Paris, they spent the entire afternoon in the Jardin des Tuileries, and on their last day out together they made a special visit to Lycée Henri IV. She wanted to show Nicolas where she and his father had met. After visiting Lycée Henri IV, they spent the rest of the day walking along the Champs-Elysées and alongside the Seine, stopping from time to time to watch the street artists make sketches and paintings of tourists. The next day—just two days before they were to depart for New York—her father took Nicolas out for the day. He said that he wanted Nicolas to experience Montmartre, a favorite place of his own, to see where many of France's best artists had lived and worked.

With the day to herself, Caroline decided to go to the place she and François loved most, the Latin Quarter. Reminiscing about their many visits, she recalled how he complained each time that St. Michel and St. Germain-des-Près, the Left Bank's main boulevards, were being taken over by fast food establishments and cheap tourist shops. She also recalled how happy he was when they were roaming the narrow cobblestone streets, which were home to scores of ethnic shops and *avant garde* theaters.

François had once told her that the presence of France's first university, the Sorbonne, was befitting for the most cosmopolitan place in the country. But his favorite among all the places they visited was the Jardin du Luxembourg. He believed the gardens were the best place to think, converse, debate important issues, admire the statues, or just relax around the pond. He once described Jardin du Luxembourg as one of only a handful of truly unspoiled places in Paris. On sunny days, elderly men could still be seen meeting under the chestnut trees to play chess or a friendly game of *pétanque*. For Caroline, Jardin du Luxembourg was a treasure trove of memories.

She finished her day with coffee and cognac at one of her and François' favorite places, a small café on Rue Racine. Afterwards, she took the Metro from Cluny la Sorbonne to

Concorde and walked the rest of the way to her father's apartment. Despite the warm days, the evenings were still mild and the gentle breeze that stirred felt good on her face. Even in the midst of her sorrow, she could feel the warm wind. It rejuvenated her, even if only temporarily.

When she arrived at the apartment, Nicolas and her father had not yet returned. In an effort to occupy her mind, she retreated to the family room and leafed through magazines. With no reprieve from a cavalcade of unsettling thoughts, she turned on the television and flipped through the channels, but it was useless. Her mind was flooding with thoughts of François. Images of him and the two of them together raced through her head. She had not had time to think properly during the past few days. It had been so hectic. But what tormented her most was the fact that she had not spoken to him before he died. She knew that not seeing or talking to him would make finding closure difficult. But she was strong-willed and wouldn't let herself wallow in misery. She knew she had to do something. She had to stay busy, occupy her mind—allow time and the pain to pass. She had to pull herself together and return to her job at Human Rights Monitor (HRM).

Her work as Vice-chair of the Children's Rights Division of HRM had always meant a lot to her. It brought satisfaction and that was exactly what she needed right now. She had worked at HRM since finishing graduate studies at Columbia University. She concluded that immersing herself in work might just take her mind off her grief.

Chapter Twenty-Seven

When Caroline noticed the time it was nearly 6:00 p.m. Before long Nicolas and her father would be returning from their outing. She could spend no more time pondering the idea of returning to work. Without hesitation, she moved over to the video-phone and put through a call to HRM.

"Roger Talbot. Children's Rights Division," she said when prompted by the computerized phone directory.

Soon afterwards, the image of a young man appeared on her screen. He was sporting a plume of dreadlocks, bunched awkwardly on top of his head. His red hair and the blue and grey plaid flannel shirt he wore summed up his views about conformity and the war waged by high-minded cultural snobs against what they considered an invasion of inferior cultural markers in American society.

"Let me guess, this wouldn't be Caroline, would it?" Roger Talbot said, smiling. "How are you? Are you holding up OK? I'm sorry about what happened to your husband. He was a highly respected…"

Before Roger Talbot could finish she interrupted. "Yes," she said. "I'm fine and thanks for asking. I'm managing," she said, producing a faint smile.

"I'm sorry," he returned. "I just thought you might need some more time to yourself before phoning the office."

"Please, Roger," she said. "I appreciate your sympathy, but don't be so apologetic. I know you mean well, but I don't know if I can handle any more sympathetic outpourings. It's making me depressed. I need to do something to change that."

"Yeah… sure," he spluttered. "Does this mean you're coming back to work?"

"Yes, it does!" she said. "Let's see… today is Thursday, the twentieth, and Nicolas will be returning to school in four days. I want to be back in the office when he does."

"OK," the young man said, confused. "Well… I guess we'll see you on Monday then," he added, spluttering once more.

"Yes, you will. Oh, and Roger!" Caroline said, remembering something else important. "Would you pass something on to Gabriel Hansen?"

"Yeah… Sure. What's the message?"

"Tell Gabriel that when I return, I have no desire to be on the receiving end of a rash of sympathy speeches. I'd appreciate it if he sensitized the rest of the division to that. I don't want to be treated like I'm made of glass. Can you do that for me?"

"Sure thing," the young man said, still puzzled.

"Nicolas and I have to get on with our lives," she added. "I know that's what his father would've wanted and it's what I want, too. I'll see you on Monday."

"I'll pass on the message. See you soon, and take care of yourself," he added and ended the call.

After she hung up, she wondered if she ought to tell her father about her decision. She knew that she would have to at some point, because he would question her about what she intended to do when she returned to New York. She wondered how he would react.

Caroline was in the kitchen preparing dinner when her father and Nicolas returned. Earlier that morning she had managed to convince him to give Muriel a few days off.

Nicolas was very happy; when he entered the kitchen, she gave him a huge hug. "Do I need to ask if you had a good day?" she said.

"No need," said Nicolas. "It was incredible," he added,

beaming. "At first I thought I would be bored to death, but when I saw the works of Salvador Dali in the Espace Montmartre and we went to the Museé de Montmartre and the Place du Tertre, it was fantastic! I had never thought of art as the past, or as part of history."

Caroline grinned. "Now why do I get the impression that you like spending time with Papa Henri?"

"I do," the boy said grinning. "He knows how to make even boring things interesting."

"I'll bet he does," she said. "But it looks like you've done enough interesting stuff for one day. So run along and get cleaned up for dinner. It'll be ready in ten minutes."

Caroline smiled inwardly. She was pleased that he was beginning to adjust. But she knew that there was every chance that he would be stricken by latent grief.

A few minutes later, she shouted, "Come on, you two! Dinner's ready!"

Within seconds, Henri and Nicolas appeared in the kitchen doorway. Henri took a long whiff of the wafting aromas and said, "That smells good! Muriel had better be careful or she might find herself out of a job!"

"No, she won't," Caroline said smiling. "Will you please stop patronizing me and open the wine!"

"Of course, *madame*," he replied, nodding and clicking his heels together.

"Only a quarter of a glass for you, young man," Henri said, as he poured sparkling water to half-fill the wine glass he had placed in front of Nicolas.

"So… Did your young explorer tell you what a great day we had? If my eyes haven't deceived me, I'd say he genuinely had fun and may have even learned a thing or two!"

"Yes, he did," Caroline said. "And thanks for all you've done."

"Are you kidding?" said Henri. "I think I had just as much fun, if not more, than he did! And how was your day?" he asked.

"Good!" said Caroline. "I went to Jardin du Luxembourg and spent most of the day there."

Henri quickly sensed that she had had a day of reflection, so he didn't pursue the subject any further.

"I've been thinking…" said Henri. "Why don't you guys stay another week? It'll do you both a world of good!"

"Yeah, Mama… Why don't we?" Nicolas chimed excitedly.

"I'd love to, Papa!" said Caroline, "but Nicolas needs to return to school and I want to get back to work as soon as possible. I don't want too much idle time on my hands," she added.

"Of course… How inconsiderate and selfish of me."

"It wasn't inconsiderate or selfish, Papa. It's just that I think that Nicolas and I both need to resume some sense of normalcy in our lives as soon as possible. Besides, young man," she said, turning to Nicolas, "you've got lots of school work to catch up on, which means there'll be no time for cycling, roller blades or soccer in the weeks ahead!"

"OK," Nicolas said, disappointedly.

"So, when are you leaving?" Henri asked.

"Day after tomorrow… Saturday… Remember? We said we'd stay one week only."

"Yes, I know," said Henri. "But I'm getting used to having the two of you around and it feels good."

Caroline sensed the onset of a charm offensive and changed the subject. "By the way, Papa, are you still seeing Madame Dumont?"

"If you mean, are we still friends, the answer is yes. She's a very nice lady."

No sooner had he replied than she weighed in with a barrage of questions. "How long have you known her? Twenty-three, twenty-four years? That's a long time!" she said teasingly. "And you're sure the two of you are just friends?"

"Hey! What do you mean by this line of questioning? There's

no time limit on friendship. You should know that!" he retorted, half smiling.

"OK! I'm sorry," she said then added, "We're a bit prickly, aren't we?"

She had caught him off-guard and he felt the need to clarify his relationship with Yvonne Dumont. "The kinds of feelings you are implying, young lady, have never existed between us," he said.

Satisfied that she had solved the mystery of his long relationship with the widow Dumont, they made their way through dinner amid conversation that was at times lively and at others routine. After dinner, Henri ordered the classic film *Cage aux Folles.* They watched the film together and went straight to bed.

Two days later, with Nicolas wearing the new wrist watch-communicator his grandfather had bought him, they left Charles de Gaulle Airport for New York to open a new chapter in their lives.

Chapter Twenty-Eight

Alexandria, Virginia

Amanda Costanti's red convertible Toyota Celica pulled away from the curb in front of the Royal Street North townhouse in Alexandria's Old Town at exactly 9:15 a.m. As it pulled away, Amanda and her friend, Beth O'Connell, waved frantically to her parents, who were standing in the doorway. A few minutes later, Amanda turned the car west onto King Street. After heading west for a short distance, she turned north on Route 1 and headed toward Interstates 395 and 295 North, before eventually joining the Beltway for Interstate 95 North to New York. It was an unusually warm day along the Mid-Atlantic coast and she and Beth had taken advantage of the beautiful weather by putting the convertible's roof down.

Amanda had driven down to Alexandria from New York the previous weekend to visit her parents before flying to Vancouver for Patty Maynard's funeral. Patty's funeral had brought her and her university classmates together again, but much sooner than they had planned. The day before she left New York, her boss, Ambassador Robert Hollingsworth, had been summoned to Washington, D.C., for meetings and consultations. But before leaving, he had suggested rather strongly that she take advantage of the slow pace at work and take some time off after the funeral. She had taken his advice and put in for leave for the entire week.

When Amanda met Beth and Kristie in Vancouver for Patty's funeral, Kristie had invited her and Beth to spend Easter in the Seattle area with her, her boyfriend, and her parents on Bainbridge Island. But Amanda turned down the offer, and so did Beth who had decided to tag along with Amanda and spend a few days at Amanda's parents' house before they headed for New York. Patty's death had opened Amanda's eyes to something she had forgotten—the importance of spending time with family. Kristie's invitation, however, had reminded her that she had important matters at work that needed to be taken care of before the Easter weekend.

The two women had been traveling north on Interstate 95 for just under four hours when they reached the outskirts of Philadelphia. After negotiating the relatively light mid-day Saturday traffic on the Philadelphia bypass, Amanda turned the car's radio off and found a classic Beatles' album on her plug-in iPod. Drive-time tunes soon flowed from all the Toyota's speakers, and the two women settled back in their seats for the rest of the journey.

Less than an hour after passing through Philadelphia, they reached the New Jersey Turnpike. Amanda took the ticket at the Turnpike entrance, settled back once more into the Celica's leather seats and began thinking of Patty and the horrible way she had died. She and Beth had spoken very little to each other since leaving Alexandria. It was a solemn time for both of them and they both found it difficult to believe that Patty was dead. No matter how hard Amanda tried, she couldn't erase the image of Patty or the expression on her face that night in Kuala Lumpur. She could still see her, arms outstretched, struggling to reach Beth and Kristie on the other side of the road. She tried, to no avail, to push the thoughts and images out of her head. *If only I hadn't drunk so much wine. Maybe I could have saved her.*

Surprisingly, for the time of day, not many cars were on the Turnpike. Mainly commercial traffic occupied the road in both directions. A stream of large trucks was dominating northbound traffic. As the Celica sped along the wide, multi-lane road toward New York, Amanda's thoughts slipped further into the past. After a few minutes, her mind was awash with memories and images of the days and years past. The song, *A Hard Day's Night*, one of Patty's favorites, was blasting from the speakers. As she drifted back from her emotional journey into the past, she noticed Beth staring at her. The look on her face said, *I know what you've been thinking about.*

But before Beth could verbalize her thoughts, a loud snap came from under the front end of the car—a sharp, clear, and peculiarly harsh sound. Amanda sprang up from her semi-reclined position. Something was wrong. Her eyes flashed across the Celica's gauges, but everything looked normal.

"Did you hear that?" she asked Beth.

"What was it?" Beth said, looking frightened.

"I don't know. It sounded like…"

But before Amanda could finish, it became clear what had happened. She could feel none of the resistance from the steering wheel normally produced by the wheels on the road. Panic struck. Her heart began to race. Suddenly, the car began to veer left from the center lane they were in toward the concrete barrier that separated southbound and northbound Turnpike traffic. It felt as if the front wheels were hydroplaning, but the road was dry.

Hurtling along at over seventy miles per hour, Amanda cursed and began fighting the wheel, trying to turn the car away from the barrier. It was useless. Her efforts to change the car's direction of travel had no effect.

"What's happening?" Beth shouted.

Neither of them fully understood the horrifying events that had begun to unfold. But what was clear from the lack of control when trying to steer the car to the right was that one of the tie rods had snapped.

As the car drifted toward the center barrier, Amanda,

running on adrenalin and hope, spun the wheel frantically. First to the right out of desperation, then to the left, but there was no response. The left wheel, now detached from the steering column, had assumed a will of its own and was veering the car toward the concrete barrier. Time seemed to slow, temporally hyper-extended. Even their frantic screams came out distorted —stretched and half-muted. For a while, it was like a film being played in slow motion. But then, as if to mark the end of the slow motion segment, the car's left fender slammed into the barrier and its wheels began to climb the six feet high, steel-reinforced, concrete barrier. It traveled with its left side half way up the barrier for nearly fifty yards before slamming down onto the road then skidding sideways to the right across two lanes. Their screams grew louder as the car changed direction and careened across traffic toward the shoulder of the road.

Amanda resumed her futile fight with the wheel. After a beat, they heard another loud snapping noise. The second tie rod had parted. Overcome with fear, Amanda slammed her foot on the brake pedal and looked to the right, only to see a large truck, an eighteen wheeler, with lights flashing, bearing down on them. She braked harder, but the car slipped into a pirouette. With the roof down the truck driver could see their panic-stricken faces. He slammed on his brakes and gave a sharp blast on the horn. He tried to swerve to the shoulder of the road to avoid them, but the car spun directly into his path. He struck the red convertible broadside and pushed it for nearly thirty yards before the truck's front wheels climbed on top of it. The full weight of the truck soon came down and flattened the car. Amanda and Beth died instantly.

Of the four friends reunited in Kuala Lumpur, only Kristie Bremmer was still alive.

Chapter Twenty-Nine

New York

Caroline and Nicolas' flight touched down at JFK International Airport at 2:30 p.m., seven hours and fifteen minutes after leaving Paris. Because of the time zone difference, they still had much of the afternoon ahead of them. They cleared immigration, collected their luggage and took a taxi from the airport to Brooklyn Heights. They already missed Henri but were pleased to be returning to everyday surroundings and daily routines.

On the way home from the airport, Caroline was overcome by a cold and empty feeling—a feeling brought on by the realization that François wouldn't be at the house to greet them when they arrived. In fact, he wouldn't be there for any future homecoming.

They arrived home just before 4:30 p.m., took their luggage to their rooms and went downstairs to the kitchen. After drinks, Caroline encouraged Nicolas to get some rest.

"Are you tired?" she asked him. "If you are, you can take a nap and I'll wake you in a couple of hours." Sensing his hesitation, she added, "It's OK, you can sleep if you'd like."

"Are you sure?" Nicolas asked.

"Of course I am. I've got lots of mail to sort through and then I'll need to go online to pay some bills. I've also got a few calls to make. You run along and I'll sound reveille in a couple of hours."

Nicolas gave her a big hug. She kissed him on the forehead and he went up to his room while she went to the front door to collect the mail from the drop basket. After nearly two weeks, the basket was full of the usual stuff—bills, statements, and junk mail. There were also lots of sympathy cards. Even though she had not asked her to do so, the next door neighbor, Mrs. Preston, had been kind enough to collect the daily and weekend newspapers from outside the front door to avoid the appearance of an empty house. Although Brooklyn Heights was a safe neighborhood, vandals and would-be burglars sometimes cased the area, looking for a target of opportunity.

Caroline took the mail from the basket, clutched the pile with one hand, picked up her mug of peppermint tea with the other and walked through the house toward the room François had converted into an office. She knew she needed to get all the domestic, financial and administrative matters sorted out before she returned to work. There would be quite a lot to do to catch up at work, since her senior researcher and assistant was away on maternity leave. Piling the mail on the desk, she slid into the chair and began sorting through it, placing bills in one stack, personal mail for each of them in one, and miscellaneous stuff in another.

As she worked her way toward the bottom of the pile, she picked up a medium size brown envelope addressed to François. The return address was from the New York office of TEARS. The postage cancellation date indicated that it had been mailed the day before he left for Kuala Lumpur. The envelope didn't have any urgent delivery notices on it, and because he sometimes received mail from the office at home, she thought nothing of it. More important, she was feeling depressed and thought it better not to open any of his personal mail just yet, as seeing and reading messages or letters intended for him would conjure up more unsettling feelings. She looked at the envelope for a moment, turning it over from front to back then placing it in the stack with the rest of his mail and heaped it all in a basket on the work table near his desk marked *Incoming Stuff.*

Caroline continued working on the mail, opening and reading several dozen sympathy cards before becoming weary of the sadness they caused. In an attempt to change her mood, she switched to the bills and statements. More than two hours had passed and it was time to wake Nicolas. But after surveying the contents of the refrigerator, she decided that a bit of shopping was needed. On most days, she would have done the shopping from the local supermarket online. But today, she felt the need to keep her mind occupied and to avoid being on her own too much. She knew that with time, her feelings would change. But for now, she needed it to be that way. She decided to leave the online bill transactions until later that evening and went to wake up Nicolas to go to the supermarket with her.

When they returned later with the shopping and everything had been put away, they sat in the kitchen and outlined what needed to be done, to include a plan of action for the rest of the weekend. She promptly decided that after dinner he would begin doing catch-up work on the lessons he had missed. She would return to the bills and then spruce up the house. Depending on his progress, he could stay up late and they would watch a film together.

"If all goes well with today's plan, tomorrow morning after breakfast we can spend the morning riding in Central Park."

"Alright!" Nicolas whooped.

A few hours later she reminded him again of the progress he needed to make on school work. "Young man, you still have more school work to do tomorrow afternoon," she said. "I've gone over what you've done so far and you've done better than I expected on the four make-up assignments. But you still have a science test to prepare for by Tuesday and several chapters of reading. We're only going to the park tomorrow because I think you can finish what needs to be done to get you ready for school on Monday."

"OK," he sighed. "None of this is negotiable, is it?"

"No! It's final!" said Caroline.

"Alright… You win!" he submitted.

Chapter Thirty

On Monday morning, Caroline dropped Nicolas off at the Brooklyn Heights Montessori School and took the subway to Manhattan. She arrived at HRM's thirty-fourth floor 5th Avenue office just after 8:30. As she entered the reception area outside her division's office, the receptionist got up from behind her desk and rushed towards her smiling. "Welcome back! We missed you an awful lot," the woman said.

"Thank you," Caroline replied. "It's good to be back."

"Oh!" the receptionist added as Caroline walked toward her office. "There's a folder on your desk with the most recent reports on children's rights and an agenda for the director's meeting at ten o'clock this morning."

"Thank you," she replied.

Caroline entered her office and immediately went over to the kettle to boil water for a cup of tea. On her way past her desk, she took the folder containing the children's rights reports and the current quarter's agenda. She glanced over the agenda first and then began reading the first report. It was on the forced recruitment of child soldiers by rebels in several African countries. Although the wars had ended some years earlier in these countries, rebel fighters had managed to sustain low-level insurgencies by going to ground after tenuous peace deals were struck between the various factions within their movements and the governments'. During the past year and a half, however, members of some of the rebel factions had re-emerged; when they did, they began instructing their commanders to abduct or recruit teenage boys into their ranks to build a force large enough to destabilize the governments that were in power.

Just as she completed the summary page, the kettle began to boil. She made a cup of peppermint tea, took a seat behind her desk, and continued reading the thirty-five page report. The note attached to the report said it had been well received by the United Nations and the governments of several Western countries, including the U.S., France, Germany, and Great Britain. Having been brought onboard by HRM two years earlier to complete a project in New Guinea, the author, Stephen Morris, was well known among non-governmental organizations and widely respected. After reading nearly two-thirds of the report, she could see that he had once again done a solid job and she wanted to arrange a meeting with him before his one-year research fellowship at HRM ended.

She knew he had been a project manager for a large non-governmental organization in Kenya and his skills as a program manager were impeccable. Besides, before she left, there had been rumors circulating that Karen Lacy, her senior researcher and assistant, might not return to work after her baby was born. She thought that Stephen Morris would make a strong addition to her team. More importantly, having also spent an extensive amount of time in the field as a researcher, he understood the nuances of the business and could help the division focus its efforts to get better results from its shrinking budget. Although she couldn't move ahead of management and begin talking to him about a permanent job, she could meet with him and assess his suitability ahead of time.

After reading the report on child soldiers she looked up at the clock then glanced again at the agenda for the ten o'clock meeting. It was nearly nine. Returning to the agenda, she noticed that manpower for her division was an item. There was also the matter of a budget review, which was no doubt linked to the issue of manpower in each of the divisions. Over the past few years, HRM had been experiencing a reduction in financial resources, which meant that projects had to be prioritized more stringently and more staff positions might have to be shifted from full-time to part-time employment.

Being the quick study and problem solver she was, she realized that Stephen Morris could be part of the solution for both problems in her division. Although she would not mention him by name in the meeting, she thought she should at least allude to the need for someone with his skills and background. She decided she would ask the Chair of the Children's Rights Division, Gabriel Hansen, to let her handle the matter.

The second report she turned to was on child labor in Mexico. Mexico's economy had taken off since it joined the North American Free Trade Agreement (NAFTA) in the early 1990s. Consequently, many opportunistic businesses began searching for the cheapest labor they could find to satisfy production needs, while significantly increasing their profits. Because statistical indicators now identified Mexico as a developing country, many politicians and watchdog organizations had become complacent about monitoring the exploitation of child labor in Mexico. But the report she was reading would bring the issue back to the fore. It, too, was well researched and well written. The quality of both reports and the praise they received from the United Nations and some politicians in the U.S. had affirmed the appropriateness of her intuitive decision to take on the two researchers.

By the time Caroline finished skimming the report on Mexico, it was nearly 9:50 a.m. She topped up her cup of tea and headed off for the ten o'clock meeting with Gabriel Hansen and the other senior staff members of the Children's Rights Division. When she reached the conference room, several of the division staffers were already seated. Each of them got up, gave her a hug, and said, "Welcome back."

It was at once evident that the cautionary advice she had given Roger Talbot to pass on to them the week before had been received and acted upon. Not a single one of them asked her how she was doing or poured out sympathetic statements to her. She felt good about that and her reply to each of them was simple: "It feels good to be back." When they were all seated at the conference table, Gabriel Hansen walked in and turned to her. "Caroline, it's good to have you back with us again. Your absence has been seriously felt. If there is anything I or any of us can do, please don't hesitate to call on us."

On cue, she repeated the words she had said to the other division heads earlier in the morning but added, "It's good to be back at work doing something important. Despite our sometimes unfortunate circumstances, the world doesn't stop when we stop."

"Well put!" Hansen replied. "Now!" he announced. "Let's get on with the meeting and the agenda items. As you can see, high atop the agenda for the divisions is the issue of budget resources."

When the meeting ended, she caught up with Gabriel Hansen outside his office. "Gabriel, can I have a few minutes of your time?" she asked.

"Sure," he said. "What's on your mind? I thought you might want to talk after the meeting," he added. I could see the wheels turning inside your head as you spoke. I believe I already know what you'd like to talk to me about, but I'll let you tell me anyway."

"Was I that obvious?" she asked.

"To me you were. I'm not sure if the others picked up on it. But what you shouldn't forget is that I've known you since you arrived and I suppose you and I are often on the same wavelength."

"Thank goodness for that!" she replied.

Caroline entered Hansen's spacious office and began pacing back and forth in front of his desk. Instead of sitting down, he stood half facing her and half looking out onto the green of east Central Park.

"OK! Shoot!" he exclaimed.

"After thinking about what the finance officer said this morning about the budget constraints we're faced with in the coming year, I believe I may have a solution."

"What? Are you planning to make a personal contribution?"

"Actually, I already have. I do every year," she retorted light-heartedly. "All kidding aside, this'll probably mean scaling back or completely cutting some of the research projects we have planned. But the way I see it, if things stay slow, we'll have to cut research expenditures by at least fifteen percent anyway."

"Your point being…?" he asked.

"I believe we can save ourselves two research positions, either permanent or fellowship-wise, by taking on Stephen Morris on a full-time basis. Look!" she said, before Hansen could interrupt. "We both know Karen is not likely to return to work for at least two or three years. It's no secret. How many times did you personally hear her say that she wanted to be at home with her child full-time until it's old enough to go to nursery school or kindergarten? Besides, I don't think it's fair for her to handcuff us this way until she makes the announcement officially. While we're waiting, we're missing an opportunity to bring on real talent to replace her."

"I get your point. But you know we just can't offer or even promise anyone the job until she has officially asked for a leave of absence, or tendered her resignation. I'm afraid this is the way it has to be."

Caroline continued. "You know Stephen Morris is an extremely good researcher and writer. He's worth at least three of our current staff researchers. Besides, he also has management skills, which means we could make him a project coordinator for several types of projects in his area of expertise! If we had Morris, we could reduce our budget straight off the bat by three research fellowship positions. Don't you agree?"

"I hear and understand what you are saying, Caroline, but we just can't bring him on board, at least not now. I also realize that we may lose him at the end of next month when his fellowship ends, if we don't act soon. But no matter how you slice it, we're going to have to wait!"

"Couldn't we extend his fellowship, or perhaps offer him a new project to keep him around?" she asked.

"I suppose," Gabriel replied grudgingly. "But just as you asked, I am going to leave this up to you to work out. Arrange it informally without causing all hell to break loose from the other staff and researchers. If you can manage that, I'll be more than glad to bless it. Was there anything else?"

"Nope!" she grinned as she strode toward the door. But before leaving his office, she spun on her heel, faced him and said sarcastically, "Gabriel, you know what I like about you?"

"What?" he asked.

"You really put up a darn good fight!"

"Go to work!" he shouted playfully.

As she walked back to her office, she could feel her old self returning again. She had found what she needed—a cause—something to focus on instead of François. The rest of the day went well for her.

Shortly after a second division and advisory committee meeting with a key member of the board of directors and Gabriel Hansen, she held a short meeting with the remainder of the division staff to pass on the minutes of the ten o'clock meeting. There were many questions and concerns about the impending reduction in the workforce. But she assured them that she and Gabriel would work together to make sure that the worst they would be hit with would be the shift of a few positions from full-time to part-time status. She promised them that if there was any way possible, they would avoid even that.

Chapter Thirty-One

Caroline arrived home earlier than usual, fearing that Nicolas might be upset and need her support. She was surprised and relieved to find him in his room, immersed in school work. Later at dinner, he told her that he had been anxious during the days leading up to his return to school. But now that he was back, it felt good. After sharing all the good things that had happened, he asked, "How was your day?"

Caroline smiled. Her son was mature beyond his years; sometimes she felt he was growing up too fast. She confessed that she, too, had been anxious about returning to work. "Do you know what I did today?" she asked.

"No," he said. "What did you do?"

"Well, my first day back at work and I think I may have saved at least three jobs."

"How did you do that?"

As briefly and simply as possible, she told him what she had suggested to Gabriel. Her smart son appeared to follow every word and argument.

"Just think, if it works, you'll be a hero!" he said, grinning.

"What do you mean, *if* it works?" she asked. "Of course it'll work!"

He looked at her and smiled. "Looks like we both had a great day. Didn't we?"

"You bet we did!" she replied.

They finished dinner and as they were getting up from the table, she told him, "I spoke to Grandpapa and Grandmama

Gordon before leaving work and they invited us down to Virginia Beach the weekend after Easter."

"What did you tell them?"

"I told them we'd be happy to come. Is that alright?"

"Yes!" he shouted. "I love her homemade pecan pie!"

"Is that all you can think about, food?" she asked teasingly.

"No! But thinking about food doesn't hurt! When are we going?"

"I figured we'll pack next Thursday evening and I'll leave work a bit early on Friday, pick you up from school and we'll drive straight down."

"That works for me!" he replied.

Chapter Thirty-Two

The next Friday afternoon, Caroline and Nicolas left New York for Virginia Beach. While there they visited Arthur and Lucy Gordon and several of her mother's relatives. They left for New York early Sunday evening. Despite the resumption of routine activities and visits with friends and family, the weeks following François' death had worn on her like a New York winter, cold and harsh, and she was still unable to escape the loneliness and sense of abandonment that frequently pervaded her mind. Nevertheless, she was determined to gain the upper hand in her struggle with what she believed was latent depression.

On several occasions when she spoke to her father, she was aware that she had shown signs of withdrawing and avoiding the issue. However, shortly after she and Nicolas returned from Virginia Beach, he called her for a private talk, during which he asked her in an empathetic and fatherly way to share her thoughts with him. It was the first time since François' death that she had opened up to him. She apologized for her behavior and explained that she couldn't understand what was happening to her.

"These last few weeks, I've been fighting to suppress overwhelming feelings of abandonment and anger," she explained. "I suppose I've had these feelings ever since he left me, but early on they seemed to come and go. But now I feel them nearly all the time. What's more unsettling is the battle that rages inside of me. I mean... I can't understand how I can love him so much and be so frustrated and angered by what his going away has done to me. Do you know how difficult it is not be able to share these feelings with anyone because they're so cruel and unconscionable? Papa, I feel so helpless. What can I do? These feelings won't go away!"

"But that's where you are wrong, *ma chérie!*" he had offered sympathetically. "This feeling *will* go away! But it will take time. Did you know that when your mother died, I too felt helpless and abandoned? I blamed her for leaving me because we had talked about and planned to spend the rest of our lives together. I felt she had broken our agreement and I could not bear the thought of living the rest of my life without her. But after wallowing in self-pity for months, perhaps years, do you know what I did? I told myself that the way your mother loved me, she would never in a million years have chosen to leave me. I realized that if she had known what was going to happen to her, she would have avoided it. She didn't want to leave me, you, or this world."

He paused briefly and continued. "Knowing and accepting that gave me the strength to go on with life. And like François, she left me with some very special things that only she could have given me, like the incredible feeling I get from having known her and shared special experiences with her. But most importantly, she left me something very, very special—a part of herself... you. I'm sure you have similar, and perhaps many more, things in which you can find joy that will sustain you. You know, each time I hear and see you, I am reminded of how fortunate I am to have met and known your mother. I am sure you have similar feelings about Nicolas. Do you not?"

She had pondered the question before answering, but her answer was yes. The conversation was in essence a turning point for her. After talking to her father, she knew she had to come to grips with the changes that had taken place in her life. The talk with him had brightened her mood and she was again grateful to him for his love and support.

On Monday, she returned to work with a stronger sense of

purpose. A few weeks later, she accomplished the goals she had set for herself at HRM, which included cutting nearly fifteen percent off projected operating expenditures for the first quarter of the year.

Her success at work and coming to terms with what her relationship with François meant helped to lift the heaviness of her grief. Still she thought of him often, especially when she found herself alone and it was quiet. But at least her thoughts no longer gave rise to anger or caused such a feeling of abandonment. Instead, they strengthened her determination to help others, because it was one of the qualities she had admired most about him.

Chapter Thirty-Three

Caroline's life at home and work had begun to take shape and direction. It was already late spring and even she was surprised at how quickly she had recovered from the loneliness that had pervaded her life only weeks earlier. Then one Friday afternoon, less than two weeks after the conversation with her father, she received an unusual call from TEARS' New York office. Because her co-workers were still discreetly concerned about her emotional well-being, the switchboard operator checked with her first to see if she was interested in taking the call. All communication between her and TEARS had ceased once her attorney and a member of TEARS' legal staff had taken care of the financial, administrative, and legal matters that remained after François' death, so she had no idea what the call could be about. But curiosity quickly got the better of her and she accepted it.

Straight away, a man with a youthful, but conservative and intelligent look about him appeared on her monitor. He wore a crisp white shirt and a burgundy and black striped tie. His hair, which was very dark, was cut short and neat and a pair of small, frameless, rectangular-lensed glasses adorned his long, thin face. He had the appearance of a young Harvard or Yale law school graduate.

"Good afternoon, Mrs. Dupré."

"Good afternoon," Caroline replied, puzzled.

"I know you are very busy. I appreciate you taking time from what must be a very full schedule to take my call, so I'll get straight to the point. My name is Antoni Miklus, and as you may or may not already know, I assumed the position of director of TEARS' New York office in mid-November. I have also been appointed acting director by the board of directors of TEARS International."

She was surveying the young man as he spoke and guessed his age to be no more than thirty-two or thirty-three. But because he spoke with such confidence and eloquence, she could see why he had been cast in the role. He was about to begin the next line of his presentation when she interrupted him.

"Mr. Miklus!" she interjected. "I don't want to appear rude, but I'm afraid I don't understand why you've contacted me. Is there something my lawyer overlooked while closing out my husband's legal affairs with the organization?"

"No, there isn't, but if you'll permit me to continue," he said courteously, "I'll explain. Prior to coming to the New York office, I was the director of TEARS' Seattle office. I knew and worked with your husband for a couple of years before that—first at Friends of the Earth then at Greenpeace International. Before the unfortunate incident in Kuala Lumpur, he proposed to the board of directors that I be appointed deputy director of the organization; however, this was not accomplished because of numerous other issues that came up after his death."

Antoni Miklus paused, cleared his throat then continued. "Realizing that I was about to be named deputy director, the board decided that I should become the acting director. But since my appointment as acting director, my powers of observation have shown that the support the organization enjoyed under your husband's leadership has been eroding quite steadily. The board seems to have failed to recognize the reason for this decline. But the majority of the area directors, myself included, realize that the causes TEARS fights for, in and of themselves, should not only guarantee a sustained level of support, they should increase and broaden that support, but this isn't happening. Mrs. Dupré, as you well know, it's unfortunate, but most people are quite fickle and tend to follow, support, and attach themselves not just to a *cause célèbre*, but to the charismatic or near charismatic leaders of those causes. Your husband was such a leader. It was his personality and manner that made people want to get involved. He made them want to do something about the environmental problems we're facing."

"Mr. Miklus!" she interjected once more. "I still don't understand what any of this has to do with me."

"I was coming to that," Antoni Miklus said. He paused briefly before continuing. "You see, Mrs. Dupré, what TEARS needs, or better yet, what those people who should be fighting to continue what your husband started need is something to ignite them—something or someone to help them believe that after the tragedy of a few months ago, things don't have to change. Myself and most, if not all, of the area directors, realize that the board of directors is just a group of men and women, few of whom really know anything about how to fight and win the struggle we are engaged in. But we on the ground know what's needed. We need someone who can step in and take over where your husband left off."

Feeling utterly astonished, Caroline responded. "Let me see if I'm reading you correctly… Are you asking me to assume leadership of TEARS?"

"Yes," he replied.

"You can't be serious! I mean… just because my husband did a great job at leading the organization doesn't mean I can do the same!"

"I can understand your shock and surprise, and why you should question such a proposal," the courteous young man replied. "But you're not being asked simply because your husband was a good leader. We're asking because he died fighting for a good cause. Your husband left a legacy, Mrs. Dupré—a legacy that tells us all that we should carry on hoping, even while striving against seemingly insurmountable odds. For so many, he personified that hope. And without him, many have lost hope. The tragedy in Kuala Lumpur touched many of us, but no one as deeply as it did you. Your picking up the torch to light the way for those who need direction would be natural. It would be as if your husband had handed it to you himself. So you see, this isn't about egos or status, Mrs. Dupré. It's about winning! We must win! And we *will* win! So please, before you reject this proposal out of hand, give it some serious thought."

For the first time during the conversation, Caroline felt her composure breaking down. "But I don't know the first thing about leading an organization like this! What could I do? What *would* I do?" she asked, feeling a bit overwhelmed.

"TEARS has offices in more than fifty countries. We, the directors, know the issues and what must be done, but not one of us has the appeal your husband possessed. It wouldn't be easy, but we could educate and prepare you. You would have the support and assistance of the entire organization."

"This is too sudden!" she said. "I need time to think."

"To be frank with you, Mrs. Dupré, none of us expected you to leap at the proposal. In fact, I would feel better if you took some time to carefully consider it. Again, let me say I appreciate your patience and willingness to entertain the offer. And I take it you'll be in touch sometime in the not too distant future?"

"Yes," she said. "You'll hear from me one way or the other."

"Good, then! And thank you again for your time and patience. I'll leave you to your work."

"Thank you," she replied then hung up.

After the call, she sat at her desk, stunned, for nearly a half hour before she realized that all the man had said about the fickle nature of human beings and the need for charismatic leadership was true. Still, she couldn't see herself at the head of such an organization, with its colossal responsibilities. Apart from anything else, she had a son to consider.

A few minutes later, her anxiety gave way to compassion and logic when she remembered something François had once told her. "If you believe the cause is great enough and important enough, you'll find the courage, energy, and desire to act." He had always told her that there was nothing special about him, other than the desire to do what was right. After thinking about the proposal, she realized that by accepting the offer and working to save and strengthen the organization, his death would not have been in vain.

Chapter Thirty-Four

When the work day ended at HRM, Caroline left her office and went straight home. It was just after 6:30 p.m. when she arrived and found Nicolas absorbed in an interactive video game. She had interrupted him; when he saw her, he rushed over to her and she gave him a hug. But before going to her room to change out of her work clothes, she told him she had something important she wanted to discuss with him.

She ordered Chinese food from a nearby take-away; when the food arrived, they sat down to dinner and she asked him how his day at school had gone. He told her he was enjoying school again and that the day before, his soccer coach had told him that after observing him practice, he was going to move him to the first string center forward position when the season opened. She congratulated him. Then he asked, "What about yours?"

"Well... mine was different," she replied.

"Different in what way?" he asked.

"Let me see... how should I put this? Today, I received a rather startling call from your father's organization."

"What did they want?"

"A lot!" she replied. "They want me to take over as director of the organization!"

"What?" he shouted.

"They want me to take on the job your father had. What do you think about the idea?"

"I don't know. I'm just a kid!"

"Yeah, I know. But you said you're the man around here now!"

"I am!"

"Then act like it!" she said jokingly.

"Well… what do you wanna do? Do you want the job?" he asked.

"I'm not sure. It's an important job, but I don't know if I can do it. Besides, it would mean I'd have to travel an awful lot."

"But didn't Papa say that after Kuala Lumpur he'd be able to spend more time at home? Anyway, there are more offices than when he started the organization."

"Yes, that's true, but you didn't answer my question."

"After what happened to Dad, I'd worry about you, but if doing it makes you happy then I'd be happy for you!"

"Do you really mean that?" she asked.

"Of course I do! Isn't that what Papa would have wanted?"

"I believe so! But I still need some more time to think about it. And I would still have to give HRM proper notification of my resignation," she replied.

"OK!" he said, matter-of-factly. "Then it's settled. You'll take the job! Next problem?" he commanded.

"I said I'd think about it," she retorted.

Reaching toward him with a smile on her face she demanded, "Give me a hug, you! You're such a man!"

With an impish smile, so like one of his father's, he said, "I know."

They finished dinner and watched television until bedtime. On Saturday, she did the shopping while he entertained two of his friends who came over to spend the night. During the next few days, she spent more and more time studying up on the issues TEARS was working to resolve. She tracked down United Nations, government, and independent studies on greenhouse gases and their effects on global warming, depletion of the earth's ozone layer, skin cancer, air and water pollution, deforestation, desertification, and a host of other environmental and ecological issues. At one point, she felt overwhelmed by the volume of information, but decided she needed to make an informed decision instead of one based purely on emotion.

Although she considered herself no expert, she concluded from the numerous discussions she had had with François and the materials he had passed on to her that the planet was in serious trouble. It had been nearly a week since Antoni Miklus had made her the astounding offer. And after careful study and a great deal of soul-searching, she knew what her answer must be. The next day, exactly one week after she received the offer, she made a short and to the point call to Antoni Miklus and accepted the position. After accepting, she told him that she would need two weeks at HRM to help with the task of filling her own position. She knew this would not be a problem, as Stephen Morris, the senior researcher she had been instrumental in hiring, was highly qualified for the job.

Antoni Miklus explained that although her appointment was a shoo-in, the board of directors would still have to go through the necessary formalities. He then informed her that her salary would be the same as François' and that there would be no debate or infighting among the leadership of the various international and U.S. offices over her appointment. He assured her that all of the sensitive issues had been resolved before he approached her with the proposal.

Caroline decided to hold off telling Gabriel Hansen about her decision until Sunday. On Sunday, she would call him at home and explain what she was planning to do, even though she had already formally accepted the position. She knew she could neutralize any claim about leaving him high and dry without a vice-chair by pointing out the fact that a highly qualified candidate for her current job existed right under his nose in the person of Stephen Morris. She would then point out that Morris's position could be filled by promoting someone from within, leaving only the latter vacancy, which could be filled by bringing on board one of the yearly research fellows.

For this position, she would recommend Melinda Sanchez, the research associate whose report on Mexico she had read upon her return to work. With her resignation strategy devised, she decided to leave work early to break the news to Nicolas and start the weekend with him a bit early.

Chapter Thirty-Five

Caroline arrived home just after 4:00 p.m. to find her neighbor, Mrs. Preston, tending plants in her tiny but well-kept front garden. Mrs. Preston voluntarily collected newspapers from her front door when she was away for François' funeral. Although a somewhat inquisitive woman, she was good to have around, as she kept an eye on the place when they were away. On school days when Caroline worked late Nicolas would be dropped off at her house, but she had also agreed to keep an eye on him when he wanted to go home. On those occasions she positioned herself in her living room so she could see the entrance to the Dupré house and watched vigilantly for any unusual activity.

Caroline exchanged greetings with the elderly woman and was about to enter her front door when the woman called out to her.

"Oh, Caroline," the woman yelled. "Do you have a moment?"

"Sure, Mrs. Preston. Is there anything wrong?"

"No. There's nothing wrong. I just wanted to tell you that a gentleman came to your house today."

"What gentleman?" she asked.

"A tall, well-dressed, and very handsome gentleman," she replied.

Caroline thought momentarily about the woman's description of the man as tall and that it might be inaccurate. Not more than five feet tall herself, the woman probably considered anyone over her own height tall.

"Is that all you noticed?" Caroline asked jokingly.

"Of course not," the woman replied smiling. "He was a white man, probably in his late forties or early fifties." Then to show off her observation skills, she added, "He had a healthy head of dark blonde hair and wore a dark suit and sunglasses."

"Did he say anything?" Caroline prodded.

"He just asked when you would be home."

"What did you tell him?"

"I told him that you usually arrive between six-thirty and seven o'clock. I asked if he wanted to leave a message and he said that he would call again when you're at home. There's no problem, is there?"

"No, Mrs. Preston," she replied. *At least not one that I'm aware of.*

Caroline pondered the reason for the man's visit for a few minutes then decided that her acceptance of the position at TEARS might have prompted it. *He might have been a colleague of Mr. Miklus.*

"Is Nicolas at home?" Caroline asked.

"Yes, he is. He arrived about an hour ago. Instead of coming here, he said he wanted to study. But I think he's playing one of those video games, because I can hear bangs and crashes coming from the room upstairs every now and then."

"Thank you, Mrs. Preston."

Just as Caroline opened her front door, Mrs. Preston shouted, "Oh! Now I remember... It was the same man who came to your house the day after you left for France. I would have told you then, but he said not to bother you. He said that he would call you or come back when you returned."

"Is there anything else, Mrs. Preston?" Caroline prompted once more, hoping for some further scrap of recollection.

"No, that's all," the woman said, clearly proud of herself.

"Have a nice evening, Mrs. Preston!"

"You too, dear."

Puzzled and disturbed by a nagging sense of something

foreboding, Caroline made her way inside, her imagination still working overtime, and tried vainly to convince her son that playing too many interactive computer games would rot his brain.

The rest of the weekend passed eerily. Caroline busied herself to avoid obsessing over what Mrs. Preston had told her. She had been thinking for several weeks that she should take François' clothes out of his closet and remove his personal items from the office. Given her mood, she thought there would be no better time than now to get those things done. She spent several hours packing coats, suits, trousers, and shoes into different boxes for the Salvation Army, Goodwill Industries, and other charities. Then she cleaned out the drawers of his filing cabinet, keeping only files she thought might come in handy after her move to TEARS.

While cleaning out the in-basket on his desk, she picked up the brown envelope that had arrived for him shortly after his death. Thinking it held nothing of importance, she had forgotten all about it. However, rather than tossing into the waste paper basket, she decided to open it. To her surprise, inside she found a small cardboard box with instructions printed by the manufacturer: *FRAGILE, CONTAINS DIGITAL DATA MATERIALS, DO NOT BEND OR EXPOSE TO HEAT.* The box bore no other markings or instructions. She opened it and found two 30-gigabyte memory sticks and a slip of paper with '*Password: NOAH*' scribbled on it.

Curious about their contents, she turned on the computer on his desk. When it was fully powered up, she inserted one of the memory sticks, touched the interactive on-screen button for the *UNTITLED* disk that appeared on the monitor, and entered the password. When the file list appeared, it contained dozens of sub-folders with names like *Global Petroleum Reserves, Greenhouse Emissions, Ozone Depletion, Polar Ice Reduction*, etc. She then inserted the second disk. It, too, was full to capacity and contained a number of similar files. She opened one of the files to find much of what it contained was data sets. The data sets on their own told her little more than the fact that someone had collected the data to perhaps prove or disprove theoretical assertions.

After examining the memory sticks, she put them and the slip of paper containing the password back in the box, placed the box inside the envelope and locked the envelope in her own file cabinet. She didn't know what to make of the information on the memory sticks, but figured it couldn't be too important because no one from TEARS had ever contacted her about it. She concluded that it was probably information sent to François by his office, in support of some research project undertaken by one of the many scientific experts who supported the work of TEARS.

Chapter Thirty-Six

On Monday morning Caroline arrived at work early. After the morning staff meeting she handed in her resignation. Although Gabriel Hansen said he understood her reasons for leaving, he accepted her resignation with reluctance and with the understanding that she would remain at HRM long enough to help Stephen Morris' transition to vice-chair and close out any unfinished business she had initiated.

Her days at HRM after she tendered her resignation were grueling. Each day, she spent ten or more hours at HRM, then went home, prepared dinner, and continued reading to familiarize herself with ongoing issues and responsibilities at TEARS. Despite what Antoni Miklus had said about the need to have her out front, she was determined not to be just a figurehead, no matter how important the cause. She decided to delve into the challenge and make herself knowledgeable and fully accountable to those she would lead and inspire.

Caroline's last week at HRM passed quickly, and on Monday, exactly two weeks after her resignation was tendered, she began moving to her TEARS office, which was located only a few blocks south of HRM on 5th Avenue. She was sad about leaving HRM, but pleased that things had fallen into place and were coming to a close. Stephen Morris had been performing the duties of vice-chair for the entire transition period and it had gone smoothly. With HRM all but behind her, she decided to celebrate the job change with Nicolas by taking him to his favorite restaurant in Chinatown.

When she arrived at home she cajoled Nicolas into finishing his science homework then went off to the bathroom to freshen up. While in the bathroom, she heard the video-phone ring and rushed out to answer it on one of the remote intercoms. Not near a monitor, she couldn't see who it was, so she asked the caller to hold until she reached the video-phone in her bedroom. She quickly put on the finishing touches of her make-up and rushed into the bedroom. As she entered the near darkened room, she could see the image of a young woman on the screen. She seemed distraught.

"Yes?" Caroline said. "With whom would you like to speak?"

"Mrs. Dupré?" the woman asked.

"Yes… This is Mrs. Dupré."

The woman sighed. "Mrs. Dupré, you don't know me but I knew your husband. My name is Kristie Bremmer. I was with your husband and his friends, Jonathan Barber and Dieter Metzger, in Kuala Lumpur."

Caroline was gripped by the mysterious nature of the call. "Is there a reason for this call?" she probed.

"Mrs. Dupré, I'm afraid I have some very bad news for you."

"What kind of bad news?" asked Caroline, her mind racing. *François was already dead. Maybe my father…? No, I would have heard from Muriel or Madam Dumont.*

Kristie Bremmer continued. "After the deaths near the Putra Trade Center in Kuala Lumpur, nearly all the media and the Malaysian government said that the shootings of all those people, including your husband, were in self-defense, but I'm not convinced. I think that all of those things were part of a plan to assassinate your husband."

Caroline shot back angrily. "Why are you calling me? Do you know what you're saying? There must be some mistake!" she snapped. "Even the U.S. government said that my husband had been caught in the crossfire between violent demonstrators and security personnel who believed that they had reason to fear for their lives. Now you tell me his death was part of some conspiracy? What are you trying to do to me? And why have you kept silent all this time?"

Fighting back tears, Kristie Bremmer replied, "I know it sounds crazy, Mrs. Dupré, but you've got to believe me. All these months I've feared for my life. I didn't know how to tell you this, but when I heard on the news that you were taking over as the director of TEARS, I knew I had to tell you what happened and warn you that you might be in danger!"

"What kind of danger and from whom?" Caroline demanded tersely.

"The day before your husband was killed he was followed by several men. I don't think these men were Malaysian security officials. One of them looked particularly menacing. He was an unusually tall man for an Asian. In fact, he looked half Asian and half American. He just didn't seem to fit in with the rest of the security people, not even the ones in civilian clothes. Mrs. Dupré, I met with your husband, Jonathan Barber, and Dieter Metzger the day before the shootings, to pass information to them about the delegates' plans to sabotage the conference. Your husband seemed very worried that day. When I left them, I spotted the tall American-Asian-looking man and several of his minions. They had your husband under surveillance."

Kristie Bremmer paused and swept away a lock of hair from her face. Taking a breath, she continued. "Even though it would have made sense to keep an eye on someone like your husband, their interest was clearly different. I believe your husband was murdered because he made some people nervous. At the start of the protest, he hinted that he was going to expose some sinister plot by rich and powerful people. At first I thought it was some kind of overstated metaphor. Then, what I saw when most of the shooting stopped convinced me something ominous was unfolding."

The girl could no longer hold back her emotions. She stopped speaking and burst into tears.

"What did you see?" Caroline coaxed. "You have to tell me!"

Still crying, the girl struggled with the words. "I saw them… I hid! I hid… and I saw them move their bodies."

"Whose bodies, Kristie?" Caroline pleaded. The girl lost what was left of her self-control. "Kristie!" Caroline shouted. "For God's sake… What bodies? Who moved them?"

The girl hung her head and buried her face in her hands. After nearly a minute, she lifted her head. She was still sobbing. "I saw the tall man, the one who looked American-Asian, take something from around your husband's waist. I couldn't see what it was because I was too far away, but it looked like a tourist travel belt. He opened it and took something from it. I don't know what, but they were two small, rectangular, shiny objects that reflected the sunlight. He looked at them, put them in his pocket, and handed the travel belt to one of the other men with him. Then those men moved your husband, Dieter, and Jonathan's bodies to different places. I saw them do it! Do you understand? I saw them! Mrs. Dupré, they were together when they died. I'm so sorry! I'm so sorry!"

"Are you sure?" Caroline asked.

"Yes!" the girl said. "But that's not all. Three of my best friends have also died under mysterious circumstances. One was killed in Kuala Lumpur before the conference, in what we all thought at first was a hit and run accident. Then, just over a week later, the other two died in a traffic accident that flattened them inside their car. Mrs. Dupré, I believe in coincidences, but these deaths are no coincidence. I don't quite know how or why exactly, but I believe they're all connected."

Caroline began to tremble. She was suddenly gripped by fear and anger. Still stunned, she tried to collect her thoughts. "Look…" she said to Kristie Bremmer. "You'd better go now. I appreciate you telling me this. But you should go!"

The girl was about to terminate the call when Caroline shouted, "Wait! What if I need to talk to you again? How will I find you?"

"I work part-time at TEARS' Seattle office, but I'm hardly

ever there," the girl replied, then added "but you can leave a message for me there and I'll call you."

"OK! OK!" Caroline replied nervously then terminated the call.

Caroline suddenly felt sick. She replayed in her mind what the girl had told her and remembered that François always used a tourist belt instead of a wallet when he traveled. Then it hit her that the rectangular shiny objects the girl thought she had seen were probably memory sticks. *Maybe they were related to the ones I found in François' mail earlier. Maybe that's why the brown envelope containing the memory sticks had been addressed to him and sent the day before he left for Malaysia. Could they be copies?* "Shit!" she said to herself. "So that's what the official-looking stiff who came here twice was looking for!"

After what she had heard from Kristie Bremmer, it was clear that the specter of some dark and sinister force was forming around her. The possibility that it was the same force that had taken her husband away roused her to a level of cold, hard fury, the likes of which she had never felt before. She vowed to find out who murdered her husband and make them pay, if it was the last thing she did.

PART III

Chapter Thirty-Seven

Galesville, Maryland

It was almost 7:00 a.m. when Richard Marsden returned from his daily five-mile run to his house on the Chesapeake Bay. He had moved to the coastal town of Galesville, Maryland, after separating from his wife of more than twenty years. He had made the move to Galesville only months before retiring from the U.S. Secret Service. He was in dire need of somewhere to live once his wife had asked for a divorce, for he knew in all likelihood that she would be awarded their marital home. He had been lucky. He had bought the three bedroom waterfront property from an old friend whom he had once worked with when he was at the CIA. It had been the man's summer home and he had had no further use for it after his wife had died.

Richard "Dick" Marsden had started his career in intelligence in the Marine Corps, but left the Corps after six years when he was recruited by the CIA as an Operations Officer. He had stayed with the Agency for ten years before joining the Secret Service to finish out his civil service career. He was already eighteen months into retirement. However, unlike most ex-intelligence and law enforcement officers, he couldn't accept the idea of sitting around doing nothing while reminiscing about the 'good old days' and watching himself grow old, fat, and inept.

A few months after retiring he started his own business,

Personnel Security Consultants, Inc. (PSCI), of which he was now president and senior partner. At age fifty-four and only slightly graying, he was a poster boy for the over-fifty retiree and the envy of many of his former colleagues. He was strong, fit and energetic. His attitude toward fitness reflected anything but the 'Johnny-come-lately' stance most men his age adopted to boost their egos. He had been obsessed with strength and fitness training since his days as a high school athlete, but he didn't fine-tune either until he entered Navy Reserve Officer Training Corps at university.

His obsession with strength training and physical fitness had enabled him to meet the rigors of the Marine Corps' elite Force Reconnaissance program and subsequent special warfare training with relative ease. Earning his third degree black belt in Tae Kwan Do while at university had also made him highly competitive. Armed with skills provided by advanced martial arts, strength training, fitness, speed, and an encyclopedic knowledge of weapons, he was a finely-tuned killing machine. This, coupled with his sharp instinct, made him one of the best in the business. Over the years, he had learned how to stay alive by spotting trouble and heading it off before it developed. It was these skills that he now relied on to keep his clients from becoming prey.

Only minutes after returning from his run, his satellite phone rang. The ringing triggered a run-through of the short list of persons who knew how to contact him on the encrypted device. After considering the list, the name he settled on gave him a disturbing feeling. For nearly two months he had been trying to shore-up a botched operation and recover a duplicate set of memory sticks containing sensitive research material for a special client known only as 'Mr. Smith.' The original copies of the memory sticks had been taken from a research laboratory to which Mr. Smith was somehow connected. They had been taken around the same time as the disappearance of one of the lab's research scientists and Mr. Smith had made it clear that there was no doubt in his mind that the renegade scientist had taken them when he left. Mr. Smith had pointed out that the lab maintained strict control over its inventory of data storage devices, permitting no new devices to be brought in or removed without the highest level of authorization.

The scientist had disappeared from the Transnational Research Group (TRG) laboratory—a high-tech facility located in upstate New York. Marsden had only seen the blueprint and aerial photos of the facility, but he knew that the laboratory constituted only about half of the rather unimposing-looking facility, which was tucked away in the forests of the Adirondack Mountains. But a single visit to the facility's laboratory by anyone reasonably familiar with research and development would have revealed instantly that it was nothing short of cutting edge. Mr. Smith had told him that the laboratory specialized in the design and development of a variety of sensitive data collection and measuring instruments for ecological and environmental research.

The few pamphlets available to the public about the facility boasted that the instruments and equipment it designed and developed enabled research scientists to measure the level of carbon dioxide and other harmful pollutants in the atmosphere, conduct oceanographic research using submersible devices that measured sea temperatures at varying depths, and monitor ocean thermal shifts and numerous other collection activities with unrivaled accuracy. But this was where TRG's work ended. Because the laboratory was not a licensed research institute, it could not engage in scientific ecological and environmental research. It could only field-test the products it designed and developed.

After the phone rang a fourth time, Dick Marsden lifted the handset. "Marsden here."

The voice at the other end was measured and confident. "Mr. Marsden! Have you found them yet?"

"Mr. Smith, I presume?" Marsden replied.

"You presume correctly," the man confirmed then added, "I can see there's no fooling you. Now, please tell me you have them!"

Marsden paused. But before he could reply, Mr. Smith resumed. "I gathered as much! Before you say anything else, like handing me some weak excuse, you should first understand that I can't and won't continue to put important pursuits on hold while you blunder about the world searching for my property. Is that clear? Now, let me see… You were about to tell me you don't know the whereabouts of my property! Is that correct?"

"Yes, sir," Marsden replied. "But I've eliminated a number of possibilities as to where Dupré might have hidden the second set of memory sticks. I know he didn't pass them on to his organization or the media."

"Why is that, Mr. Marsden?"

"Because if he had, I wouldn't be talking to you now, would I?" Marsden quickly replied.

"And pray tell, Mr. Marsden, what makes you think those memory sticks would somehow be incriminating?"

"You seem to forget that I have ears and I listen carefully with them," Marsden retorted then continued. "My guess is that he hid the second copy of the memory sticks some place obvious. He probably left them with his wife and she hasn't figured out what they are, or he sent them to a place he thought would be safe. I'm convinced he did both. Which means the place he would have sent them is to himself. It's a very old trick," Marsden added. "It would explain why nothing about them has surfaced."

"So you're telling me that his wife may have them but doesn't really know she has them, or at least what they are."

"Right!"

"But don't you think all this will change now, with her taking the job at TEARS? Perhaps she didn't know before she took the job, but if she hasn't already started crawling around and opening up things belonging to him or the organization that look official, she'll soon start. However, if you're convinced that this is where you should be looking, then get on with it! Do whatever it takes to find and return my property! Do you hear me, Mr. Marsden? And when you learn something important, I want to know about it. I want to know what she finds and when she finds it. As soon as you know, Mr. Marsden! Is that clear?"

Marsden was becoming annoyed with the man. Not for telling him how to do his job, but for repeating his name *ad nauseam* and for his condescending manner.

"Sir..." Marsden said firmly. "I've already thought of this and I've already begun putting the necessary mechanisms in place to find out what and how much she knows."

"Does she know about you, Mr. Marsden?" Mr. Smith asked arrogantly.

"No! She only knows that someone dropped by her house a few days ago. I'm certain she doesn't know why."

"Good, Mr. Marsden. Then I trust the next time we speak you'll have good news for me. I'm sure I don't need to remind you that you're being paid a hell of a lot of money for your services. I'm only being generous because I was told that you're the best in the business."

"I *am* the best!" Marsden interjected cockily.

"Well then... it's time for you to prove it! Try not to disappoint me, Mr. Marsden. I don't like disappointments."

Before Marsden could reply, Smith interrupted. "Good day, Mr. Marsden," and hung up.

Marsden was revisited by the doubt that had crept into his mind shortly after he accepted the job and the installment of two and a half million dollars. When an intermediary initially contacted him about the job, he was told that there could and probably would be complications. However, he didn't suspect that recovering the memory sticks would require him to slip into the gutter alongside a host of cutthroats and back-stabbing opportunists. After all, Mr. Smith appeared to have a legitimate legal claim in wanting to recover his stolen property. He also understood that for someone willing to pay eight and a half million dollars to recover a couple of memory sticks, they must be pretty damned important. But for that kind of money, the contents of the memory sticks didn't concern him. And although he had seen no red flags or anything else to warn him of sinister activity, he couldn't help being suspicious. With or without red flags, he remembered the adage '*If it sounds too good to be true, it probably is.*' However, in the end he reconciled his concern with another old cliché: '*Never look a gift-horse in the mouth.*'

Chapter Thirty-Eight

Dick Marsden was eager to conclude business with the enigmatic Mr. Smith and collect final payment. His divorce had left him nearly broke. When the dust settled, his ex-wife had walked away with their $750,000 home in Reston, Virginia, and most of its contents. She was also awarded half of their investments and half of his pension. All he had left was his individual retirement accounts, most of which contained stocks that had disappeared or failed to recover from the international banking crisis a half-decade earlier, an equal share of their other less valuable investments, the older of two cars, and the outstanding balance on their joint credit card accounts. His wife's lawyer claimed that while married to him, she had sacrificed numerous opportunities for a successful career to be with and support him during his assignments as a military officer and as a CIA employee. The lawyer had gone on to argue that the move to the Secret Service after ten years with the CIA substantiated this, because Marsden had made it known to his colleagues that he was making the move to the Secret Service in order to bring stability to his marriage.

His wife's lawyer had stressed to the judge that by the time he had moved to the Secret Service, it was already too late because his wife was nearly forty years old, and the knowledge and skills she had acquired with her advanced degree in marketing, and the experience she had gained during the few years she had worked, were all but irrelevant. This, the lawyer had argued, would have forced her, if she resumed her career, to start at the bottom, with only a limited earning potential and meager retirement benefits. The female judge ruled in his wife's favor.

Marsden knew that after the tragic financial effects of the divorce, he needed to make a quick recovery—one that would allow him time to enjoy the retirement he had envisioned. The TRG contract was the right ticket. Even though he had three partners with whom he would have to share the wealth, he knew his share of the contract would resolve all his financial woes. He had figured that of the eight and a half million dollars he would get roughly three million; he had calculated that with it, his partial pension, and a few smaller contracts, he would be in good enough shape to retire fully in three years' time.

He hadn't expected things to turn out the way they did in Kuala Lumpur, nor had he expected the complications that ensued. The Kuala Lumpur operation was supposed to have been textbook stuff. It should have only involved identifying the target, surveillance, overcoming security challenges at the recovery location, and a quick and tidy recovery operation. Common sense had told him that without the memory sticks, whatever François Dupré had masterminded would have been thwarted. Even when he found out about the copies of the memory sticks, he was certain there would be enough time to conduct a similar or near-simultaneous operation to recover them. Unfortunately, there had not been enough time to determine their location and arrange the second operation. Nevertheless, he was confident that François Dupré and his two colleagues would have led him to the second set, had they not been killed.

Marsden was confident that his plan was a good and safe one —one that required no strong-arm tactics, at least not like the carnage that got splashed onto television screens around the world, or the deaths of the three girls, whom he had not seen as a threat to the recovery operation. Nevertheless, he knew when he drew up the plan that there would have to be weapons involved as part of a backup strategy if things went wrong. He also knew that there would have to be a legitimate reason for those executing the plan to resort to the use of deadly force, if the need arose. At the time, however, he didn't think that the man selected to lead the operation in Kuala Lumpur would turn out to be an overzealous, trigger-happy idiot. The man had been a liaison officer for the Special Branch of Malaysia's National Security Service. He had retired and had begun operating a security firm that contracted its services to the Malaysian government. Any concern about the man's professionalism had been dispelled because he had been highly recommended by a PSCI partner, who had worked with him when he was posted to the U.S. Embassy in Kuala Lumpur as a CIA case officer. Using the Malaysian had made good sense. He fitted the profile needed for the job perfectly—he had excellent access and was an indigenous insider, even though his English mother's genes made him a bit taller and American-Asian in appearance.

Marsden knew now that the carnage in Kuala Lumpur would make the job of recovering the second set of memory sticks more difficult. The extreme measures taken by their contractor had turned a textbook operation into one where operatives were allowed to run amok and was now unraveling. Marsden knew all too well that the loose ends had to be tied up quickly and quietly. Anything or anyone revealing information that might lead back to him or PSCI would have to be dealt with, permanently. To do this, there would undoubtedly have to be more killing, something he had hoped to avoid altogether. But for now, the immediate task was to determine exactly who was involved and precisely what they knew. And no matter how bad things got, he knew he could never use the idiotic, trigger-happy Malaysian contractor, not ever again.

Chapter Thirty-Nine

Dick Marsden was still fuming from the conversation he had had with Mr. Smith; the latest call from him confirmed the gut feeling he had had from the outset—that Smith was a micro-manager, someone who would have his fingers in everything. He wasn't accustomed to working that way and he knew that he couldn't allow it to continue. Millions of dollars or not, from now on, his mysterious employer would only be apprised of important developments. He would only be given periodic progress reports and he would only deviate from this if an issue developed that required his authorization to proceed.

To prevent fall-out from the botched Kuala Lumpur operation from drifting his way, and to put things back on track, Marsden turned to his number two at PSCI, Marcus Anderson. Anderson was a first rate professional. He had helped Marsden get out of a sticky situation a few months earlier. 'Mack' as he was called by friends and colleagues, was not only a top-notch professional, he was easy to work with.

Like Marsden, he was a former military officer and a member of the special warfare community. He had been a U.S. Navy's SEAL. But after ten years of service that included operations in Iraq and Grenada, he left the Navy and went off to graduate school, where he was recruited by the CIA. He had spent his entire career working in the Middle East and Africa. It was during his early years in the Middle East that he and Marsden met.

Born to an African-American Chief Petty Officer in the U.S.

Navy and a Moroccan mother, Anderson had been an excellent Middle East operative. As a young boy, he was eager to learn and his mother had taught him to speak, read, and write Arabic and French.

He had earned the nickname 'Mack' when he was working at the CIA because of his calculated and at times cavalier style in dangerous situations. A story that circulated widely in operations circles suggested that when he was Deputy Chief of Station at a post in the Middle East, he had stormed into a deadly counter-intelligence operation to save a junior case officer and an important asset that had been compromised. Unable to contact the young case officer and warn him of the impending danger, Anderson showed up at the rendezvous location and snatched the officer and his agent from the jaws of death. It was said that he came onto the scene out of nowhere, 'like a Mack truck.' The operation thus earned him the name Mack—a moniker that stuck to him.

For Marsden, knowing Anderson and his reputation for getting the job done made his selection a no-brainer. Mack was, without a doubt, the only person to help him deal with the complexity of the TRG job. TRG was the PSCI's most lucrative contract to date and Marsden couldn't afford to have it botched by any more reckless, amateurish operations. Since its start-up, the PSCI had relied on each of its partners to market the firm and bring in contracts. Prior to the contract with TRG, most of the jobs that had been drummed-up involved the sale of secure communications equipment and training of security personnel charged with protecting corporate interests, to include executives and their families. On a few occasions, PSCI was asked to do security assessments, as well as accompany senior corporate executives when they traveled to dangerous overseas locations. In cases where these demands exceeded PSCI's in-house manpower, sub-contracts were out-sourced to other tested and reliable firms. But Marsden knew that in order to meet the provisions laid out by TRG in an efficient and timely manner, he would have to stop using sub-contractors. This was another reason for turning to Mack Anderson. He trusted Anderson more than anyone to watch his back when the going got tough; he had a feeling that this was about to happen.

Chapter Forty

Nearly two months had passed since the fiasco in Kuala Lumpur and Dick Marsden needed a break in the recovery operation in order to get Mr. Smith off his back. By the time he contacted Mack to help him, his frustration was already deepening. Most people who knew Marsden knew that frustration was something the normally cool, level-headed security expert had always managed to keep under control. It had only been a week since he had received the last annoying call from Mr. Smith. He had contacted Anderson the next day and instructed him to return to the U.S. as soon as possible. Anderson had been accompanying a senior executive from one of the major oil companies on a trip to the southern part of Chad to inspect a project in the Adoba oil field.

Two days after the call, Anderson showed up in Galesville, Maryland. Anticipating his arrival, Marsden was standing on the front porch when his hydrogen-powered BMW pulled into his driveway. Even though the car was considered a major feat of engineering and had been applauded by most environmental groups, a number of them were still criticizing governments for their limited use of hydrogen fuel cell technology and the automobile and petroleum industry for perpetuating fossil fuel dependency by making only a half-hearted attempt to apply the technology more broadly.

Despite years of testing hydrogen power for automobiles, there were still dangers associated with using the highly volatile fuel source, particularly where refueling and high impact collisions were concerned. But Anderson had calculated that the risk of being killed by an explosion during refueling, a collision or a mechanical failure was significantly less than that he had experienced as a Navy SEAL or a CIA case officer.

Mack Anderson clambered from the black sport sedan with a broad grin on his face. "You ought to get yourself one of these!" he joked, striding coolly toward Marsden's front porch.

"No thanks!" Marsden said, smiling. "I saw what happened to the Hindenberg!"

Anderson chuckled. "What's up? What was the big rush for me to return all about?"

Marsden got straight to the point. "I fucked up, Mack! I fucked up! I took Dave Bearsden's word when I took on our Anglo-Asian friend to handle the operation in Kuala Lumpur. Regardless of what Bearsden said about having worked with the guy, I should've checked him out myself."

Mack Anderson hesitated then let out one of his high-pitched, staccato laughs. They were like nothing Marsden had ever heard. They were Anderson's trademark and he was well known for them. By the time Anderson's prolonged 'I told you so' laughter subsided, Marsden's face was showing the embarrassment he felt about the situation.

"I could've told you that idiot was going to screw things up," said Anderson, adopting a more serious demeanor. "From what I heard about this guy, he's always been overzealous—a real fan of 'over-kill.' The guy must've thought he was on a movie set! If you ask me, I think he got his rocks off doing the whole thing. I could've told you he was gonna fuck things up, even your textbook recovery mission. Before you chose him, I was gonna suggest that you and one of the partners do the job."

"Me and which partner?" Marsden asked jokingly.

"Me of course," Anderson replied, grinning. "So what now?" he asked.

"We clean up the mess and get things back on track. Come

on inside. I've got something to show you."

Once indoors, Marsden handed Anderson the file on the Kuala Lumpur operation and he began to skim through it.

"You want some fruit juice or ice tea?" Marsden asked.

"Yeah... A glass of cold orange juice would be good," Anderson said, not taking his eyes off the folder's contents.

Marsden wandered off into the kitchen and after a short time returned with a glass of orange juice. He sat in silence for nearly ten minutes while Anderson pored over the entire contents of the folder. When Anderson finished, he looked up at Marsden and said, "You've got problems!"

"No shit!" Marsden said.

"According to this report and from what Smith says, there are still a few loose ends that need to be taken care of immediately. There's the woman, Kristie Bremmer, who surveillance picked up meeting with Dupré in Kuala Lumpur, plus her contact working with the U.S. delegation at the conference. Amanda Costanti, I believe her name is?"

"Was..." Marsden interrupted.

"What do you mean *was*?" Anderson asked.

"She's dead! Constanti and two of her friends, a Canadian woman named Patricia Maynard and a woman named Elizabeth O'Connell, all bought the farm."

"Eliminated?"

"Yep. Costanti and O'Connell met their maker on the New Jersey Turnpike. It looks as if someone was getting nervous about the relationship between Bremmer and the three dead women. As far as I can tell, there was only direct contact between Dupré and the Bremmer woman, so the elimination of the other three might be unrelated." Marsden paused for a moment. "Look at it this way... they weren't really part of the problem, at least not ours. But it seems that whoever was concerned about them decided to make it look as if it was part of our operation."

"You mean they used our operation to mask their own?"

asked Anderson.

"They must have," Marsden replied, looking puzzled. "The surveillance reports from Kuala Lumpur indicate that only one of the women, Amanda Costanti, was connected to our man Dupré through the Bremmer woman. So I don't see anything that would've made killing the other two, Maynard and O'Connell, necessary."

"At least not yet!" Anderson replied then added, "Don't forget, two of them just happened to be working for two of the men who scuttled the conference. That's something, and I think it's important, but there's not enough to connect all the dots yet. I think we can still say with some confidence that their deaths weren't the work of our trigger-happy contractor. It's not his style. Besides, he doesn't have the reach to pull off an operation in the U.S." Anderson paused to contemplate the situation then added, "So tell me, will the deaths of these women affect what we're doing?"

"I don't see how they could." Marsden said, not quite sure of himself. "At least not now, anyway," he added. "Other than the fact that they died suspicious deaths, there seems to be no cause for us to be alarmed. For now, we should stay focused on the memory sticks and on controlling the damage caused by the idiot in Kuala Lumpur."

"OK!" Anderson said, sounding a bit more confident. "So the deaths of these women aren't an immediate concern, but this Dr. Joseph Mescheler that Smith mentioned, the renegade scientist from TRG; he is, right?"

"That's affirmative," said Marsden.

"I'll bet you a month's pay he's gone to ground and will be hell to find," said Anderson. "We're probably gonna need some help from your man Smith in getting what we need to track Mescheler down. As for the Dupré woman, she's gonna need special handling. I say we get to work on her right away."

"That's about what I figured!" said Marsden. "But how do we go about it?" He stared at Anderson momentarily then offered a solution. "I paid her a visit several weeks ago when she was at work in order to check out the lay of the land. You know, type of house, neighborhood, neighbors, etc. She's got an old biddy for a neighbor. She's nosy as hell and at home all the time."

"That's good to know," said Anderson. "So, the first thing we need to do is get surveillance set up on her, twenty-four-seven, to find out what she knows so far and what she's planning to do. Then we get on to the Bremmer woman. No matter what the Bremmer woman may have learned, or who she decides to share it with, it won't mean squat without whatever is on those memory sticks. Agreed?"

"I agree!" said Marsden.

"Anderson continued. "I'll get the technician to put together whatever we need. When we get all the surveillance equipment set up, me and fat ass Bearsden can do the monitoring."

"Forget about Bearsden!" Marsden interrupted. "I'll do the monitoring myself. He's already fucked us once! Besides, you should start tracking down the Bremmer woman."

Anderson broke in, "I thought we just agreed that those women and what happens to them is none of our business."

"We did… But after thinking about it, I realized that if the Bremmer woman knows something and it gets out, it may not damage Smith, but it might link PSCI to the Kuala Lumpur carnage, and neither of us wants that. Do we?" Marsden asked bitterly. "The Bremmer girl shouldn't be too difficult to find. She works part-time at TEARS' Seattle office." Marsden paused and gave Anderson a penetrating look. "Look, Mack, this isn't at all what I wanted, but you know it has to be done."

Marsden paused again, this time running his fingers through his already disheveled hair. "If we handle it this way, we break the link between PSCI and the mess in Kuala Lumpur. It'll put us back in the driver's seat."

"OK!" Mack replied, nodding. "It makes sense. I'll meet you in New York tomorrow evening."

"I'll grab a couple of rooms for us at the Sheraton near La

Guardia and pick you up at the airport when you arrive," Marsden said then added, "It'll be like old times again, won't it?"

Anderson got up from his chair, walked out onto the front porch, and down the steps to his shiny BMW. Marsden stopped on the porch behind him. "Just be careful that the damn thing don't blow up underneath you!" he shouted jokingly.

Without turning around or looking back, Anderson threw up his right hand in a waving gesture and said, "See you tomorrow!"

Chapter Forty-One

La Guardia Airport, New York

Marsden picked up Anderson at La Guardia Airport just after 2:00 p.m. and they drove straight to the Sheraton Hotel. Having arrived earlier that morning, Marsden brought all the equipment and tools needed to cut and polish the fiber optic cable that carried communications in and out of the Dupré residence and tie-in a transmitter. He had also brought along an assortment of miniature transmitters, which could be placed at various locations throughout the woman's house. Since the Dupré woman's nosy neighbor had already seen and spoken to him, Anderson suggested that it would attract less attention if only one of them was seen near the house and that a disguise should be worn.

Marsden decided that he would be the one to handle the job because he was familiar with the neighborhood and he knew where he needed to go. But as backup he downloaded the modified blueprint plan the woman submitted to the Preservation Commission when she renovated the brownstone. For the occasion, he chose a disguise consisting of beige overalls, a long grayish-brown wig, which he planned to wear pulled back in a ponytail, and a pair of Ray Ban Wayfarer sunglasses. To avoid arousing suspicion from other neighbors, he would go to several residences along the street under the pretext that he was checking the impact of a damaged booster amplifier, which was intermittently disrupting broadband service to some subscribers in the area.

Anderson's job was to go to Manhattan, wait for Caroline Dupré to leave her office, tail her and inform Marsden when she was approaching the house. When she got home, Dick Marsden would turn up and ask to check the strength of the broadband signal entering her residence, explaining that her house was just one of several he needed to check in the neighborhood and that the job would take only a few minutes. The plan was watertight.

Chapter Forty-Two

Less than two weeks into her new job, Caroline was feeling overwhelmed by the volume of information she had to read and absorb on pressing environmental issues. Still, she made a point of getting home before or only a few minutes after Nicolas' friend's mother dropped him off from school. Aware of her schedule, Anderson arrived at just before 5:00 p.m. on Friday and took up his position across the street from her 5th Avenue office building. Less than twenty minutes later, Caroline Dupré emerged from the building and headed toward the 5th Avenue subway station. He immediately called Marsden and alerted him of her departure then began tailing her on foot. He followed her into the station, boarded the train in the next car after she entered and got off with her when she left the train in Brooklyn. When she left the station in Brooklyn, he phoned Marsden and told him that she was ten minutes away from the house.

Within fifteen minutes of her arrival, Marsden rang the doorbell. When she answered the door, he showed her his fake employee identification card and explained the reason for his visit. Once inside he asked for the location of each of her video-phones and her broadband router. He then asked her to show him the telephone jack where the router was connected. He removed the cover of the junction box and slipped in a tiny transmitter which picked up and relayed the digital signal to the receiver he had left in his vehicle. He also placed tiny transmitters on the back of a book case in the sitting room, one under her dining room table, one in the kitchen, and one under a chair in her bedroom in order to monitor general conversation.

Placing the transmitter in the kitchen had been the trickiest, as there was no router there, but he had said that he wanted to check the broadband signal strength in the room. For this part of the house he had brought along the perfect device. He asked to be taken into the kitchen; when they entered he pretended to be thirsty and asked for a glass of water. Caroline went over to the cupboard to take a glass from it; as soon as she turned her back, he attached a tiny transmitter under the bottom edge of the cabinet near the sink. The transmitter was about the size of a pencil eraser in diameter and its hard stem, which could be embedded in wood, gave it the appearance of a thumb tack.

With all the devices in place, he thanked Caroline Dupré and left the house. The whole job had taken him less than fifteen minutes. After leaving the house, he went straight to the van he had parked down the street. He had rented the vehicle when he arrived that morning and had placed removable logos for Northern Communications, one of the area's leading high speed communications service providers, on its sides.

Dick Marsden climbed into the van and drove a few blocks down the street before stopping to activate the monitoring equipment. He checked the quality of the signal from each device. Each of the tiny transmitters was producing its maximum signal. He switched from one to the other, checking each, one last time before calling Anderson. When Anderson answered, Marsden said, "We're in business!"

"Are we gettin' a good read on everything?" asked Anderson.

"All fivers!" Marsden responded. "Meet me here in half an hour. I'll keep the car when you arrive and work from it. You can take the van and head back to the hotel. It'll attract too much attention if it stays here. I'll stay until she's tucked away for the evening and when she's off to work, I'll call in at the Sheraton and get some sleep."

"Solid!" Anderson replied.

Chapter Forty-Three

Brooklyn, New York

Marsden and Anderson had been monitoring Caroline Dupré's calls and movement for only two and half days, but Marsden's frustration was beginning to rise. He had begun asking himself how much more waiting he could handle. Then at 8:30 p.m. on Monday, less than sixty hours after they started surveillance, they got the break they needed when her video-phone rang. She had been in her bathroom brushing her teeth when the unit sounded. But because of the running water, Caroline didn't hear the first few chimes. When she finally heard it, she dashed into the bedroom and answered. It was Kristie Bremmer.

"Kristie? Where are you?" she asked anxiously.

"Mrs. Dupré?" Kristie asked, not sure if she had the right person.

Caroline could sense fear in the girl's voice and thinking it might help calm her down,

she said, "My name is Caroline. Call me Caroline."

"I'm in Seattle. I can't talk very long," the girl said nervously. "I don't believe this is over yet."

"What do you mean? What's not over?"

"Do you remember the friend of mine who worked for Robert Hollingsworth, the U.S. Ambassador to the UN, who I told you was killed several weeks ago?"

"Yes," Caroline replied.

"Well, the week before she was killed, she told me Ambassador Hollingsworth had become unusually nervous after the incident in Kuala Lumpur. She said he seemed frightened and had begun taking a lot of calls on his personal cell phone. A couple of times, he seemed angry with whoever he was talking to. I think my friend's death was somehow linked to those phone calls."

"What makes you think this? Maybe he was having an affair. It may have been just a lover's quarrel or some other sensitive matter."

"That's possible, but just days before your husband and his friends were killed, Patty Maynard, a good friend of mine, was killed in Kuala Lumpur. She was one of the three I told you about last time. What's odd is that she was killed the day before the start of the conference."

Kristie Bremmer paused to regain her composure then continued. "I know that all of the official reports say she was the victim of a hit and run by a drunken driver, but that's not true. Her death was an accident alright, but not the kind reported. I believe that whoever killed her made a mistake. They killed the wrong person. I think it was Amanda Costanti, who was killed about a week later, who was meant to be the target in Kuala Lumpur. She and Patty looked almost identical. From a distance even I couldn't tell them apart. Don't you see? They killed the wrong person! That explains why they killed Amanda not long after the so-called accident."

"What leads you to believe all of this? You think they were killed because they both worked for ambassadors who walked out of the conference?"

"Yes... at least Amanda Costanti, anyway. Killing Patty Maynard was a mistake."

"But wouldn't the fact that they both worked for representatives who walked out of the conference be enough of a reason for someone, maybe some deranged radical, to target either or both of them?"

"Maybe, but it was Amanda, Ambassador Hollingsworth's staff assistant, with whom I kept in closest touch. And before the conference, she had begun providing me with information about Hollingsworth's role in the plan to sabotage the conference. Also, Amanda told me before she was killed that she believed someone had something on Hollingsworth and was using it to pull his strings."

The girl was about to continue explaining her theory when Caroline interrupted. "I see what you're saying, and maybe it does make sense, but what about the American-Asian-looking man who removed the travel belt from my husband's body? Where does he fit in?"

"I'm not sure," said Kristie Bremmer. "Your husband never mentioned anything to me about this man. I gather there was no need to."

"Well, I think I know where he fits in," said Caroline. "Several weeks ago, I found something just like the objects you said the man removed from my husband's money belt, but I didn't know what to make of them."

Kristie Bremmer suddenly realized that far too much had been said over the line already. "Don't say any more, Mrs. Dupré," she warned. "I think it would be better if we discussed this another time. Look, I live on Bainbridge Island, in Puget Sound, but I'm in Seattle now. I'll be coming back into the city again Saturday morning. I don't put in much time at the office any more, but I still go in a couple of times a week to check messages and to see if they need me for anything. The office is normally open a half day on Saturday. So, I'll check my messages and give you a call around 1:00 p.m. my time, which is 10:00 a.m. for you. If you have a cell phone, I'd feel safer talking to you on it."

"Yeah, sure," Caroline replied and gave the woman the number.

"I'll call you from a pay-phone or from my cell phone."

"OK," said Caroline. "Look after yourself. I've been thinking about you and what you said ever since you called the first time. I'm glad you called again."

"I'll be careful, and you should, too," said Kristie Bremmer. "I've gotta go now. I've got a bit of work and some other things to do and I don't want to have to take the last ferry back home. I'll speak to you on Saturday."

Marsden could hardly contain the excitement he was feeling about what he had just heard. As soon as the call between the two women ended, he shouted "Bingo!" He had heard everything he needed to hear from the Dupré woman, except the cell phone number she had given to the Bremmer girl. As bad luck goes, Caroline Dupré had gotten up and gone into the bathroom to turn off the tap when she gave the girl the number and the sound of the running water had momentarily drowned out her voice. Nevertheless, he was pleased with what he had heard. He flipped opened the case containing the satellite phone and called Anderson.

Chapter Forty-Four

Marsden was beaming when he told Anderson that his hunch about Caroline Dupré having the memory sticks had been right. While he was summarizing what he had heard, his brain slipped into high gear. He explained to Anderson how the Dupré woman had confirmed that Kristie Bremmer had seen her husband's assassination and that the girl's own description of her relationship with Ambassador Hollingsworth's staff assistant, Amanda Costanti, and the Canadian staffer Patricia Maynard, substantiated what he had, to some extent, suspected about the death of the two women. Where the O'Connell woman was concerned, it looked as if she was in the car with Amanda Costanti simply for the ride, which was the wrong place at the wrong time. And while there was still some concern about the women's deaths, Marsden felt they had the information they needed to stop the trickling wound to their operation from turning into a hemorrhage. By the time he finished talking to Anderson, they had devised the first part of a plan that would bring the operation under control.

Marsden knew that he and Anderson needed to act quickly and that the plan they devised would have to be implemented immediately. The plan required Anderson to go to Washington and deal with the Bremmer woman. He would remain in New York and put things in place to recover the memory sticks. He was especially delighted that the Dupré woman still didn't fully understand what was on the memory sticks, which meant that unless things changed, he could get them without having to add her to the rising body count. They agreed that Anderson would catch an early flight to Seattle on Friday; once there, he would find the Bremmer woman and silence her.

Anderson arrived at La Guardia airport at 7:30 a.m. and took United Airlines' 9:05 a.m. to Seattle. To avoid leaving a paper trail that could be followed to either him or PSCI, he traveled in disguise and under an alias, used a fake drivers' license and retired military identification card, and paid for his ticket with a pre-paid cash card. Although he knew that Kristie Bremmer lived on Bainbridge Island, he still hacked into the Division of Motor Vehicles' database and got her address. Knowing the girl would be traveling to and from Bainbridge Island by ferry, he had obtained a copy of the schedule from the Internet before leaving New York.

Chapter Forty-Five

Seattle, Washington

The United Airlines flight from New York landed at Seattle-Tacoma Airport at 9:50 a.m. Pacific Time, just three hours and forty-five minutes after it left La Guardia. After checking into the airport's Marriott Hotel, Mack Anderson ate an early lunch and took a taxi to the ferry boat terminal on Pier 52 to familiarize himself with the facility. He also purchased a return ticket and made the thirty-five minute crossing to Bainbridge Island. He wanted to assess the level of security on the boats and see if he would have enough time to move against his target during the crossing.

At the terminals in Seattle and Bainbridge Island, he noticed there were no metal detectors and the only security personnel aboard the boats were assigned to the vehicle transport deck to guard against vandalism and theft of property from unoccupied vehicles. After surveying the situation, he concluded that there were several convenient places on the boat to move against unsuspecting prey, but because the boats transported between 1,200 and 2,500 passengers, it would be difficult to isolate the woman from the other passengers. When he returned to the terminal in Seattle, he collected a diagram of the terminals from the ticketing area and went to his hotel.

After identifying several locations aboard the ferry where he could launch a surprise attack, he needed to devise a way to coax her to move to one of the locations. If that failed, he would have to have a back-up plan. He knew he could do one of two things: on Saturday morning, he could tail her from Bainbridge Island to Seattle and hope for an opportunity; or he could wait and catch her when she left Seattle in the evening. From his notes, he knew the girl was planning to spend the day and evening in Seattle and return to Bainbridge Island sometime before or just after midnight. He decided that her return trip would offer the advantage of darkness and perhaps a boat that probably would be less crowded. But to pull it off, he would have to stick close to her without being spotted and without attracting the attention of the other passengers.

Anderson had acquired what he considered to be the right tool for the job, a sufficient quantity of the highly lethal drug Etorphine—a drug commonly referred to by veterinarians as 'elephant juice' for its use in sedating elephants. With the right dosage, a human target could be taken out quickly and quietly, possibly in less than a minute. But because even a very small amount of the drug was lethal to humans, he had acquired the antidote, Naloxone, in case he accidentally stuck himself with the needle while administering the concoction. If the opportunity to use the Etorphine didn't avail itself on Saturday, he would have to stay until the job was done.

If the Etorphine couldn't be used, Anderson decided he would use the .45 caliber Mark 23 pistol and silencer, which he had disassembled and sent in three separate shipments to himself at his Seattle hotel via express courier service the same day he left New York. He had had several copies of the pistol made. They were weapons that couldn't be traced if they were discarded. The knock-off Mark 23s were almost perfect, as they matched the performance of the Heckler & Koch original in nearly every way. Anderson was confident that one way or another, Kristie Bremmer would be eliminated.

Chapter Forty-Six

On Saturday morning, Kristie Bremmer arrived at the Bainbridge Island ferry terminal and purchased a foot passenger ticket for the 8:40 a.m. ferry to Seattle. Knowing that the girl had told Caroline Dupré that she would be arriving at TEARS' Seattle office before noon, Anderson went to the terminal around 8:00 a.m. It was an unusually warm spring morning, so he bought coffee and a newspaper at a kiosk and took a seat outside on a bench. When he arrived at the terminal, he went into the toilet and donned a disguise different from the one he had used when he traveled from New York. This time he chose a false beard and a conservative pair of eyeglasses. He wore a casual outfit, complete with photographer's vest and walking shoes. He also carried a large photographer's bag slung over his shoulder. To the casual observer, he looked like any other tourist waiting to catch the ferry to Bainbridge Island.

At 9:15, the Bainbridge Island ferry arrived. A few minutes after it docked, a flood of foot passengers and vehicles began disembarking. After fifty or so foot passengers had streamed past him, he spotted Kristie Bremmer. He glanced down at the photo of her he had tucked inside the newspaper to confirm her identity. It was her. She was wearing jeans, a T-shirt, hiking boots and a beige sweater, draped over her shoulders and tied loosely around her neck, and a pair of sunglasses on top of her head. She also carried a backpack slung over her right shoulder.

As the woman moved past him, Anderson downed the last of his coffee, rose to his feet and tucked the newspaper under his arm. Maintaining a careful distance behind her, he followed her to the bus stop and lingered among the other passengers until the bus approached. When the bus pulled up to the stop, Kristie Bremmer boarded and he followed. Anderson moved all the way to the back of the bus so he could see when the woman got off. She was completely unaware that she was being followed.

The bus lumbered along its route, making scheduled stops, until it reached downtown Seattle. When it arrived at Wall Street and 5th Avenue, Kristie Bremmer rose from her seat and moved toward the exit door. Her stop was next; it was just two blocks from the TEARS office. After she and several other passengers had disembarked, Anderson got up and made his way to the exit. Keeping a safe distance behind her, he followed her until she crossed the street to enter the building where TEARS' office was located. He elected not to cross the street behind her. Instead, he remained on the opposite side and kept a close eye on her. When she entered the building, he took out his cell phone and called Marsden.

"The pigeon's in the nest."

"Good work! I'll keep my ears open," said Marsden then he added, "I'll be expecting a call from you later."

Kristie Bremmer remained in the office until just before 1:00 p.m. When she emerged from the building, Anderson spotted her from the position he had taken up at a coffee shop across the street. After leaving the building, she went a few doors down the street to a newsstand and bought a newspaper. She then took up a position along the facade of a building a few feet from the newsstand and pulled her cell phone from her back pack. Anderson took out his phone and alerted Marsden, who was stationed just down the street from Caroline Dupré's house.

"She's on air," said Anderson.

"I'm on it!" Dick Marsden replied.

Before Marsden could hang up from the call with Anderson,

he heard Caroline Dupré's cell phone ringing. Both women were under the impression that their avoidance of landlines gave them privacy from listening ears. They were at least half right. Only Caroline Dupré's side of the conversation could be heard in full. Their conversation would have been completely secure if Caroline had moved outside the house to take the call, as monitoring was being facilitated solely by listening devices planted inside the house and by tapping into her communications lines before voice and data left the junction box and entered into the broadband stream. From the tiny microphones planted a few days earlier, Marsden heard Caroline Dupré answer her phone.

"Hello! Is that you, Kristie?"

"Yes," the woman replied.

"Where are you?"

"I'm in Seattle. I've just come from the office. There were no messages from you. Are you alright?"

"Yes. I'm fine, thank you, but I'm still worried," said Caroline.

"We both have reasons to be worried," Kristie replied then went straight to the purpose of her call. "A few days ago, you mentioned that you had found a couple of memory sticks like the ones you believe were taken from your husband's body. Can you tell me more about it?"

"I'm not a hundred percent certain about the connection," Caroline began, "but shortly after I accepted the position at TEARS, I started going through my husband's things. You know… his clothes, sports equipment, and some mail he'd received from TEARS after his death. In one of the envelopes from his office, I found two 30-gigabyte memory sticks he had apparently mailed to himself the day before he left for Malaysia. I didn't know what to make of them until you told me what happened. Then I remembered my neighbor telling me that a man had been looking for me just days after his death. I suppose it all began to make sense. Which means that the memory sticks must either be duplicates, or part of whatever they took from his body."

"Have you seen what's on them?" Kristie asked.

"Yes. I had a quick look when I opened them. They're both full of some kind of statistical data on petroleum, sea levels, the climate, and other stuff. Most of it I can't make head or tail of, but it must be important."

"Shit!" said Kristie, stunned by what she had just heard. "Your husband said several times during his speeches that if the conference didn't bring about a solution, he'd expose a behind-the-scenes plot to undermine international efforts to arrest global warming and climate change. It looks as if those memory sticks had something to do with what happened in Kuala Lumpur. I wish I knew exactly what your husband had been planning."

"So do I," said Caroline. "Somehow, I have to find out what all this means. Because he didn't send the memory sticks to his office, he must have already put something in motion. I've gotta find out what that was."

"Be careful!" Kristie said. "Someone killed your husband because of this, and I believe they also killed my three best friends. And when they find out that you've got the memory sticks, they'll come after you too."

"I'll keep my eyes open, but I think they're already on to me," Caroline replied.

"Just please be careful," the woman warned again. "Look, I've gotta go now. I've got errands to run then I'm meeting some friends for drinks and dinner. I'll call you again in a couple of days."

"Thank you again for your help, Kristie. I know it hasn't been easy for you and I'm sorry about the way I treated you when you called the first time."

"No apology is necessary. I understand how you must have felt. I'll call you again soon, I promise."

The two women said goodbye and hung up. And although

Marsden could hear only one side of the conversation, he was satisfied with what he had heard. The Dupré woman's conversation with the girl had confirmed that she had the memory sticks and he now knew that she realized that they were important, but had not yet figured out what to do with them.

Marsden rang Anderson back and told him he had collected more of what they needed. His instructions to eliminate the girl were therefore simple and to the point: "Proceed as planned."

Chapter Forty-Seven

Anderson maintained surveillance of Kristie Bremmer for the rest of the day and into the evening. He had been hoping that an opportunity to move early against her would have presented itself, but it didn't. In the evening, the girl joined several of her friends for a couple of hours in a cocktail bar. Afterwards, they all went to dinner at a Vietnamese restaurant. Just after 10:00 p.m., they left the restaurant and went their separate ways. Kristie Bremmer said goodbye to her friends and made her way to the bus stop to wait for the bus to the ferry terminal. As she moved toward the bus stop, Anderson remained on the opposite side of the street and walked briskly in the other direction.

Just four blocks ahead of him and on the same side of the street as the Bremmer woman, was another bus stop. To avoid raising suspicion, he decided to board the bus at the earlier stop so he would be on it when she got on. As he approached the bus stop, he could see the bus in the distance heading toward him. When it arrived, he asked the driver if the ferry terminal was on the route. The driver told him it was and he purchased a ticket and settled near the back of the bus, unfolding the newspaper he had been carrying in front of his face.

When the bus pulled up to the stop where the Bremmer woman was waiting, she boarded and took a seat near the middle of the bus. The trip from downtown to the ferry terminal took less than fifteen minutes. Earlier that morning, Anderson had purchased a return ticket for the Seattle to Bainbridge Island ferry. His ticket for the 11:15 p.m.

sailing, but he was concerned about restrictions on the use of the ticket. The man in the ticket office had assured him that because it was a weekend, the boat was not likely to be full and he should have no problem using the same ticket for an earlier crossing, if he desired.

Minutes before the bus arrived at the ferry terminal, Anderson withdrew a small black case from his pocket containing the hypodermic needles with the deadly dose of Etorphine and the antidote Naloxone, to make sure they were ready. Other than Kristie Bremmer and himself, there were only eleven other passengers on the bus when it left downtown Seattle. By the time it reached the ferry terminal on Pier 52, seven of the passengers had gotten off.

When the bus arrived at Pier 52, Kristie Bremmer and the other passengers got off. Anderson tailed her onto the pier and they both boarded the ferry. Although the boat making the crossing could carry up to 2,500 passengers, fewer than 800 foot passengers were onboard.

It was a clear, calm evening on Puget Sound and a dozen or so passengers, mostly young couples, made their way to the boat's upper deck to take in the lights and Seattle's skyline as the boat moved away from the shore. The Seattle Needle was a favorite sight among tourists and area residents on an evening outing.

Kristie Bremmer had made her way into the passenger cabin on the main deck; Anderson could see that she was restless. After only a few minutes inside, she left the cabin and went out onto the main deck. He followed her. There were a considerable number of passengers on the upper deck taking in the view or making out, which prompted her to move aft on the main deck to an area just below the pilot house. The huge 328 foot long boat had identical pilot houses on the upper deck at each end, which were used interchangeably, depending on the direction the boat was traveling. The area below the pilot house was deserted, which suggested that she wanted peace and quiet.

When she reached the place on the port side, below the aft pilot house, she stood there leaning against the railing, staring out onto the waters of the Sound.

The ferry boat moved swiftly away from Seattle's shore; pretty soon the glow of passenger cabins and the running lights of a few other marine craft were the only things penetrating the darkness of Puget Sound.

Anderson had followed Kristie Bremmer as closely as he could. He didn't want to approach her too soon or from the same direction she had come from for fear that she would suspect him of following her. He therefore turned around and moved quickly up the port side of the boat, climbed the ladder to the upper deck, and went down the starboard side. As he rounded the upper aft deck area near the unoccupied pilot house, he almost stumbled over an object on the deck. He looked down and in the near darkness he saw a piece of chain, approximately three and a half feet in length. Given the task before him, he thought it might come in handy. After all, a good operative must always be ready to improvise.

He looked down at the illuminated face of his wrist watch and realized that the ferry would be arriving at Bainbridge Island in less than twenty-five minutes. He knew he had to move quickly, if he was going to finish the job. Having nearly circumnavigated the upper deck, he quickened his steps and descended to the main deck. After walking up the starboard side, he crossed over to the port side, walked through the passenger cabin and headed toward the aft end of the boat. As he approached the aft section of the boat, he spotted the woman. She was leaning against the railing, looking out onto the Sound. Rather than startle her, he turned around, re-entered the passenger cabin and climbed to the upper deck to retrieve the length of chain. Although using the chain was not a part of his original plan, finding it had proven to be a bonus.

Inside his oversized camera bag he carried a large 35mm digital camera and lenses, a small digital camera, a cell phone, a

Mark 23 Pistol, silencer, and several other electronic gadgets. Realizing there was not enough room in the bag for the chain and its current contents, he threw everything except the cell phone and the Mark 23 pistol and silencer over the side. He quickly affixed the silencer to the pistol and tucked it into the waistband of his trousers and closed his photographer's vest over it. He surmised that the chain weighed somewhere between eight and ten pounds, which would help with his improvised plan.

After tucking the chain inside the camera bag, he looked down at his watch once more and saw that he had just under ten minutes to complete the job and dispose of the girl's body at the mid-crossing point in the Sound. With a camera bag that looked heavier than normal, he re-entered the passenger cabin carrying the bag in front of him and exited on the port side. He walked briskly until he came upon the Bremmer woman. As he moved toward her, he slowed his steps and took a couple of deep breaths to regain his composure. When he reached where she was standing, he stopped and asked politely, but showing some concern, "Miss! Is there a problem? Is anything the matter?"

Kristie Bremmer's gaze was fixed on the Sound and she didn't hear him at first. Suddenly, she became aware of his presence and looked in his direction. "No! No! Thank you. Everything is fine," she replied.

Sensing her confusion, Anderson moved to take control of the situation. "I saw you standing there alone in the dark and thought you might be contemplating something grim. I always believe it's better to be safe than sorry, so I decided to enquire."

"You're right! It is better to be safe than sorry," she said, "but I'm fine. Thank you though for your kindness and concern."

"Any time," Anderson said beaming then added, "Oh look! I run a photography business back east and if you're ever on the east coast, give me a call and I'll buy you a coffee."

He did a quick scan of the area and saw that they were

completely alone. With darkness to conceal his actions, he set the camera bag down on the deck, reached into the pocket of his photographer's vest as if searching for a business card and withdrew the small black case containing the deadly hypodermic needle filled with Etorphine. Before Kristie Bremmer knew what was happening, he had placed his hand over her mouth and injected the lethal concoction into her neck. She tried to struggle, to scream, but he was far too strong for her. As she twisted and wriggled, the drug sped more rapidly through her veins. In less than half a minute, her body had gone limp.

When she stopped struggling, he slipped his arms around her waist and up to her diaphragm and squeezed several times to expel as much air as he could from her lungs. As he squeezed, his eyes scanned the area to make sure they were still alone. He lowered the woman's body onto the deck and took the chain from his camera bag. Racing against time, he straightened her body out, wrapped the chain around her ankles, and fastened its ends together with a plastic gripper tie he had taken from his camera bag.

After taking another look around to make sure no one else was in the area, he rolled the woman's body over the side and watched it plunge into the water. He kept his eyes on her, watching impatiently as the waters of Puget Sound enveloped her. Because of the chain around her ankles, her body sank immediately and raced like a dart toward the bottom.

Romantic inspiration, lust, noise from the boat's engines, and the churn of its propellers ensured that the passengers at the aft end of the boat remained ignorant of what had just happened. To avoid suspicion being cast on him if someone was waiting for the woman at the terminal and reported her missing, he tossed the unused Mark 23 and the silencer into the Sound.

Satisfied that the mission was complete, Mack Anderson straightened his clothes, gathered up his camera bag, the empty hypodermic needle and case he had dropped to the deck and moved with deliberate quietness up the port side of the boat. With just over five minutes remaining until the ferry reached Bainbridge Island, he re-entered the passenger cabin, took a seat and began calmly reading his newspaper. When the ferry docked at Bainbridge Island, he called Marsden and told him that all had gone better than he had expected. He returned to Seattle on the 00:50 a.m. ferry and took a taxi to the Marriott Hotel. The next day, at 9:25 a.m. Pacific Time he boarded a United Airlines flight to New York.

When Kristie Bremmer failed to come home, as she had told her parents she would, they reported her disappearance to the police. But an extensive search of the Seattle area failed to locate her or uncover any sign of foul play. She had, for all intents and purposes, vanished from the face of the earth.

Chapter Forty-Eight

New York

A week had passed since Kristie Bremmer's disappearance; although the media had reported the incident, there was no attempt by anyone involved in the investigation to look for a connection between her disappearance and the deaths of Patty Maynard, Elizabeth O'Connell, and Amanda Costanti, given that the four of them had been close friends. It was as if the distance separating each of the incidents had somehow precluded a logical attempt by the police and the press to make such a connection.

As he had vowed, Marsden prepared a complete progress report for Mr. Smith. Because he could not contact Smith directly, he followed a set of established protocols and left a message for Smith at the TRG laboratory. The arrangement required him to contact the laboratory and the laboratory would pass his messages on to Smith. Smith would contact him within an hour after receiving the message.

Less than thirty minutes after Marsden put the call through to TRG, Smith called him on his secure satellite phone. Smith was pleased that several of the potentially dangerous loose ends had been tied up. But what surprised Marsden most about his contact with Smith was his knowledge of the courses of action that had often just been taken. He seemed to know far too many details. Nevertheless, again he shrugged off the discomfort Smith's knowledge of the developments caused him.

He told himself yet again that it was simply the man's meddlesome nature.

Smith wasted no time after Marsden answered. In his usual efficient but arrogant style, he got straight down to business.

"Mr. Marsden," he boomed. "You're quite a resourceful fellow! I see you've taken care of at least one of your immediate problems."

Marsden couldn't help but notice Smith's emphasis on the word 'your' when he referred to problems associated with the operation.

"Don't overestimate my present mood, Mr. Marsden," Smith continued. "Underneath the thin veneer of what may seem to you like my satisfaction about the progress that has been made, my patience is still wearing thin."

Marsden tried not to show the disdain he felt about the man's meddlesome behavior and the condescending tone in which he spoke to him. Yet, despite his frustration, he listened attentively to his lecture before delivering a forceful but diplomatic reply.

"Sir… I have fresh information that confirms that Caroline Dupré is in possession of the memory sticks you are looking for. More importantly, it confirms that she has not shared, nor is she likely to share them with anyone else."

Marsden's confidence about his ability to recover the memory sticks wasn't shared by Smith. In his typical arrogant fashion, Smith admonished against using risky methods to recover the memory sticks. "If you deal with this Dupré woman in a crude manner, like breaking into her house or roughing her up or some other heavy-handed tactic, she might panic and turn the material over to someone. This would be most unproductive, not to mention that it would frustrate me immensely. And because you're not a common thug, I trust there won't be any more tactics used like those you used with the Bremmer woman."

Marsden agreed resentfully with Smith's analysis of the

situation, declaring that, "Any actions we have taken during the course of the last few weeks are the results of blunders someone else made while trying to save their own neck. I'm specifically referring to the deaths of two UN staffers and the young female professor. Need I say more on the subject?"

"Those matters shouldn't concern you, Mr. Marsden. But the fact is that the Bremmer woman was dragged into this saga because she saw what your man in Kuala Lumpur did, which gives rise to speculation as to why all four of the women who shared the experience of having been in Kuala Lumpur have all ended up dead." Mr. Smith paused before continuing. "Because of the potential for this little side-show to spiral out of control and distract you in your efforts to recover my property, I've taken the liberty of seeing to it that nothing further comes of it."

The revelation of Smith's influence in the matter of the women's deaths left Marsden momentarily speechless. After recovering from the shock, he declared, "There will be no distractions and you'll be pleased to know that through surveillance, I've learned that the Dupré woman desperately wants to know what the data on the memory sticks means. It's clear that she knows that without that knowledge, she can't determine an effective course of action."

None of this seemed to impress Mr. Smith, as he went on to remind Marsden that the situation was still much more serious than it appeared because the renegade scientist, Dr. Joseph Mescheler, was probably still alive and very much at large. "If Dr. Mescheler is still alive, and I believe he is, he now knows about the Dupré woman's rise to the head of TEARS. Mr. Marsden, I have every reason to believe that Mescheler will try to contact her. After all, it's the only way he can save his skin and come in from the cold. He's been out there a long time. So you see, we not only need the memory sticks, we need him too. Is that clear, Mr. Marsden?"

"Perfectly clear!" Marsden said, sternly. He was hoping that his gung ho reply concealed the surge of anger and frustration he felt about having Smith add yet another complication to the job—that of tracking down Mescheler. *What else is he going to throw into the mix?*

Smith continued. "The deaths of Kristie Bremmer, Patricia Maynard, Elizabeth O'Connell, and the Costanti woman have without a doubt unsettled Mrs. Dupré. Put yourself in her place for a moment, Mr. Marsden. By now, she must be feeling pretty darn scared and alone. So you can see, whether revealing that she has the memory sticks makes her look foolish or not, sooner or later she'll want to rid herself of the risks associated with them. She's very aware that death has become inextricably linked to those memory sticks, and she's a mother too, don't forget. That'll make her all the more determined to stay alive. I am therefore convinced that all it would take for her to break her silence is for Mescheler to contact her and tell her what she's holding or for you to deal with her incorrectly. This cannot and will not be allowed to happen! There can be no doubt in your mind about my position on this! Do I make myself clear, Mr. Marsden?"

"Crystal clear, sir!"

"I suggest you cast your net wider and bring Dr. Mescheler in as well. I don't think I need to elaborate on this any further. I want him returned to the TRG facility, alive, Mr. Marsden."

"I understand fully, sir!"

"Oh!" Smith interjected, almost as an afterthought. "Time is of the essence. This has been allowed to continue far too long. I'll be in touch soon," he added and hung up.

After each conversation with Smith, Marsden felt more and more like he was not fully in charge of his own operation. Smith was omnipresent and omnipotent. He seemed to have access to everything and everyone and had eyes and ears everywhere. This made Dick Marsden even more curious about the true identity of the man. Still, once again he managed to convince himself that everything Smith had said was true; the money he was being paid was more than sufficient for him to tolerate the man's meddlesome behavior until the job was finished.

Chapter Forty-Nine

Immediately after Smith's call Marsden put through a secure call to Mack Anderson to apprise him of Smith's reaction to the progress report. Anderson had not long returned from Seattle and was at the LaGuardia Sheraton, preparing for surveillance duties the next day in Manhattan. When the phone rang, he answered in his usual boisterous manner.

"Mack here…"

"Did I wake you?" Marsden asked.

"Nope. I was just catchin' up on the baseball scores. What's shakin'?"

"Nothing new," said Marsden, somewhat unsettled. He paused then asked, "Have you noticed that Smith seems to be on top of everything? In fact, he seems to be planning this thing for us. He knows everything before I tell him."

"Don't sweat it!" said Anderson. "With the kind of money this cat seems to have, he's probably got connections everywhere… the police, FBI, Washington, who knows. The guy's a heavy hitter."

"You're probably right. But his meddling still makes me uneasy. Yet I suppose he's only telling us what we already know —that we've gotta round-up Mescheler, before he makes contact with the Dupré woman. What's puzzling though is he wants Mescheler alive and delivered to the lab."

"So what's the big deal?" Mack asked. "We already know he's part of the package. What Smith does with Mescheler is of no concern to us. Our job is to pick him up, and to do that, we stay closer to the Dupré woman than her thongs and we'll know when Mescheler makes his move. And when he does, we'll grab his ass."

"Problem is though, Mack, this guy could be anywhere. And besides, we don't even know what he looks like."

"That's already been taken care of."

"What do you mean?" Marsden asked.

"After you left this morning, 'fat ass' called from the office."

"Who? Bearsden?"

"Yeah. He said he'd just received some photos sent for your attention. He opened the Federal Express envelope and found a memory stick containing photos of one Dr. Joseph Mescheler. Someone from the TRG lab sent 'em! He uploaded 'em straight away and sent 'em to me via e-mail. Already got 'em. Gotta give it to your man Smith, he's thorough!"

"Yeah! He is, isn't he?" Marsden replied, perplexed.

"We'll know if Mescheler tries to contact her at home," Marsden continued. "But if he gets hold of her at work, we're fucked! We're gonna have to find some way to tap into her phone at work, preferably her extension and not the switchboard. We'll also need access to TEARS' e-mail server, as well as the one with their home page, since it's interactive. He might try to post a message to her through web mail. I can handle getting into her phone line, but you'll need to get the technician back up here to get into the servers."

"Consider it done!" Mack replied. "I'll get hold of the tech as soon as we hang up and have him come up this evening."

"OK," Marsden said, continuing his instructions. "I'll have to create some kind of communications problem to get into the electrical and communications infrastructure work area. I'll start on it this evening. In the morning, they'll put in a trouble call. I'll intercept it and go in for the job. As soon as the tech arrives, I'll need you to come over and relieve me at the house so I can get things in place for tomorrow. Have I left anything out?"

"Nope!" Mack replied. "But why don't we have the tech hack

into the phone company's computer and disable the lines into the office's switchboard? And while he's at it, he can cook up a little communications problem for the 'rent-a-cop' security guards in the building. They'll notice their communications problems straight away and use their cell phones to put in a trouble call to the phone company. The tech can intercept and divert the call to you and you can waltz right in. The security guards should take you right where you need to go. It'll save you a trip back to the building in the morning."

"That sounds like an even better plan!"

"I'll call you when I'm headed your way," Anderson added.

"Roger that," Marsden replied and hung up.

Chapter Fifty

The PSCI technician arrived at the Sheraton during the early evening hours with a specialized laptop computer and another miniature computer he used for deciphering passwords. The small but powerful computer could process several hundred thousand random password combinations every minute and bypass normal system lock-out measures while attempting them. The technician, who only moonlighted with PSCI, had created the program, which he called The Wizard, only a few months earlier. The program essentially allowed anyone monitoring activity on accounts and databases to look over the user's shoulders.

Less than fifteen minutes after his arrival, the technician had hacked his way into TEARS' web and e-mail servers and found each of Caroline Dupré's user identifications and passwords. With general access to the servers, Marsden and Anderson could now search, explore, and exploit e-mail accounts, data bases, and confidential files at will. Because they were only interested in gaining access to Caroline Dupré's outgoing and incoming communications, the technician set up an alarm that notified anyone monitoring her accounts when messages were sent or received and when the accounts were accessed.

As soon as the technician began work, Anderson left for Brooklyn. When he got on the road, he called Marsden. A short while later he pulled up around the corner and a few streets down from Caroline Dupré's house. He had been reminded by Marsden to bring along the duffle bag containing the disguise he would need to enter the building on 5th Avenue. Anderson parked the new vehicle he had rented, a mid-size Toyota sedan, around the corner and walked the two blocks to the tinted-windowed car where Marsden was conducting surveillance. He approached the driver's side and tapped on the window. Marsden lowered the window partially and asked sarcastically, "What took you so long?"

Anderson moved around to the passenger side. As he climbed in he let out a subdued chuckle. "That piece of Japanese shit I'm driving handles worse than a tank!" Referring affectionately to his hydrogen-powered BMW, he lamented, "If I'd been driving the Silver Streak, I'd have been here in half the time. How on earth do folks drive around in these rickety pieces of scrap metal?"

"Yeah, yeah, yeah! We can't all be superstars like you," Marsden replied, jokingly. "Besides, some of us just naturally have poor taste!"

Anderson broke into his familiar staccato laughter. "That's for sure! How's it going?"

"Well," said Marsden. "I just got a call from the technician. He tells me we're in business with the web and e-mail servers. He says we'll be able to monitor with a portable laptop setup as long as it has a wireless, cellular modem. I thought we'd eventually have to do some communications surveillance on her at work, so last week I had 'fat ass' rent a small office over a bookstore across the street from her building using a front name."

Anderson interrupted. "I see you've started calling Bearsden 'fat ass' too!"

Marsden chuckled. "You're a bad influence. Seriously though, we can set up in that office and it'll give us full coverage on her." He paused. "I'll tail her in every morning from here until she reaches work, you can take over from there. I'll double back and pick up the car and head for the hotel, get some sleep or give you a hand if you need it. Hopefully, something will break and we won't have to do this too long."

"I hear that," Anderson replied.

"OK!" Marsden chuckled. "Here we go!"

Marsden took the disguise he had used to enter the Dupré residence from the duffle bag and dressed on the back seat. As he opened the door to leave, he told Anderson, "I'll call you when everything is in place. I should be back in two to three hours."

"Don't forget to call the technician and let him know when you reach the building, so he can work his magic," Anderson reminded him.

"Got it!" said Marsden.

Chapter Fifty-One

Everything went according to Dick Marsden's plan. The PSCI technician disabled the security guards' communications network and minutes later the guards put in a trouble call, just as Marsden predicted they would. The technician then intercepted the call and passed it to Marsden. Twenty minutes later, Marsden was in the building.

When Marsden arrived one of the guards at the main security station on the ground floor met him in the lobby and took him to a downstairs room with a sign on the door that read *Engineering Room, Technical Equipment, Staff Only.* They were met outside the room by the building's duty electrical engineer, who had brought along the schematics for the building's communications lines.

The walls of the technical equipment room were covered with junction boxes and several powerful servers. Most of the equipment relied on fiber optics, but a few outdated coaxial cables jutted from one or two junction boxes, possibly to be used as part of a backup system. Within minutes, Marsden announced that he had found at least one of the problems. He then put in a call to the technician who immediately cleared the communications disruption he had created only minutes earlier.

After clearing the security guards' communication problem, Marsden located the fiber optic cable that supplied basic communications to TEARS offices. He told the duty engineer that he suspected that there was another disruption in a junction box on the 32nd floor, where several fiber optic cables converged into a bundle. He then explained to the engineer that he suspected that the solution would require no more than cleaning and polishing the fiber optic cable ends and reconnecting them. The engineer understood the problem, but explained that because those types of office connectivity problems were not his responsibility, he would have one of the security guards escort him to TEARS' office spaces.

Once inside, Marsden fiddled with the main junction box as if to test the connections. He then asked if he could check in the other offices to see if there were other boxes. He was taken into two other offices before being led into Caroline Dupré's office. The guard soon grew comfortable with him and left him to go raid a candy dish on the receptionist's desk he had locked his eyes on when they entered. It was just the break Marsden needed.

Since a number of businesses still used conventional telephones as backups for video-phone services, he removed the cover from Caroline Dupré's telephone and installed a tiny listening device. He reassembled the telephone and for good measure, he placed another device under her desk. When he had finished, he yelled out to the reception area and asked the guard for access to the conference room. Still busy devouring sweets from the candy dish, the guard simply pointed in the direction of the room.

Marsden moved quickly inside the conference room. He placed three tiny listening devices under the long conference table. Then, on his way back to the reception area, he spotted the office of Antoni Miklus, the Deputy Director. Afterwards, he peered out into the reception area and saw the guard, who was still sitting on the corner of the receptionist's desk, chomping on an assortment of miniature candy bars. Marsden ducked quickly inside the Deputy Director's office and planted a listening device in his telephone, one under his desk, and another under a coffee table on the other side of the room. Miklus' office was a bonus and he smiled inwardly as he

191

finished and made his way back to the reception area.

"You're all set!" he told the security guard.

"That was quick!" the guard replied.

Marsden smiled. "I'm in a hurry. I wanna get back in time to catch the baseball scores on ESPN!"

The guard escorted him downstairs to the lobby, where the guard at the main post signed him out of the building. As soon as Marsden left the building, he called Anderson. When Mack Anderson answered, he said, "We're in business," then asked, "Is everything in order at your end?"

"Yep! All's quiet. It was lights out about thirty minutes ago."

"Good!" Marsden replied. "I'll see you in about forty-five minutes."

He then called the technician and told him that his job would be finished as soon as Anderson returned to the hotel and reviewed the surveillance setup.

Chapter Fifty-Two

Marsden drove back to Brooklyn Heights and took over surveillance at the Dupré residence. But before he relieved Anderson, they went over their strategy and agreed that they now had enough coverage on Caroline Dupré to follow all of her activities. Just as Anderson was opening the door of the surveillance car to leave for the hotel, Marsden again mentioned his concern about the enigmatic Mr. Smith.

"You know, Mack, this Smith character is a very clever customer."

"What do you mean?" Anderson asked.

"I've been thinking. What kind of connection could there be between him and an environmental organization... a not so radical one at that? I mean, there are several organizations that engage in far more radical activities than this TEARS outfit. They've never gone to extremes to undermine any government policies, nor have they ever engaged in any destructive activity, like ripping up genetically modified crops or endangering lives by blocking nuclear waste transfers. And this guy Dupré, he was as clean as a whistle. All the demonstrations he organized were carried out without breaking any major laws."

Anderson sat quietly for a moment. "If you ask me, I think all this revolves around your man Mescheler. He's the guy who made off with the data or whatever dark secrets Mr. Smith wants to keep hidden that's on those memory sticks. He took 'em and gave 'em to Dupré."

Marsden interrupted. "He trusted the guy. And with Dupré's

193

record as a straight shooter, he knew he'd do something about it. So, whatever is on those memory sticks must be pretty damaging—something our Mr. Smith doesn't want made public. I think it's more than a matter of private property, or a case of Smith not wanting the competition to know about some major scientific breakthrough. My gut instinct tells me that there are a lot of people involved in this thing... important people."

"You may be right," Anderson replied. "But we don't know any of this for sure. As it stands now, Smith has a legal right to recover his property—property that was taken illegally by an employee who violated the confidentiality agreement he signed which said he wouldn't disclose information about his activities inside the organization nor details about his relationship with his employer."

"Then why not get the police or the FBI involved?" Marsden asked.

"Good question, but maybe he doesn't want to attract attention to whatever it is the lab is working on," Anderson suggested.

"Yeah! But this thing has already gotten nasty. Dozens and dozens of people have already paid with their lives for mistakes on all sides, including ours."

Anderson chuckled. "As true as this may be, none of it can be linked to our man Smith. We're the ones he contracted to recover the memory sticks, and all the deaths you mentioned are on our hands. He pays us in cash, remains anonymous, and there's no paper trail. There's no link. Not even to us! The man has plausible deniability. He's untouchable... as pure as a newborn babe in all of this. It's our nuts that are in a vice if this thing blows up. So it's in our best interest to see that it gets cleaned up and brought to a rapid close. I say we finish the job, get our money, and say goodbye to the likes of Smith, or whoever he is. We've come too far and we're in too deep to start worrying about the whys and wherefores of this thing. We're in business and this is a job. I say we get on with it."

"I hope you're right, Mack. I hope you're right," Marsden replied wearily.

After returning to the Sheraton, Anderson tested the portable monitoring equipment and reviewed the procedures with the technician before turning in for the night. After his shower, he lay in bed replaying the conversation he had had earlier with Marsden about Smith. As he gave more thought to the matter, Marsden's growing obsession with Smith's identity and his comments about the killings began to trouble him. He began to wonder if what he had heard and seen could jeopardize the success of the operation. Then he reminded himself that there was too much riding on the success of the operation for Marsden to be getting a case of cold feet. He had known him a long time, which went far in convincing him that Marsden would remain committed to fulfilling any contract he had seen fit to accept. And given Marsden's past behavior, which had been consistent over the years, and the amount of money involved, he concluded that his attitude probably was born of concern about keeping PSCI alive and in business. After all, he was its president and founder and wouldn't want himself or the business to be tainted or stigmatized as a murder for hire organization.

After carefully weighing up the situation, he was convinced that Marsden's attitude would change as things began to smooth out and move closer to completion. But despite the logical conclusions he had arrived at, his better judgment demanded that he err on the side of caution; in the end he decided that it might not be a bad idea to keep a close eye on his long-time friend and colleague.

Chapter Fifty-Three

Caroline arrived at her office on Monday in a stoical mood. She said the usual hellos to the receptionist and the other employees, but it was obvious to anyone who had come to know her that the vibrant personality she had consistently displayed from the day she arrived had taken leave of her. However, what they didn't know was the reason for the change in her mood. No one knew of the fear and trauma that had gripped her after she learned what happened to Amanda Costanti and Elizabeth O'Connell, and how her fear had grown when she learned of Kristie Bremmer's disappearance. She was horrified—certain that whoever killed her husband and the four women would stop at nothing to get what they wanted. It was now clear that they were willing to eliminate anyone who got in their way.

Unknown to her, the nemesis driving her fear was just across the street. Above the Vintage Bookstore on 5th Avenue Mack Anderson and Dick Marsden were hunkered down in a small office, waiting for the laptop Anderson was monitoring to tell them when there was activity on any of her e-mail accounts. As Anderson fixed his gaze on the computer screen, Marsden sat in front of a receiver with headphones on, ready to listen in on her office conversations or any calls she received.

Dick Marsden and Mack Anderson were cramped, but they were settling in. The small office, which probably had not seen much use in months, if not years, was musty and its walls were stained and peeling. They sat on folding chairs, each with a playing-card-size table in front of him that held eavesdropping or computer monitoring equipment. Along the back wall of the room was a fold-up cot bed, which they used to take turns sleeping on. There was also a toilet at the back, to which the door remained partially opened because its bottom edge dug into the uneven floor. The blades of a big, caged electric fan hummed as it swiveled in front of a half-opened window to combat the stale air that permeated the room. An antiquated ceiling fan also swirled overhead, its blades biting into the musty air like helicopter rotor blades. It was only late May and daytime temperatures were already climbing as high as mid-summer levels. By 9:30 a.m., it had reached nearly 80 degrees Fahrenheit. The exceptionally warm weather so early in the year was only a sign of things to come. In the months ahead, it would get significantly worse.

Back across the street at TEARS Caroline Dupré made her usual cup of peppermint tea and prepared for the weekly meeting with senior TEARS officers. She couldn't help thinking about what had happened to all four of the women. Her instincts told her that Kristie Bremmer was dead and this touched her personally. Although they had never met, she felt as if she had known her a long time. She knew that what she and Kristie had stumbled onto was potentially dangerous, but until she vanished, she hadn't fully grasped the magnitude of the danger. Yet despite her growing fear, she couldn't tell her colleagues what had happened. She knew that if she tried to explain to them, they would probably recommend that she take some time off and might even suggest that she seek psychiatric help.

Sitting behind her desk, her thoughts drifted back to the last conversation she had had with Kristie Bremmer. The more she thought about the girl's mysterious disappearance, the more she began to ponder her own fate. She also found herself pondering an even grimmer and previously unthinkable notion. *What would become of Nicolas if anything happened to me?* She couldn't bear the thought of him being left without a father and a mother. Surprisingly, he had been coping and adjusting well to his father's death.

In just over a week's time, Nicolas would begin his summer break. She knew she had to act soon to minimize the risk of him being hurt. In order to avoid the same fate that befell Amanda Costanti, Patty Maynard, Beth O'Connell, and Kristie Bremmer, and keep Nicolas safe, she would have to identify, elude and maybe even draw those responsible out in the open so she could see them coming, at least until she could find out what was on the memory sticks that was worth killing for.

She decided the best thing to do was to get Nicolas out of New York as soon as he was out of school. She knew that taking him to Paris to stay with her father or to Virginia Beach to her grandparents was far too risky. He'd be too easy to find if anyone wanted to abduct him and use him as a bargaining chip. She concluded that the safest place for him would be with Debbie Creighton, a childhood friend she had played with during her visits to her grandparents' house.

Not wanting the receptionist sitting in the outer office to know what was going on, she excused herself and told the receptionist that she was going to the cafeteria several floors below for tea bags. When she reached the cafeteria, she called her friend from a pay-phone and arranged to drop Nicolas off on Saturday morning. She knew she would only be able to devote her mental energies to uncovering the secrets of the memory sticks and the identity of the person or persons responsible for her husband's death if she knew that he was out of danger.

Satisfied with the arrangements made with an old friend, she returned to her office and began checking her e-mail. As soon as she logged in, the alarm sounded on Anderson's computer and the words *ACCESS ALERT* flashed up on the screen.

"Here we go!" Anderson shouted.

"What's up?" asked Marsden.

"She's just logged in to one of her e-mail accounts. It doesn't look as if there's anything new, though. I skimmed through it earlier and found only routine stuff. She hasn't had anything new come in since."

Anderson sat and watched the screen as she opened and read each message. Less than fifteen minutes later, she stopped reading and locked her computer. While monitoring the listening devices for conversation, Marsden heard her tell her secretary that today's staff meeting would be extended and would probably last at least forty-five minutes to an hour longer than usual. Marsden then spent the next hour and forty-five minutes listening to regional and international reports coming in from what turned out to be a video-tele conference. At the end of the meeting he was exasperated. "It'll be hard going if it continues like this. I honestly don't know how much more of this kind of crap I can take."

Chapter Fifty-Four

When Caroline Dupré returned to her office, Marsden and Anderson resumed their monitoring of her e-mail, office, and telephone conversations. Anxious for further developments, Marsden was again starting to show signs of impatience. He was beginning to think that they had gambled too much on Mescheler making contact with the woman and that they might be fishing in depleted waters. Then at 10:45 a.m. she received a web e-mail via TEARS' interactive site from someone using the name *Puzzler*. She was still in the meeting when the message appeared in her inbox. Minutes earlier, Anderson had taken advantage of her being away from her desk and had slipped into the toilet. When the alarm sounded, he had dashed out of the cramped facility, hitting his shoulder on the half-opened sticking door and swearing profusely. As soon as he hit the *ENTER* key on the keyboard, the message appeared.

Mrs. Dupré:

You don't know me, but I knew someone who was very near and dear to you. It's unfortunate that he was taken away so abruptly and so violently. You may or may not know this, but his untimely death was no accident. There were powerful forces involved in his demise—people who knew he had something that could hurt them. They are onto you as well. I too am in grave danger. Thus far, I have managed to stay a few steps ahead of them, but I suspect it won't be long before I am discovered. I believe you are in possession of something very important—something that could liberate us both from our secret prisons. But you'll need my help in understanding exactly what it is and what must be done with it. I suggest we meet. I'll get back to you when I have arranged a place and time. Until then, say nothing of this message or my contact with you. I've selected the address I have used to contact you for one-time use only, so it won't do much good trying to reply to it. Just stay put and I'll contact you.

The Puzzler.

As Anderson's eyes moved down each line of the message he began to chuckle. "It's him... He's made contact!"

"Who?" Marsden asked.

"Our man... Mescheler! He wants to arrange a meeting with her, but he's gonna contact her later with the details. He's a smart one, this Mescheler!"

"What do you mean?"

"He obviously suspects that her communications are being monitored, so he used a throwaway e-mail address. He also bounced his message off several internet servers no doubt at different locations around the world, so that the place he sent it from can't be traced."

"This means he could be anywhere!" Marsden interrupted.

"Perhaps, but I've got a hunch he's hiding somewhere not too far away. We're onto him! And it won't be long before his ass is caught!"

Relieved but still puzzled, Marsden asked, "So all we have to do is wait 'til he makes contact again, right?"

Anderson let out one of his thunderous staccato laughs. "That's right! And it won't be long!"

At 11:15 a.m., Caroline returned from her morning meeting and logged on to her computer. A small window was displayed on the screen informing her she had several new e-mail messages in her webmail inbox. As soon as she accessed the account, the alarm on Anderson's laptop sounded and he began monitoring her activity. She opened the incoming e-mail file and scanned the subject line before opening and reading two authoritative but very sarcastic messages sent as feedback to the Director.

When she opened the message from The Puzzler, the first two lines sent a chill through her body. At first, she thought it was a cruel joke. But as she continued to read, her thoughts changed. Remembering the determination of the people who killed her husband and the four women, she thought the message might be from them. After all, it wouldn't be beyond them to try to draw her out in the open by offering to help her.

Suddenly, she felt confused and frightened. She wondered why someone she had never spoken to, met, or even heard of, was contacting her with an offer of help. But what frightened her most was the idea that she might have no other choice but to meet with him, if she was going to find out why the memory sticks had caused so much death and destruction.

As soon as she closed her webmail account, Anderson sighed. "The ball's in motion! This could either be our big break or our worst nightmare!"

"I know," said Marsden.

"Now that Mescheler has made contact, she'll want to know," said Anderson. She'll want to know everything, especially what's on the memory sticks. And I'm sure he's just itching to tell her. We'll have to take care of him first!" he added.

"Not just yet," said Marsden. "We need him! We need him alive, remember? So, we'll let him go through with the meeting because we have to get her out in the open. If we play this right, we can bag 'em both at the same time."

"Yeah! But we'll need some insurance. What about the boy?"

"Who? Her son?" Marsden asked.

"Yeah! Nicolas, I believe his name is. If we grab him before she meets with Mescheler, we'll have some leverage, if she decides not to play ball."

"No!" Marsden snapped. "We'll do this without adding kidnapping to the list of crimes we've already committed. We'll grab her and Mescheler when they meet. I'm sure we'll have no trouble getting her to hand over the memory sticks. If we show her a couple of photos of the boy and tell her we know where she lives, that should be enough to convince her that we mean business." He paused. "For now, we stay on her and find out when and where the meeting will take place."

Although confused about the message from the man calling himself The Puzzler, Caroline was also somewhat relieved—relieved because she had anticipated that there might be danger to her son and had removed the threat. In a few days, she would meet her friend at a shopping mall in Baltimore and hand Nicolas over to her. But because of what had happened to Kristie Bremmer, she was certain that someone was already watching her.

The plan she devised to get Nicolas out of harm's way required her and Nicolas to split up once inside the mall. He would go into a shop and wait for her friend. Once he was picked up and at a safe distance from the mall, her friend would call her and confirm that they were safe and on their way to Virginia. With Nicolas out of harm's way, she could return to New York and get on with the business of exposing her husband's killers.

Chapter Fifty-Five

Marsden and Anderson maintained surveillance on Caroline Dupré around the clock, just as they had planned. Then two days later, on Friday, she left her office at 1:30 p.m. without warning and headed to Brooklyn Heights. Both Marsden and Anderson were caught off-guard. They had had no indication that she was planning to leave work early. This was because she had passed a note to her secretary at lunch-time, asking her to remind everyone in the office that she would be off a bit early because it was Nicolas' last day at school, and she wanted to pick him up to get a head start on their weekend together. To avoid any discussion of her plans in the office, she had arranged her early departure with Antoni Miklus earlier in the week. As Deputy Director, he was eager to help out.

When Caroline exited the building onto 5th Avenue Marsden leapt to his feet, ripped off his headphones, and threw them on the table. "What the hell?" he shouted. "Where's she going?"

"Who?" asked Anderson.

"Dupré!" Marsden barked, with a surprised look on his face that quickly gave way to panic.

Answering his own rhetorical question, he shouted, "Mescheler! Damn him! I've gotta catch up to her!" Marsden said, bolting for the door. "You stay put and keep the lid on things here!" he shouted as he ran down the stairs. "I'll call you when I get a fix on what's going on!"

Marsden dodged and wove his way through the crowded streets before spotting the woman. She was about to enter the subway station for 5th Avenue. Searching for the ticket he used to trail her daily to her home, he scampered down the stairs behind her, went through the barrier, and onto the platform. When the train arrived, he entered the same car as her and sat at the opposite end. When the train stopped in Brooklyn Heights, he got off and followed her at a careful distance.

When she turned on to Remsen Street he slowed his pace. But after she disappeared around the corner, he quickened his steps and arrived at the corner just as she entered her front door. She couldn't have been inside more than ten minutes before she and the boy emerged and got into her car. Biting his lower lip in puzzlement, he wondered aloud, "What the hell is she doing?" Realizing she was about to drive off, he turned and ran back toward the surveillance car he had left up the street. As he ran the two blocks toward the car, he muttered to himself, "What a hell of a way to earn a living!"

Marsden made it to the car, started the engine and was waiting near the bottom of Remsen Street when she pulled away from the curb. Running on pure adrenalin, he leaned forward, turned on the car's global positioning system and connected it to the laptop he used to monitor the mobile transmitter he affixed to her car when their surveillance began. With the laptop connected to the car's GPS, he could track her vehicle at a distance of up to five miles.

Marsden followed carefully as the blue Honda Accord with Caroline Dupré at the wheel made its way through the mid-afternoon traffic out of New York, onto Interstate 95, and into New Jersey. Less than half a mile behind her, and still puzzled, Marsden was determined not to let her slip away from him. From time to time he increased his speed and moved in close enough to gain a visual on her car. He had phoned Anderson earlier and told him that he suspected the unannounced trip south was probably for a rendezvous with Mescheler. If so, he would have to improvise—come up a plan which had to be implemented immediately.

Chapter Fifty-Six

Dundalk, Maryland

After nearly six hours, the blue Honda arrived on the outskirts of Baltimore. When it reached the junction with Interstate 695, Caroline Dupré took the I-695 exit and headed south toward Dundalk, Maryland. Just outside Dundalk she turned on to Merritt Boulevard and headed for the East Point Mall. Marsden wondered aloud why she had driven all that way with the boy for a meeting with Mescheler. Then he realized the move made perfectly good sense. *Being cautious and perhaps suspicious, she had probably insisted on meeting on neutral territory, a place far from her home with lots of people around. Having the boy along simply created an appearance of normalcy. The boy could also raise the alarm if anything went wrong.* Marsden was already convinced that Caroline Dupré was no slouch. It was clear that she was a real thinker.

As Marsden closed out his analysis of Caroline Dupré's behavior, her car swung into the entrance of the East Point Mall and headed for the multi-story car park. Once in the car park, she and the boy clambered from the car and walked briskly across the covered pedestrian bridge toward the Mall's entrance. Marsden had driven in closely behind her, but she hadn't detected him and he didn't want that to change. Still, he knew he had to stay on top of her or he'd lose her when she entered the crowded Mall. If he lost her, it would all be over.

He gave her only a brief head start; as he followed her and the boy into the Mall, the two of them stopped abruptly near a bench in the middle of the shopping area on the third floor. He watched keenly as she asked the boy a question, in response to which he shook his head. Nicolas then took a seat on the bench and Caroline strode briskly in the direction of the toilets. Marsden grinned with satisfaction after concluding that she must have asked him if he needed to use the toilet.

Seconds later, she disappeared. After she disappeared, the boy got up and walked in the same direction and began peering into shops on the opposite side of the promenade. Marsden watched intently as he drifted farther and farther away before entering a shop. The shop was too far away for him to see exactly where he had gone. But because he was interested primarily in the boy's mother, the boy's wanderings were of little or no concern to him. Marsden therefore kept his eyes fixed on the bench, knowing Caroline Dupré would return to collect her son.

Minutes later, she emerged from the toilet and headed back to where she had left the boy. Realizing he had wandered off, she began scanning the area. After peering into several shops and not finding him, the look on her face changed from confusion to frustration, then fear. Marsden maintained the position he had taken in a small coffee shop halfway along the promenade when she went to the toilet. As the woman's frustration mounted, Marsden began to chuckle to himself. He was sure the boy was fouling up her plans. He was still chuckling when she spun on her heel and started walking toward him. Soon, she was going from side to side of the promenade, glaring into shops.

Trying to make his interest in her appear less obvious, Marsden retreated to one of the coffee shop's high pedestal tables, away from the promenade. From his new position, he was able to maintain a line of sight to the area where she was walking. For several minutes he watched as the search for the boy switched from peering into shops, to entering and asking questions. When she had entered all the shops at the end of the promenade where he was now holed up, she turned and went back toward the bench where she had originally left him. She paused near the bench then began working the shops farthest away from where Marsden stood. Marsden was again beginning to make light of the situation. But this time his smugness was interrupted by a disturbing thought—he realized that the boy's disappearance might have been a distraction to allow the woman to meet with Mescheler inside one of the shops.

It had been a full twenty minutes since the boy's disappearance and once again, the woman started making her way back to the bench where she had left him. The look on her face seemed to reflect genuine fear. When she returned to the bench, she flopped down as if her body had been drained of all its energy. Marsden watched her glance at her watch and put her head in her hands. He was becoming more and more puzzled. *Could something have gone wrong? Had the boy disobeyed her and run off, or had he been taken by the person she was supposed to be meeting?*

The scenarios building in his head were suddenly interrupted by the ringing of the woman's cell phone. He watched as she withdrew the phone from her purse and put it to her ear. Seconds later, she leapt to her feet and shouted, "Yes!"

As she turned in his direction and began walking toward the exit, he could see that her mood had become jubilant. What was worse, her jubilance seemed to be the result of her son's disappearance. He then realized that he had been duped. The boy had obviously been whisked away by someone while he was being distracted by her seemingly anxious searching. By now he was probably well on his way to some unknown place, perhaps even out of the country. The trip to the Mall had been an arranged hand-off. Caroline Dupré was clearing the way to deal with whatever she had to deal with.

As she made her way past Marsden, he turned his back to her and cursed through clenched teeth. "Damn it!" As he turned to follow her, he reached for his cell phone and called Anderson. As soon as Anderson answered, he exploded. "Bad news! The whole damned thing was a set-up, a ploy designed to look like a meeting with Mescheler that turned out instead to be a meeting to hand the boy over to someone. I don't know who, but she obviously wanted him out of the picture."

"What?" Anderson shouted. "You mean this amateur of a woman managed to dupe you into losing what might have been our only insurance? Tell me you're joking!"

"It's not a joke. I wasn't focusing on the boy! I thought she'd arranged a meeting with Mescheler, so I kept my eyes on her. Hell! Nobody can be two places at once!"

"I guess you're right," Anderson replied apologetically. "I guess we'll deal with this later. Has she left the rendezvous location yet?"

"Yeah, and I'm on her! My bet is she'll come straight back to New York. But I'm not taking any more chances. I'll stick closer to her from here on. The last thing we need now is for her to make contact with Mescheler."

PART IV

Chapter Fifty-Seven

Brooklyn, New York

It was nearly 5:00 a.m. on Friday when Caroline Dupré's blue Honda Accord entered Brooklyn Heights. She was tired. She had driven throughout the night, but she had accomplished what she had set out to do—deliver Nicolas to someone she could trust to keep him safe. Her body ached and her eyes burned. Still, she felt a sense of relief knowing that no matter what happened to her, he would be safe.

During the drive back to Brooklyn, Dick Marsden had followed her as closely as possible. Only once did the distance between his car and hers increase to more than a quarter of a mile. That was when she pulled into a large gas station in Maryland. He had followed her into the station, filled up his car, and watched from several pumps away as she did the same. Knowing that he could track her from his vehicle, he had taken his time. In order to avoid detection, he had let her drive out of the station and get far ahead of him. But he was careful not to let her give him the slip and disappear for a rendezvous with Mescheler.

After following her into Brooklyn, he returned his car to the place along the street where he had been conducting surveillance. He could see the house from where he was parked, and as her car pulled to the curb, he picked up the handset of the secure satellite phone and called Anderson. Anderson had stayed in the office in Manhattan to monitor the woman's communications for any sign of contact from Mescheler. He had been napping on the cot bed at the back of the room. When the phone rang, he bolted upright, jumped to his feet, and grabbed it.

"Yeah! What's up?"

"I'm back in Brooklyn Heights," said Marsden. "She just got in. She's gone inside and I expect she'll be going straight to bed. If she's anywhere near as tired as I am, she's wrecked. What's happening where you are?"

"Nothing much… So far, there's been nothing to suggest that Mescheler has tried to contact her. It has actually been kind of quiet since she left. Speaking of which… what the hell happened at the Mall?"

"She pulled a fast one! Plain and simple… It was planned. It was a ruse to throw us off track, to hand the boy over to someone. She went to the toilet and left the boy in the middle of the Mall to wait for her. He wandered off into one of the shops and when she came back and started looking for him, I kept my eyes on her and the rest is history."

"Do you have any idea who took him and where they may have gone?"

"Not a damn clue! I don't think she's stupid enough to have her grandparents take him. She knows that would be one of the first places someone would look."

"How about Paris? Her father lives there. It would definitely be far enough away."

"Paris would be a good place, but I don't think she'd take the risk of stashing him somewhere that obvious. No, the boy will be kept somewhere in the U.S., most likely along the east coast. If we have to, we can have Bearsden track him down. But for now, we need to keep our eyes on little Miss Smarty Pants. There won't be much going on over at her office today, so why don't you come and baby-sit her for a bit while I go back to the hotel, grab a shower, a bite to eat, and get a few hours sleep."

"I was just about to suggest that," said Anderson. "I'll see you in about an hour."

"You might want to use the van, if you still have it. Even though I've parked the car at several different locations, the folks here might be getting a bit suspicious about the same vehicle hanging around the neighborhood."

"Sure thing… I'll even wear overalls," Mack chuckled.

Just after 6:00 a.m., Anderson pulled up to the curb in the earlier used white van with *NORCOM* logos on its sides and parked about twenty-five yards behind Marsden's car. Marsden watched as the vehicle pulled up behind him then he got out and walked back to it. As he approached the vehicle, he could see Anderson sitting behind the wheel, wearing sunglasses and a New York Yankees baseball cap. He went to the driver's side and Anderson lowered the window.

"What can I do for you today, sir?" Anderson joked.

"Open up!" Marsden said, looking exhausted.

Anderson flashed a smile, slid out of the driver's seat, moved through the van and opened the rear doors. As Marsden climbed in, he handed him a folding camping chair. Marsden sat quietly for several minutes then launched into a diatribe on what impact the loss of the boy might have on their plans.

"Mack, I don't have to tell you how much we need the boy because you already know," he declared wearily. "We still may be able to get along without him for a while. But just having him somewhere where she knows we could have gotten to him, would have been enough to get her to co-operate. Now, that option has been eliminated. So, in the meantime, we're gonna have to stay on her like white on rice until we get our hands on Mescheler and those damned memory sticks. Oh!" he added, "I almost forgot! There is a bit of good news."

"What's that?"

"The memory sticks she's got can't be copied."

"How do you know that?" asked Anderson.

"When Mescheler made copies, it appears he inadvertently

placed a 'write protect' on them, which makes them read-only. So if she tries to bluff us by saying she has other copies, we'll know that's bullshit."

"How'd you find out about this?"

"Miss Smarty Pants told the Bremmer woman during their last conversation that the memory sticks wouldn't copy or download. My guess is she was planning to hide a few copies for insurance," Marsden said smiling. "Who knows, maybe she was even planning to upload them and put the information on the Internet. At least now we know our problem won't suddenly multiply."

"That's good news for a change," Anderson said, sounding somewhat reassured.

"My guess is that Mescheler will be contacting her soon," said Marsden. "I think they're both starting to realize that time is running out. Just stay on top of things here and I'll be back to relieve you around 5:30 p.m. I doubt she'll go anywhere before then. She's gotta be beat from the roundtrip. But if she does leave the house, you'll have to tail her with the van. The tracking device is still on the Honda. Just don't let her out of your sight."

"Sure thing…" said Anderson. "But how easy do you expect that to be, given the antics she's pulled?"

"Not easy at all. Not even for you, Mack," Marsden said, teasing. "Remember… I know you. If it can be done, you'll find a way to do it."

Chapter Fifty-Eight

Things remained quiet at the Dupré house for most of the day. The only thing that caused excitement for Anderson was a call from the woman's father, which lasted about half an hour. He had hoped that the call would give him some clue as to the whereabouts of the boy. But he knew deep down inside that she wouldn't make such a simple and foolish mistake. The precautionary measures she had taken when she arranged to get the boy out of New York showed just how clever she could be. And when the boy's grandfather called and asked about him, she told him that the boy was spending the weekend with a neighborhood friend.

Caroline only left the house on two occasions during the rest of the weekend. The first time was Sunday morning, when she came into her front yard to pick up her newspaper, at which time her nosy neighbor, Mrs. Preston, invited her to have tea later in the afternoon. And the second time was at 4:15 p.m., when she went to visit the elderly woman.

Anderson was unaware that sometime before Caroline Dupré visited her neighbor, she had gone online to check her office webmail account. After the hand-off of her son in Maryland, he and Marsden had temporarily abandoned the listening post near her office and focused on her house. The mistake had cost them, because it gave her time to receive the message from Mescheler and arrange a meeting. The message she received from Mescheler bore the word 'Frenchy' in the subject line. It was a short message and the sender's address was an arbitrary combination of letters and numbers. The message read:

We must talk! Call me in precisely fifty minutes at (212) 555-4094.

She had called Mrs. Preston only minutes after reading the message, to inform her that she was coming over for a short visit. Anderson had heard the conversation between her and the elderly woman, but prior to the call, he thought he had heard the faint sound of fingers striking a keyboard. In the end, however, he dismissed it as nervous or restless tapping by the woman.

During Caroline's visit with Mrs. Preston, exactly fifty minutes from the time the webmail message was received, she called the number sent to her from her cell phone. She had told Mrs. Preston that she had forgotten to leave instructions for her administrative assistant to cancel a Monday afternoon appointment.

Just as the pay-phone on the east side of Central Park was about to ring a fourth time, a man, nearly out of breath, picked it up but didn't answer and Caroline didn't speak. She didn't want to risk being identified if someone other than Mescheler was at the other end of the line. After several seconds of silence at both ends, the man who picked up in Central Park asked, "Is this Caroline?"

"Yes, it is," she said cautiously.

In a gentle, middle-class English accent, he instructed, "Don't talk. Just listen. I'm The Puzzler. I'm the one who sent you the e-mail. My name is Dr. Joseph Mescheler. I'm a geophysicist and an employee at the Transnational Research Group laboratory in Hamilton County, or at least I was until a few months ago. But the long and short of it is that I worked there and was involved in the collection of data and conducting research and analysis which shows that ecologically, terrible things are happening to the Earth, and they're happening much quicker than anyone ever thought. The problem is, there are powerful people who want to suppress this information. I don't know who they are, but I have my suspicions. Before your husband left for Kuala Lumpur, I gave him something very important—the scientific data that would blow the lid off this cover-up. Unfortunately, that information led to his death."

Dr. Mescheler paused a few seconds then continued. "I believe you're holding a copy of the same information. I've been on the run for nearly four months now, skirting and hiding from faceless, nameless henchmen sent to find me. The running has to end or they'll soon catch me. They'll stop at nothing to get their hands on me. But you can help me end this and find out who's behind it and who killed your husband."

Despite being told by Mischeler to listen and ask no questions, she interrupted. "How can I help?" she asked. "I'm no better at dealing with these people than you are. What can I do?"

"Probably much more than you think," Mescheler responded, temperately. "From the looks of it, there are people in very high places involved. I'm sure those same people are responsible for your husband's death. If you want to help, meet me tomorrow at 12:30 at Alonzo's Bistro. It's on East 51st Street. If you have a cell phone, I'll need the number."

To avoid arousing suspicion about whom she was actually calling, Caroline suddenly announced, "Angela, this is Caroline. I have an urgent message for you. If you have any questions, call me right away at home or on my cell phone at 555-0919."

Mescheler's voice returned. "I won't contact you before our meeting, unless it's absolutely necessary." Then he hung up.

After the call ended, Caroline tried to keep a straight face. She sighed and then whispered to the elderly woman. "It was her answering machine. But just to be on the safe side, I think I'd better leave her a message at work in case she gets home too late this evening to call me. It'll only take a minute." She dialed the number for her office and hung up before it began to ring. After a few seconds, she pretended to speak to her office's answering service.

"Hello. This is Caroline Dupré. I'd like to leave a message for Angela Thompson." After a slight pause, she began. "Angela. This is Caroline. This is urgent. I need you to cancel my Monday 1:30 p.m. appointment as soon as you can reach someone at the other end. Please extend my apologies. Something urgent has come up. See you tomorrow. Thanks."

After finishing the call, Caroline spent the next forty-five minutes making small talk with the elderly woman, then went home and stayed there for the remainder of the evening. Marsden returned and relieved Anderson at 5:30 p.m.; throughout the rest of the evening, the only sounds he heard inside the woman's house were voices from the television and several hours of classical music. Behind the walls of the Brooklyn Heights brownstone, however, Caroline Dupré was gripped with fear and anxiety—fear over what had happened to the four young women and anxiety about the possibility that she could be walking into a deadly trap.

Chapter Fifty-Nine

The next morning, Dick Marsden was still exhausted. The nights he spent sleeping on the seat of a hot car were taking their toll on him. Nevertheless, when Caroline Dupré left her house for work, he continued the routine of following her until she reached her Manhattan office. As usual, when she entered the building he broke off foot surveillance and went to the room above the Vintage Bookstore. When he entered the small upstairs room, Anderson was already at his post.

"You look like shit!" Anderson teased.

"I *feel* like shit! Any coffee made?"

"It's in the usual place," said Anderson, pointing to the drip coffee maker at the back of the room. "You sure you wouldn't rather have something cold?"

"Coffee's fine… I need it to get my blood circulating." He paused. "Something's gotta give soon, Mack. I don't know how much longer I can cope with sleep deprivation. Anything new here?" he asked.

"Yeah!" said Anderson. "Interesting you should ask," he added, drolly. "I found out this morning that Mescheler contacted her yesterday at exactly 3:30 p.m."

"And…?" Marsden prompted, filling his coffee cup.

"He sent her another one of those untraceable messages to her webmail account. According to the time stamped by the server, she accessed the message from her house yesterday at 3:50 p.m. But that's not the worst of it. He gave her a phone number, which I was able to locate in the telephone company's database. The number was for a pay-phone in Central Park. I interrogated the phone company's records and found that a call was made to that pay-phone at exactly 4:20 p.m.—fifty minutes from the time the message was delivered to her… the exact time Mescheler told her to call. The call to the pay-phone came from a cell phone. I couldn't get the number because the woman withheld it."

Frustrated, Marsden shouted, "Damn it! You say the call was made to the number at 4:20 p.m.?"

"Yep!" Anderson replied. "That's around the time she went to the old biddy's house next door. She obviously suspects her place is wired. That's why she went next door—to make sure she had a clean line. You gotta hand it to her… this woman is even smarter than I thought she was."

Marsden stared at Anderson. "If she made contact with Mescheler, I'm sure they set up a meeting. So far, she's had too many damned breaks!" Marsden barked. "From now on, we don't leave anything to chance. You hear me? Nothing! If we have to we'll man the office here and her place in Brooklyn Heights, twenty-four-seven!"

As if to defend himself, Anderson retorted, "Shit, man! There's no way we could've known she'd do what she did, especially using the old biddy's house to call Mescheler from her cell phone." He shot Marsden an icy look. "Neither you nor I saw this one coming. We fucked up again, Dick! Pure and simple… But that don't mean we're out of the game. It's not over. In fact, it's just beginning!"

Marsden and Anderson had been duped again. Stone-faced, they took up their posts in silence. Meanwhile, across the street from them, Caroline Dupré was preparing for her 9:30 a.m. staff meeting. A few minutes later, on her way to the conference room, she slipped the receptionist a note informing her that she would be leaving for lunch at 11:45 a.m. and to mention her lunch plans to no one because she was arranging a surprise for one of the girls on her staff. If anyone asked, she should tell them that she had a few errands to run.

At 11:45 a.m. Caroline rose from her desk and without announcing her departure or plans, she left the office. She exited the building, walked south on 5th Avenue until she reached 51st Street then turned west and continued the few blocks to Alonzo's. It was an unusually hot day. The temperature in the city was already nearly 90 degrees Fahrenheit, but there was almost no humidity. Because it was a nice day, she walked at a leisurely pace and arrived at Alonzo's at 12:15.

Anderson spotted her when she left the building and shouted to Marsden. "She's on the move! Let's go!" Still suffering from fatigue brought on by the weekend chase and sleeping on the car seat, Marsden scrambled from his post and followed Anderson down the stairs and onto the street. Although her sudden departure had taken them by surprise, they stayed close on her tail. The moment she arrived at Alonzo's, the two of them split up. There were tables with umbrellas outside the restaurant near the sidewalk and the woman took a seat at one of them.

Marsden continued walking past the bistro and took a seat outside another eatery next door. Meanwhile, Anderson crossed the street and took up a position at a kiosk. From their locations, they could observe her every move. They knew that they had the advantage of not having been detected.

When the waiter came over, Caroline ordered a glass of fruit juice and a bottle of water. She told the waiter that she would order food when the friend she was waiting for arrived. Marsden and Anderson were feeling confident—smug in their belief that the trap they were about to spring would net their prey.

Some twenty yards from where Mack Anderson was standing, a homeless man stood over a garbage can. He seemed to be foraging for food or some other jettisoned item that might bring him a few pennies if traded. Despite the man's long, matted, graying hair and dirty clothes, his eyes reflected a quiet intelligence. The matted hair, dirty clothes and schizophrenic behavior were the only things that masked Dr. Joseph Mescheler's true identity from his would-be captors. As he shuffled along the street from one trash receptacle to another, he mumbled to himself, lifting his head occasionally to survey his immediate surroundings and the area across the street where Caroline Dupré was sitting.

Within minutes, he recognized Mack Anderson's intense interest in Alonzo's Bistro. When Anderson was spotted, he was aimlessly perusing the items on offer at the kiosk with no apparent interest in buying. He stuck out like a sore thumb. As Mescheler approached him, Anderson's cell phone rang. Grabbing it quickly, he put it to his mouth and turned in the direction of Alonzo's Bistro. Following Anderson's gaze, Mescheler scanned the area in the vicinity of the bistro. Seconds later he spotted Richard Marsden, who also had a phone up to his ear. Less than a minute later, Marsden lowered his phone and put it away; the man he had been observing at the kiosk did the same.

Mescheler surveyed the area for nearly ten minutes, trying to determine how many other predators lay hidden in nearby lairs. When he was certain there were only two, he moved off down the street nearly two blocks before stopping at a pay-phone.

Mescheler was already fifteen minutes late for his rendezvous and Caroline's patience had just about run out. Just as she called the waiter over to inform him that her lunch plans had changed and she needed her bill, her cell phone, which was on the table in front of her, began to vibrate. She grabbed it nervously.

"Hello?"

Mescheler's voice erupted in her ear. "Mrs. Dupré. Don't say anything! Just act normal and listen carefully. You've been followed! I was across the street from Alonzo's when you arrived. Seated outside at the restaurant over your left shoulder is a distinguished-looking, casually dressed, middle-aged white male with dark hair. He's unusually fit, I might add. Across the street at the kiosk is a smartly-dressed, middle-aged black man, who is also very fit and muscular. Please don't look in either direction just yet, but these men have undoubtedly come for me and most likely for you as well. Given the situation, I can't meet you here and now. I suggest you continue with your lunch and return to the office as you normally would. I'll be in touch soon to arrange another meeting. If I were you, after I hang up, I would pretend I was talking to someone from the office. One other thing; never, ever speak to me on your cell phone indoors, regardless of where you are. Is that clear?"

"Yes," she replied nervously.

"It isn't safe!"

After Mescheler hung up, Caroline remained on the phone, holding a fictitious conversation for nearly five minutes. After hanging up, she ordered a Caesar salad and another glass of fruit juice. When she had finished eating and paid her bill, she withdrew a compact mirror from her purse and pretended to reapply her lipstick. Using the small mirror to look over her shoulder, she spotted the man Mescheler had described. She couldn't see his entire body, but she could make out his face. It was now etched in her memory.

After applying her lipstick, she rose slowly from her seat and left. As she stepped onto the sidewalk, she took a brief look in the direction of the kiosk. Her subtle but careful glance failed to grab Anderson's attention, but it was enough for her to make out his face and commit it to memory. The realization that she was being followed frightened her. But strangely, she found comfort in seeing at least two of the people she was up against. It was also comforting that Mescheler seemed genuine and was handling the situation carefully.

Although she had not met Dr. Joseph Mescheler, her confidence and acceptance of what she had to do grew from knowing that he was on her side. As she walked back to her office, she could feel her courage growing, despite the fact that her enemies now knew she had taken up the gauntlet.

Chapter Sixty

After returning to the surveillance post above the Vintage Bookstore, Dick Marsden sat in silence. Anderson stood next to the purring fan with his shoulder against the window frame, staring at the street below. Like Marsden, he realized that delivering a *coup de grace* against Caroline Dupré and the renegade scientist wasn't going to be as easy as they had thought. He knew from the way the woman had behaved during the planned rendezvous that she had been alerted to their presence.

The fiasco at the bistro had again raised questions in Anderson's mind. How could Mescheler have identified them? And where had he been when they moved into the area? They certainly hadn't caught a glimpse of him, and that was worrying. He was also troubled by the stealth and cunning of the Dupré woman. For the third time, she had shown an ability to outwit them. Anderson thought they were beginning to look like fools, a couple of amateur sleuths. Despite the fact that they had had little warning of the meeting at Alonzo's, this latest failure was proof positive that they needed to change their tactics.

After staring out of the window for nearly a quarter of an hour in silent frustration, Anderson finally spoke. "Are you thinking what I'm thinking?" he asked abruptly.

"What's that?" Marsden asked.

"This woman is making us look like a couple of idiots! What the hell is going on? We looked like the Keystone Cops today.

Mind you, it didn't just start today. First she gave you the slip in Baltimore then she went on to set up the rendezvous with Mescheler right under our noses. This woman seems to have found all the weaknesses in our surveillance."

"It's just luck!" Marsden retorted. "She's just lucky. That's all! She's clearly no fool. After finding out what happened to her husband, which she obviously has, she simply started exercising more caution. Jeez! What would you do? Wouldn't you start to suspect that someone is listening in on your calls and probably even following you? Did we really expect her to retreat into a shell after learning that in addition to her husband and his friends, four other people with links to Kuala Lumpur have turned up dead or gone missing? I say she got lucky! It's as simple as that."

"Twice, Dick?" Anderson barked.

"Yes, twice, Mack! But she obviously had help today. If you ask me, I think she was just following instructions. She's just going with the flow."

"Following instructions or not, I say it's time we get tough with her. I say we take the gloves off. This damned thing has been drawn out for far too long. We should've wrapped it up weeks ago!"

"So what do you suggest? We grab her and beat her until she tells us what she's done with the memory sticks? Is that what we should do? I say we proceed as normal! Besides, Smith gave strict orders: no rough stuff with her. He's probably worried she'll open her mouth to someone, or even worse, run to the press. No… I say we proceed as normal, but we up the stakes a bit."

"How?" Anderson demanded.

"Even though the boy is in hiding, we call her and let her know we can find him and take him. My guess is she'll panic and contact whoever has him. She'll lead us right to him! It can't be that difficult. Besides, we've already got Bearsden working on tracking the boy down."

As Marsden talked, he fixed his gaze on Anderson, who was still standing near the window. "Look, Mack," he said. "I don't like the way this is going any more than you do. Sure, we've got holes in our surveillance and I admit we may have lost a couple of battles, but the war is ours to win. And believe me, Mack, we'll win it. You hear me? We'll win!"

"Alright!" Anderson grunted. "It's your ball game!"

"Wrong, Mack. It's *our* ball game! *Our* ball game... So what do you say we pull our act together and finish this thing? We can't afford to let it fall apart and we certainly can't afford to be at each other's throats. There's a hell of a lot of money riding on this thing and I'm ready for pay day and for it to be over!"

Anderson's mood seemed to lighten and his concern about what had happened at Alonzo's appeared to fade. He returned Marsden's gaze and smiled. "Now you're talkin'!"

"Here's what we do, Mack," Marsden instructed. "We keep the surveillance as it is and we stay on top of her. We know Mescheler's watching. So next time we just have to do a better job and not crowd her. If we do, we'll spook Mescheler again. We gotta let 'em make contact. I've got a gut feeling he'll be getting in touch with her again real soon to arrange another meeting. He's running scared too. He wants to get whatever he has for her off his chest and it's obvious he won't go to the police or the FBI because he's paranoid and doesn't know who he can trust."

Just two days after the aborted meeting at Alonzo's bistro, and just as Marsden had predicted, Mescheler made contact. Just before 11:30 a.m. he called Caroline Dupré at her office via her cell phone. It was the big break Dick Marsden and Mack Anderson had been waiting for. To avoid arousing suspicion, Caroline answered immediately after the phone began to vibrate and left TEARS' office space and made her way down to a coffee shop on the twenty-ninth floor. As she passed the receptionist and exited the main door to her office, she began to speak.

"This is Caroline," she said.

The line was quiet for a few seconds then she heard Mescheler's voice.

"Where are you? Are you alone?"

"Yes, I'm outside my office near the elevator. I'm going three floors down to the coffee shop."

"Good!" he replied. "Surely you must know by now that your video-phone, your telephones, as well as your home and office spaces, are bugged. And even if they're not, you must assume they are. You mustn't take any chances. I assume the cell phone you're using is clean?"

"Clean?" she asked. "What do you mean by clean?"

"I mean, is it possible that they could've gotten your number, say from your secretary or someone in your office?"

"I don't think so, but I can't say for sure."

"Then I strongly recommend you change your service provider today or get another disposable SIM card. In fact, get a couple of extra SIM cards. That way, if what I have planned falls through again I'll be able to contact you on a clean line. If the meeting I have planned for today falls through, I'll send you a message like before, telling you how and when I will contact you. It'll be short notice because I have to keep moving."

As she stepped off the elevator on the twenty-ninth floor and made her way to the coffee shop, Mescheler began to deliver his instructions.

"As I said… we'll meet today. As before, don't look for me, I'll find you. Go to Central Park today at 3:30 p.m. and take a seat on one of the benches near the Turtle Pond. Sit there for exactly fifteen minutes then walk toward Central Park West and up toward the Jacqueline Kennedy Onassis Reservoir."

"Why there?" she asked.

"Listen… Don't ask questions!" he admonished sharply. "However, if you must know, it'll be busy. Lots of people about, which means, it'll be safer. I'll have something for you. And if time permits, I have something to tell you. If anything threatening should happen, we should split up—go in separate directions. If we have to make a run for it, run toward a crowd of people. They won't harm you in front of witnesses. After all, they only want what you have. Me, I think they'd just as soon shoot on sight. What I have inside my head is just as dangerous to them or whoever they're working for. But no matter what happens, you mustn't worry about me. What we're about to do is far more important than either of us, but it'll be worthless unless it's delivered to the right people—honest, trustworthy people," Mescheler stressed then added, "I'll see you at exactly 3:45 p.m." He hung up.

When Caroline returned to her office, she gave a handwritten note to her administrative assistant informing her she would not be going to lunch today and would be leaving work sometime shortly after 3:00 p.m. Less than half an hour later, her administrative assistant received a call from one of TEARS' assistant regional directors requesting an impromptu meeting with her at 3:00 p.m. She informed the caller that Caroline would be leaving the office for the rest of the day at around 3:00 p.m. As soon as Marsden heard the administrative assistant, he chuckled and an ear-to-ear grin swept over his face.

"We're in business again! She'll be on the move sometime around 3:00 p.m. Another meeting, no doubt! Remember what I said… Give 'em some room. Give 'em some time to connect with each other. We can't afford to spook 'em again. If we play this right, we can get 'em both!"

Anticipating Caroline Dupré's departure from her office building sometime before three o'clock, the two men changed into less conspicuous clothing. Anderson put on a pair of casual slacks and a polo shirt. Over his shoulder he carried a small backpack containing a radio, a small pair of binoculars, his cell phone, and a pistol with a silencer. He completed his disguise with a moustache. Marsden donned a false beard and a moustache and put on running gear. Around his waist he wore a pack in which he carried his weapon; like Anderson, he also carried his cell phone, a small pair of binoculars, a semi-automatic pistol with silencer, and a small two-way radio.

Chapter Sixty-One

At exactly 3:00 p.m., Caroline Dupré left her office building and turned left on 5th Avenue. Marsden and Anderson, who had been waiting just inside the door of the bookstore, fell in behind her at a cautious distance. Caroline walked at a leisurely pace. After walking a few minutes on 5th Avenue, she turned onto East 79th Street then headed into Central Park. As instructed, when she reached the Turtle Pond, she took a seat on a bench. As soon as she sat down, Marsden quickened his pace and began jogging. To avoid raising suspicion, he continued past her, heading toward Central Park West. Anderson remained on the 5th Avenue side of the park and took up a position where he had an unobstructed view of her through his binoculars.

It was only a few minutes before 3:20 p.m. when Caroline took her position on the bench. She remained there for exactly fifteen minutes, thumbing through a magazine. At 3:35 p.m., she got up and began walking north toward the Onassis Reservoir. As she approached the south side of the reservoir, she began a meticulous scan of the landscape on both sides and in front of her. Because of the unusually warm weather there were many people in the park. Some were jogging, while others cycled, strolled, walked dogs or enjoyed picnics.

Marsden maintained visual contact on her from a safe distance—first running past her going east and then briefly south on Central Park West Drive. He then reversed course and headed north. As Caroline drew nearer the reservoir, she could see scores of people moving toward her. After a while, one among them seemed to stand out, mainly because he looked like a bum or a homeless person. As the distance between her and the homeless man closed, she could see that his hair, although graying, was long and matted.

As the homeless man continued toward her, she noticed that he was wearing a thin raincoat and his clothes were oil-stained and dirty. By now, it was clear to her that he was asking people for money, but only after offering them what appeared to be a very modest arrangement of artificial poppies, heather, and violet posies. Most of the people he approached ignored him and she could see a look of hopelessness on his face.

As they approached each other, the man stared directly into her eyes. She noticed instantly that his eyes were particularly striking, given his unkempt appearance. They looked like blue sapphires and exuded an intelligence that had earlier been concealed by the disappointment on his face. When he drew to within a few feet of her, he began to speak.

"Sister," he said in a sinking voice, "you look like a very kind-hearted soul. Could you spare a few coins for a fella who has fallen on his luck and has nowhere to lay his head and hasn't had a decent meal for nearly a week? The look on your face tells me you understand my misfortune. Mind you, I'm not asking for a handout," he said. "No ma'am," he added, with what sounded like a slight hint of an English accent. "I've got these flowers you can buy if you want. The poppies are especially good for wearing on the lapel of your jacket."

For a brief moment, Caroline wondered if the man in front of her might be Dr. Mescheler, but quickly dismissed the notion and decided to give him some money to get rid of him. As the homeless man continued his sales pitch, she glanced at her watch, realizing that Mescheler was already several minutes late. She wondered if he had seen the man approach her and decided to pull a no-show like he had done at the bistro. She fumbled quickly through her handbag until she found her wallet. Without removing it from the handbag, she pulled out a ten dollar bill and handed it to him. The man's eyes grew large with excitement and he reached into the small dirty, cloth bag he carried slung over his shoulder and withdrew an unflattering arrangement of heather and violet posies. He returned his hand to the bag a second time and withdrew a rather sizeable piece of foil and proceeded to carefully wrap it around the short stems of the flower arrangement. As he handed the bunch of flowers to her, he muttered, "Thank you kindly. I could tell from your face that you are a kind and thoughtful soul. I believe there is much you can learn by studying the contents of this wrapper."

Still anxious about her meeting with Mescheler, she failed to grasp the significance of the comment. Instead, she replied in a somewhat impatient voice, "You're welcome. It won't provide a place for you to sleep, but it'll help you find something nourishing to eat." Then, in a glib tone she told him, "Sir, I would truly love to spend more time talking to you, but I have to go. I have an important appointment. I wish you the best of luck."

She glanced at her watch once more as she began walking away from the man. The time was 3:53 p.m. *Joseph Mescheler has pulled another no-show. Except this time he hasn't bothered to call.*

When she had walked some fifteen feet away from the homeless man, she heard a voice behind her. "Take care of yourself, Mrs. Dupré and don't look back. Enjoy the flowers!" he added. "By learning more about flowers we learn more about ourselves. They have a great deal to tell us about what life on earth has been like, what it's like now, and what it will be like in the future."

Chapter Sixty-Two

Dick Marsden and Mack Anderson had been observing the interaction between Caroline Dupré and the homeless man and were thrown off by her checking her watch several times. Her concern about time had caused them to dismiss the actions of the homeless man as genuine. But as the homeless bum began moving north in the park, Anderson had a memory flash. He remembered he had seen a homeless man dressed the same as the man on the street near the kiosk across from Alonzo's bistro. Although he had not paid much attention to the man foraging through the trash cans, he remembered that it was not until the man left the area that the Dupré woman received a call—a call that apparently aborted their meeting. Anderson realized that the man's appearance near Alonzo's and now in the park was no coincidence. It was an ingenious plan.

As soon as he correlated the incidents, he pulled out his radio and called Marsden.

"Dick! You there?"

"Yeah! What have you got?"

"It's Mescheler!"

"Where?" Marsden asked, alarmed.

"The bum she was just talkin' to! He's the same guy I saw when I was at the kiosk across the street from Alonzo's. A few minutes after he left where I was, her phone rang. It's too convenient to be a coincidence!"

"Are you sure?"

"You're damned right I'm sure! He handed her something,

didn't he?"

"If you're wrong, we don't get another chance. We're screwed! You know that, don't you?"

"It's him, I tell you! I still have him in sight! He's headin' north in the park. I'll go north on the 5th Avenue side, cut across 97th Street and head him off. You take the girl!"

Anderson made his way up 5th Avenue and into the park, first walking briskly, then breaking into a trot, and finally running at full speed. Unaware that he was being followed, Mescheler walked at a steady pace. After a few minutes Anderson was less than a hundred yards behind him on 97th Street. As Mack Anderson closed on the renegade scientist, he slowed to a brisk walk, removed the silencer from his backpack and fixed it to his .45 caliber Mark 23 pistol.

Mescheler was starting to feel confident that the hand-off he had just made would soon bring an end to his running and hiding. But before the thought could wind its way through his head and begin to settle, it was interrupted by loud footsteps approaching him from behind.

Before he could turn to investigate, he felt a sharp pain in the lower part of his back. Anderson had caught up with him and thrust the gun up against him.

"Doc, you ever see what a .45 caliber Mark 23 with hydra-shock ammunition does to a man at this range?" Anderson asked, breathing heavily. "It'll turn your insides to mush! So, if you wanna' keep breathin', keep your eyes in front of you and your mouth shut."

To emphasize the point, he thrust the gun, which concealed under a jacket carried across his arm, tighter against the Mescheler's back.

"What do you want from me?" Mescheler asked nervously.

"Shut up!" Anderson commanded through clenched teeth. "I'll ask the questions!"

"It's just that I don't know what use a homeless man might be to anyone," said Dr. Mescheler. "I have nothing. I have no money, except the ten dollar bill the nice lady just gave me for my flowers, a few singles, and some change. It's yours if you want it."

"Shut up, you old fool! If I have to tell you again to shut your mouth, I'm gonna squeeze one off into you! Do you understand me?"

"Yes," Mescheler said, nodding.

"Homeless man, my ass!" Anderson muttered. "Now, you just continue walkin' beside me as if we were long lost friends. When we get to Central Park West, we're gonna take a ride somewhere. And I want you to behave yourself. 'Cause if you don't, my finger might just slip and end you. You read me?"

"Loud and clear," Mescheler replied nervously.

"So you're the infamous Dr. Joseph Mescheler?" Anderson asked rhetorically. "I've gotta give it to you, Doc. You're a pretty clever fella! You've managed to evade capture for over four months. Hanging out on the streets, eating out of trash cans, begging for money and food just like a real bum. Shame on you! A man with all your education surely could've done better. But I suppose, as a man of science, you probably looked at it in a more pragmatic way. You're probably thinkin' that it kept you alive," Anderson said chuckling. "Doc, you've caused me a hell of a lot of inconvenience these last few weeks. But your runnin' days are over, my friend."

As they neared Central Park West, Anderson lifted his two-way radio, now clipped to his belt, and called Marsden.

"Dick!"

"Yeah! What's up?"

"I've got him!"

"Mescheler?"

"Yeah! He's right here beside me. I'm headed over to pick up the van and get him bundled up all nice and cozy."

"Good idea!" Marsden replied.

"What about the girl?" Anderson asked.

"I'm in pursuit! It looks like she's headed back to her office.

She's ahead of me somewhere. I lost her in the crowd after she exited the park. You stay with Mescheler and I'll take care of her. I think it would be wise to get him home as quickly as possible. It'll be one less problem to deal with."

"You read my mind! We'll head out as soon as I pick up the van. I'll call you again when I'm on the road taking this runaway home. Good hunting!"

Chapter Sixty-Three

As soon as Anderson arrived at Central Park West with the renegade scientist, he hailed a taxi. Less than an hour later, he had reached the LaGuardia Sheraton Hotel. On the way to the hotel, the taxi driver had asked who his friend was; Anderson had told him that Mescheler was the down-and-out brother of a friend with whom he had served in the military. He had been asked by his friend's family to find him and bring him home, because his friend was terminally ill and wanted to see his brother before he died. The driver accepted the concocted explanation, lock, stock and barrel.

When the taxi reached the LaGuardia Sheraton, Anderson had the driver drop them off in the parking lot near the van. Within minutes, Dr. Joseph Mescheler was bound, gagged, and on his way to the TRG laboratory in upstate New York.

Back in the city Marsden continued his pursuit of Caroline Dupré, but he had failed to catch up to her. Somewhere along 5th Avenue he had lost sight of her; the next time he laid eyes on her she was entering her office building. Thinking on his feet, he raced across the street to the room above the Vintage Bookstore and headed straight for the laptop they had been using to tap into her e-mail accounts. Acting on his hunch that she would contact whoever was holding the boy if she thought he might be in danger, he had called her office from his cell phone when he and Anderson were in the park waiting for her to make the rendezvous with Mescheler.

Knowing she was out of the office, he had told her assistant that he was a friend of her late husband who was passing through New York and wanted to say hello. Her assistant had felt the call important enough to give him Caroline's cell phone number.

After setting up the laptop to interrogate the telephone company's call-handling computer, he rang her office on one of TEARS' commercial lines. Because it was now well past 5:00 p.m. and all but one or two staffers had gone home, she answered the phone herself.

"Hello... Caroline Dupré."

"Mrs. Dupré," the voice said then fell silent.

"Who is this?" she asked.

"Never mind who it is. You have something that doesn't belong to you. Something I want."

"I don't know what you're talking about!" she replied.

"Don't play games with me, Mrs. Dupré, or should I call you Caroline? You have a couple of memory sticks which your friend Dr. Mescheler stole from his place of employment several months ago. The owner wants them back."

"I'm sorry. I believe you have the wrong person."

"Look, lady!" Marsden shouted angrily. "Don't play fuckin games with me!"

"You've clearly contacted the wrong person," she said. "I haven't a clue what you're talking about!"

"OK! If that's the way you wanna' play it! You see, we caught up with your friend in the park after you left. No doubt by now he's beggin' to tell us about what he gave you and what you already had. By the way, earlier today an associate of mine also picked up your son. Nicolas, I believe his name is? So don't get smart with me."

"What?" she shouted. "My son... What have you done with him?" she pleaded. "Please don't hurt him! Please, mister, please. He's all I have in the world! He's innocent. Don't hurt him! Please!"

"He won't be hurt if you keep your mouth shut and do exactly as I tell you."

"I'll do anything! Just don't hurt my son!"

"First, you'll say nothing to anyone about this call. Second, you'll keep your mouth shut about the memory sticks and whatever Mescheler gave you today. Third, you'll do absolutely nothing until you hear from me, at which time I'll tell you the place and time for an exchange—the boy for the memory sticks and whatever else Mescheler gave you. Is that clear?"

"Yes," she replied, fighting back the tears forming in her eyes.

Before hanging up, Marsden reminded her that she was not to discuss anything about what was happening with anyone, if she wanted her son back safely.

As soon as Caroline hung up, she grabbed her cell phone and made her way down to the coffee shop on the twenty-ninth floor. Once outside her office, she frantically dialed her friend in Virginia Beach where Nicolas was staying. Her hands trembled as she searched the phone's directory. The phone rang four times before it was answered.

"Debbie? Is that you?" she asked.

"Caroline? What's wrong?"

"Is Nicolas OK?"

"Yes, he's fine. He's here with me and the kids. I was planning to take them to the beach. Is anything wrong?"

"Yeah! There's lots wrong! Don't go to the beach or take him anywhere until you hear from me."

"What do you mean? What's happened?"

"The people who killed François are looking for me. They told me they had Nicolas. I had to know he was still safe."

"As long as I have him, he's not going anywhere! You hear me?" the woman said, cockily.

"Thanks, Debbie. I know you'll take good care of him. In the meantime, I've gotta find a way to get out of this mess. I'm gonna have to disappear for a couple of days. You won't hear from me until I've figured this out. I don't want them to connect me to you. I'll call when I know what needs to be done next."

"Why don't you call the police, the FBI or somebody?" the woman suggested, clearly worried.

"I can't. It's too dangerous! Besides, it looks as if some powerful people are involved in this. So even if I did go to the police or the FBI, I couldn't be sure what would happen when the people controlling things discover what's going on. They probably have people in the police department, the FBI, and who knows how many other agencies. There's no way of telling who is and who isn't a part of this. Right now, the last thing I need is to have every law enforcement agency in the country on my tail for some trumped-up charge. I just need to lay low for a few days. I've gotta get a handle on what this is all about."

"Please take care of yourself," said Debbie. "Be careful. You hear me? And don't worry about Nicolas. I'll keep him safe. Just get through this so you can be with him."

"I will. I promise," Caroline said. "Look Debbie, I've gotta go. I'll be in touch as soon as I can. But if you haven't heard from me in seventy-two hours, get hold of somebody and tell them as much as you can. Someone from the media probably would be the safest bet," she added. "I'm sorry I can't tell you where I am because it'll only make trouble for you. Tell Nicolas I love him very, very much and that I want nothing more right now than to see him and hold him. Tell him I'll see him as soon as I can. OK?"

"I'll explain things so he'll understand. I'm sure he knows you love him," the woman said reassuringly.

"I've gotta go. Take care of my baby."

Although Marsden wasn't able to hear both sides of the conversation, he was able to hack into the telephone company's call-routing computer and identify the number Caroline had called. She had failed to heed Mescheler's advice about getting a new SIM card; it had made her phone vulnerable to hacking.

Because she was calling a land line, Marsden was able to locate the call activity from her phone while she was still talking. By the time she hung up, he knew that she had been speaking to a Deborah Creighton in Virginia Beach, Virginia. He then interrogated the telephone company's subscription database, got the address and passed it to Dave Bearsden. Already playing on his hunch, he had sent Bearsden to Virginia Beach; Bearsden was already scouring neighborhoods in the area where the Dupré woman's parents lived.

When Caroline made the call, she had had no idea she was exposing her son to the very danger from which she had sought to protect him. And now that Mescheler was in the hands of the people whom she suspected had killed Kristie Bremmer, Amanda Costanti, Beth O'Connell, and Patty Maynard, her problems had suddenly multiplied. The killers were now training their sights on her.

Chapter Sixty-Four

By the time Caroline mustered the courage to leave her office, it was 6:30 p.m. Troubled by the call she had received from a man threatening her son's life, she had sat at her desk for nearly an hour, wondering what to do. She was too frightened to go home and wondered if she should call someone from work and tell them what was happening. Even though she'd just been assured of Nicolas' safety, she knew there was no way of guaranteeing he would stay that way. Thoughts of what could happen to him flooded her head. She couldn't help thinking about how the memory sticks she had locked in her office file cabinet had become a source of deep fear and anxiety. It was becoming clear that they were tied to something sinister—something dark and deceptive, something conspiratorial. She wondered what would have happened if she'd never opened the envelope containing the memory sticks. *Would the people looking for me still be after me, threatening my life and the life of my son?*

Through the agony and fear that consumed her thoughts, she realized that not knowing of the existence of the memory sticks probably would have made little or no difference. They still would have believed that her husband had hidden them among his personal things. And without knowing about the memory sticks, she and Nicolas would have been unwitting targets of the same relentless, intrusive, and dangerous activities carried out by the same people.

As she raised herself from her chair her eyes caught the

bunch of flowers Mescheler had given her. Overwhelmed by the call and the fear it caused, she had forgotten about them. Staring at them, she felt anger rising. As her memories of the encounter in the park with Mescheler began to crystallize, the words he spoke as she walked away struck her. 'By learning more about flowers, we learn more about ourselves,' he had said. The words rang in her ears as she began to remove the thin sheet of aluminum foil he had wrapped carefully around their short stems.

From the outside, the wrapping looked like a piece of foil sheeting. But as she unfurled it, she could see that a piece of thin paper had been rolled up inside it. The paper contained a message—a message carefully and cleverly written in small, neat handwriting on both sides. As she began to read its contents, her knees weakened and she recoiled back into her chair and away from her desk.

By the time you read this, I'll either be the victim of an unfortunate accident or counting down the hours to freedom. As for you, a monumental task lies ahead. Your husband lost his life over what you are about to learn. If you succeed, you'll not only avenge his death, you'll also save millions of lives.

Over ten years ago, an unknown number of philanthropists set up a laboratory in the Adirondacks called the Transnational Research Group, or TRG. On paper, the lab was supposed to design and develop equipment for measuring levels of carbon dioxide and other pollutants in the atmosphere, submersible devices for oceanographic research and other equipment for studying and analyzing the environment. In reality, the lab collected data using its own equipment. It also received environmental data on the 'state of the planet' from other 'credible' organizations, with particular emphasis on global warming, rising ocean and sea levels, thawing of the polar regions, trends in climate change toward extreme weather and other ecological phenomena, as well as fossil fuel deposits and reserves world-wide.

After more than ten years of data collection covering thousands of years of climatic events, twenty of the world's best scientific minds employed by TRG found evidence that supports environmental theories which say that the earth is experiencing a greenhouse effect, and that shifts in climatic conditions and increases in skin cancer due to the destruction of the earth's ozone layer, are directly related to the emission of greenhouse gasses into the earth's atmosphere. The scientists also made another astonishing discovery: that globally, fossil fuel supplies—so-called reserves—are some forty percent below the estimates of geological survey experts from the most developed countries, and at the present rate of consumption, supplies will be exhausted within the next half century.

This work was done by groups or teams of scientists from different disciplines, according to the interrelatedness of the issue. I joined them some eighteen months ago. The work was compartmentalized so that none of us had any idea what the big picture looked like. Because TRG is a private laboratory, we all signed a confidentiality agreement that forbids divulgence of any information. I and the other team leaders were told from the beginning that whatever our 'parallel' research revealed, the findings would under no circumstance be made public. They would instead be presented through the appropriate channels to governments. This would give these governments sufficient time to prepare the appropriate course of action and put mechanisms in place to manage any ensuing public reaction. As the senior geophysicist and team leader, I had access to the work of geological, oceanographic, and meteorological scientists because I was in a managerial position. It wasn't easy to compile the data from the other two group leaders, but I managed. The memory sticks you hold contain nearly 60-gigabytes of that valuable data.

From what I can make of it all, revelation of this information would be financially devastating to the interests of the petroleum industry, since governments would respond by shifting efforts to find safer alternatives and undoubtedly renewable sources of energy. But what's worse, we discovered that massive irreversible damage has already been done and the planet's still growing population will make life on earth environmentally unsustainable for the projected population over the next four to five decades. In short, the earth is dying and its death will spread exponentially with increases in fossil fuel use, global warming, and population growth.

My gut feeling is that there's more to this than meets the eye, because one of the other scientists, an astrophysicist who regrets his less than ethical role in this undertaking, told me that he recently learned of a stepped-up private effort to increase the capacity of artificial habitats, currently being researched for colonies on Mars by NASA and the European Space Agency. I can't quite link TRG and its activities to this, but I have a feeling that more than a few rich and powerful people are involved.

I need not tell you to be careful because I know you will. You know what must be done. So I will simply say 'good luck.'

As Caroline's eyes moved across the last line of the carefully scribed message, she could feel her heart pounding. Her pulse quickened and her anxiety spiked. She had heard and witnessed her fair share of deviousness during her life, but those experiences paled in comparison to what she had just read. Caroline Dupré suddenly found herself breathing even deeper and more rapidly. She was hyperventilating. She had not imagined before reading Mescheler's message what she was up against. Her first instinct was to make a dash to the media with the information. She knew that they would know exactly what to do. Then she thought… *What if they get to Nicolas? What if they do something to him as revenge for my actions?* She knew she couldn't take that risk. First, she would have to make sure he was completely out of danger. And because of what Mescheler had said about the people behind what was apparently some diabolical plan having the power to influence decisions made by NASA and the ESA, she knew there had to be some very powerful individuals involved.

Her mind began to race. But this time, her thoughts were

clearer. Many of the earlier, seemingly insignificant events that she had ignored at the time, all of a sudden became relevant. First, there were the positions taken by the American, Australian, and Canadian Ambassadors at the conference in Kuala Lumpur and the policies adopted by the leaders of those hold-out states, specifically their decision not to support the environmental commitments laid out in the advanced round of the Kyoto Protocol and the Protocol's subsequent renewal. Months earlier, there were the statements made by the American Vice-president, who, as head of NASA, promised a more vigorous approach to research on Mars and spacecraft propulsion systems, with particular attention given to the use of matter and anti-matter. Finally, there was the support and participation of European countries in the ESA in the aggressive pursuit of interplanetary space travel. She could only wonder how many were involved and who they were?

The mere thought that the people behind this could do just about anything they wanted, sent a chill through her body. With seemingly unlimited power and influence, they would have no enemies they couldn't either bribe or eliminate. Because of this, they would have no fears, except maybe one: exposure. This meant that whoever they were, they wouldn't want the information she was holding to reach the media. Thus far, they had managed to keep everything under wraps. And if what Mescheler said was true, they had probably paid huge sums of money to just about every politician, scientist, or public figure willing to make his or her services available to them.

Then it dawned on her that in his last message, François had intimated that the need for him to travel so often would decrease once he had exposed the sinister activities of corrupt, self-serving politicians and ruthless industrialists that threatened life on earth. Suddenly, the Bremmer woman's comments in relation to François' statement about having something on some important people that could damage them began to make sense.

249

Having assembled a number of the pieces of the puzzle, she concluded that whoever was behind this would not hesitate to kill her son if she refused to co-operate. But logically, she knew it wouldn't make sense for them to kill her or him before they got their hands on the memory sticks. It was clear that they knew that without the memory sticks, or at least someone like Mescheler to verify her story, and without the names of any of the conspirators, it would be absolutely ludicrous for her to go to the media with such a story.

While Caroline was busy making sense of all the information she had been given or had heard about the TRG laboratory and its connection to her husband's death, Dick Marsden was across the street making sure that he had the ultimate bargaining chip. Less than forty-five minutes after his call to her office, he had received a secure satellite phone call from Dave Bearsden telling him he had run down the Virginia Beach address and the boy was there. Bearsden had also explained that the Dupré woman's friend had gone so far as to dye the boy's hair to conceal his identity. Paradoxically, what he had told Marsden next caused both excitement and trepidation. An unexpected opportunity had presented itself when the woman had gone out with the boy and several other kids, so Bearsden had taken advantage of the situation and had snatched him.

Despite his value as a bargaining chip, kidnapping the boy was the last thing Marsden wanted to do. He would have preferred to use the threat of kidnapping to force Caroline Dupré to co-operate. But in the belief that it would bring about a quicker end to the operation, he instructed Bearsden to take the boy to his house in Galesville, but to make sure that he didn't know where he was being taken. Bearsden had followed Marsden's instructions; he had blindfolded the boy and taken away the wrist communication device he was wearing.

As uneasy as Dick Marsden was with the idea of kidnapping, he knew that with the boy in their possession, things could be wrapped up in another forty-eight to seventy-two hours; he would have his cash and Smith would be off his back.

Chapter Sixty-Five

By the time Caroline Dupré left her office, she had mustered the courage and determination to get on with the task before her. Although still frightened, she decided to go home. With the memory sticks hidden away in her office, she instructed the senior security officer on her way out not to allow anyone, for any reason, to enter TEARS' office space without her express permission.

Across the street, Dick Marsden continued to monitor the activity in her office and when she left, he followed her, keeping a safe distance as she entered the 5th Avenue subway station. He continued to wear the false beard and moustache he had donned hours earlier. And as always, when she arrived at the subway station in Brooklyn, he lagged behind and was among the last passengers to leave the train and the station. He exercised similar caution as he followed her to her house. When she neared the house, he broke off and went to the car he had left around the corner. Inside the car he set up the eavesdropping equipment and resumed surveillance of her residence. He also set up the satellite phone he had brought with him.

Only minutes after he set up the secure phone, it rang. Thinking it was Anderson, he answered in his usual brusque manner.

"Yeah, Mack! What's up?"

"I beg your pardon! You were no doubt expecting a call from your colleague, Mr. Anderson, it would seem."

It was Smith. Marsden tensed up. "That's correct," he replied.

"Sorry to disappoint you. But never mind. I'm sure he will call in due time. But in the meantime, I hear you've managed to lay your hands on Dr. Joseph Mescheler and that he is, as we speak, on his way to the TRG facility. Excellent! It certainly took you long enough. Nevertheless, you deserve a modest 'well done'."

Marsden was once again surprised by the speed at which Smith acquired information about his activities. He thought the only way the man could know these things was if Anderson was telling him. However, if Anderson was not the informant, then Smith probably had some kind of observer force monitoring their activities. Either way, the manner in which Smith dealt with him infuriated him and the moderate concern he had had shortly after he accepted the contract was becoming a thing that was more worrisome. He liked being in control of his operations, especially the dissemination of information about how they were proceeding.

Mr. Smith continued. "I also hear that you have the Dupré woman's boy and plan to arrange a swap—the boy for my property. Mr. Marsden, I won't congratulate you on this stroke of genius until the seeds you have sown bear fruit, but I do feel it pertinent to remind you that my property must be returned immediately. No matter what the cost. I've been extremely patient up to this point. Now I expect results."

"Yes, I understand."

But before Marsden could finish, Smith interrupted. "Here's what I want you to do, Mr. Marsden. It appears that the woman received something from Mescheler, or that he told her something during their meeting. It's imperative that I know what it was. I suggest that when you arrange your swap and you have the material in your possession, you inspect it first to determine its authenticity. You will do this by using the Open File command and typing in the word NOAH. While there are files that can be accessed by using the Open File command, the password NOAH will open several hidden files—files with titles like oceanography, atmospherics, geology, etc., each of which contains sets or quantitative data readings by year."

"But how do I determine then and there what else she knows? Do I even need to? After all, without the memory sticks, which we know she can't copy, she has nothing."

"I can see that time has taxed your patience and perhaps sapped your logic, Mr. Marsden. I suspect that by now the woman knows quite a lot. But I want you to exercise caution when extracting the information from her, even though I doubt that she'll be in the mood to make any confessions to you that will reveal what and how much she actually knows. And even if she did confess certain things to you, they probably wouldn't make any sense. I therefore suggest that once you have authenticated the memory sticks, you take full advantage of the situation and snare her and the boy and bring them both to the TRG facility. Once at the facility, I'm sure her desire to co-operate will increase significantly."

"Look, Mr. Smith, or whatever your name is, when I took this job, you told me you only wanted to recover your property. But in the process of doing this, there's been nothing but death and destruction. A massacre in Kuala Lumpur, the death of four young women, possibly a scientist too, and now you're telling me that two more people may have to die?"

"Don't be so melodramatic, Mr. Marsden! Are you telling me that when you accepted this job you had no idea that things might get a bit ugly? Well, let me remind you of a couple of things. I've already paid you a very large sum of money in advance. Like any *quid pro quo* arrangement, I expect and will get my desired results! And must I also remind you that the killing of all those people was your doing, not mine? Although you weren't directly responsible for the death of the UN staffer, the young professor, and her friend, your blunder in Kuala Lumpur had a significant bearing on their demise. And your latest stroke of genius, kidnapping the boy, was nothing short of overzealousness on your part—an effort to fulfill your dream of a financially comfortable retirement. Had you not blundered your way through this entire undertaking, some of these atrocities, as you call them, might have been avoided. And one other thing, Mr. Marsden, it's your face and that of your colleague this woman has seen, not mine. Oh yes! Despite your clever five and dime disguises, she knows who you really are. Are you comfortable with that, Mr. Marsden? Are you willing to pay the price that the divulgence of your identity will cost you?"

Somewhat subdued, Marsden replied, "No, but the killing has to stop somewhere and if I can find another way to get the job done, I'll do it."

"Mr. Marsden, I can assure you that we have no intention of harming the woman or the boy. Remember, she has broken the law by accepting stolen property. But because of my desire to maintain discretion where TRG's scientific pursuits are concerned, I simply want to impress upon Mrs. Dupré the need to respect the organization and its investors' right not to have efforts costing years of research and billions of dollars handed to competitors on a platter. Is that asking too much?"

"No. It isn't."

"Then it's settled. You'll recover my property and bring the woman in so we can see just how much damage she is capable of inflicting on us. I expect the next time we talk you'll be able to tell me that all is well."

Marsden was about to reply when Smith hung up.

Chapter Sixty-Six

It took Marsden several minutes to calm himself down after the surge of anger that followed his conversation with Mr. Smith. Once his anger had dissipated, he picked up the phone and called the number for Caroline Dupré's cell phone. She was in the kitchen when the phone rang and had to run into the living room to get it from her handbag. When she answered, she was startled to hear the voice of the man she had spoken to before she left her office.

"Mrs. Dupré," Marsden said calmly.

"How did you get this number?" she shouted angrily.

"It wasn't very difficult. Let's just say a little birdie told me!"

"How dare you call me to deliver more threats!"

"Mrs. Dupré, my call to you earlier this evening was no threat. We do have your son. A colleague of mine picked him up this evening in Virginia Beach. He was with a friend of yours, a woman named Deborah Creighton, I believe."

"You bastard!" she shouted. "He's just a boy! Have you no sense of decency? What have you done to him?"

"He's safe and well and I can assure you he's in no danger, unless you refuse to co-operate. When we've finished talking, I'll have my colleague call you so you can see for yourself that he's alive and well."

"There's a law against kidnapping, or aren't you aware of that?"

"There's also a law against accepting stolen property!" he retorted. "Believe me, Mrs. Dupré, I didn't want it to come to

256

this. If you had agreed to return the memory sticks when I contacted you earlier today, this whole thing could have ended and your son would be with you now. Look!" he shouted. "Don't make this any more difficult than it already is!"

"Any more difficult?" she snarled. "People I know and don't know are being exterminated like insects and you call me and threaten my life and the life of my son and then tell me 'don't make it any more difficult'! *You* made it difficult, Mr. X, or whatever you call yourself!" Through clenched teeth, she added, "You listen to me, you bastard! I want my son back and I want him now! Do you understand me?"

"You can have him, if you do exactly as I say. We know you have the memory sticks and whatever else Mescheler passed to you. I want all of it—the memory sticks and whatever he told you or gave you in the park today. You'll bring the items and meet me tomorrow at the Brooklyn dockyards. There's an abandoned warehouse on Pier 14. Meet me there tomorrow afternoon at 3:00 p.m. with everything. And don't get cute! Bring everything! And if I get even the slightest, I mean the slightest, inkling that there's a third party around, you can forget about ever seeing your son again. Do I make myself clear?"

"Yes," she replied nervously. "But how do I know you'll keep your word?"

"You don't! You'll just have to trust me; for whatever it's worth, I'm not into hurting women and children."

"Yeah… Tell that to the mothers and fathers of the young people massacred in Kuala Lumpur and those four women you killed!" she retorted, angrily.

Marsden paused momentarily then shouted, "Just be there!" and hung up.

Chapter Sixty-Seven

While she was talking to the man who had become her nemesis, Caroline felt a return of the rising anger that was triggered earlier by his call. But this time, it was so intense that it made her sweat and feel nauseous. Without realizing it, she had gripped the phone so tightly during the conversation that her fingers had gone numb. But before she could recover from the shock and anger of the call from the stranger, her cell phone rang again. It was Dave Bearsden, calling to provide proof that her son was indeed in their hands.

Still trembling, she picked up the phone and answered. "Hello."

There was silence for several seconds then she heard Nicolas' voice. "Mama! Mama! Help me, Mama! Please help me!"

A man's voice suddenly interrupted. "Do you still think this is a game?"

"If you hurt one single strand of hair on his head... so help me God, I'll..."

"You'll do what?" the man interrupted. "You'll do just what you're told to do!" he added and hung up.

After the second call, Caroline could feel her heart racing, pounding like it was about to rip through her rib cage or explode inside her chest. She started to get up from the sofa where she had slumped during the first call, but her legs wouldn't co-operate. Her whole body ached and she trembled from anger and fear. From the moment she realized what she'd become involved in, she knew things might get dangerous, but she hadn't expected it to be anything like this. Taking on a powerful and unknown adversary who seemed to be able to reach her anywhere and anytime, frightened her even more. And although she had set eyes on two of them, she knew there were others, but how many? Dozens? Hundreds? Who were they? High ranking politicians, judges, law enforcement officials… Who? But what troubled her most was the fact that she didn't know where they were. If she went to the police or the FBI about the kidnapping of her son, would it jeopardize his safety? She knew the only place for her to go was to the media. But with her son's life at stake, such a move would almost certainly prove fatal for him. It was therefore out of the question. She would have to go it alone.

For the second time in a single day she found herself groping for what remained of her courage and her resolve. She had fought off the urge to give into the pressure, knowing that if she did, her son would perish. The choice was simple: do something or become a victim. The latter was not an option. Drawing solely on her determination to save her son, she lifted herself from the sofa and made her way back to the kitchen. Still shaking, she managed to prepare a pot of green tea. Her eyes filled with tears as she stood in front of the kitchen sink.

As she nervously drank her tea, she thought about how she had failed her son and how cavalier she had been about his safety. She even questioned how she ever came to consider putting his life at risk to respond to an appeal from a stranger who, for all she knew, might be a lunatic. What was worse, she had refused to inform her father, because she believed that the fewer people involved the better. Now, she wondered how she would tell him if something happened to his only grandchild. How would she be able to explain that it was her actions that led to the death of his beloved grandson? The thought of having to reveal such a tragedy was just as painful as the danger Nicolas was facing. She knew she couldn't fail him.

As she moved back toward the living room, she noticed for

the first time the flashing red light at the top of the video-phone monitor. She moved quickly over to it and pressed the 'activate' button. The device sprang to life and the image of a distraught woman in her mid-thirties appeared. It was Debbie Creighton.

"I'm so sorry, Caroline! I'm so terribly sorry," she babbled tearfully. "They took him! The people you told me were looking for you took him! We were just out to get ice cream and this fat man was standing near a car. Nicolas was the last one to decide what he wanted, so he was a few yards behind us when we walked back to the car. When he walked past the man, I heard him scream and I turned and saw the man hustling him into the back of the car before speeding off.

"I tried to get the kids into the car so I could follow him and call the police, but he got away too quickly. Oh God! What have I done? What have I done? How do I live with what I have done? Please, Caroline! Where are you? Please call me! I'm so sorry. I'm so terribly sorry."

When the message finished, she chose to save it, thinking that it might prove useful if something happened to Nicolas. She then requested that the call to her friend be returned. She wanted to reassure her that she wasn't to blame for Nicolas' kidnapping.

"Debbie, it's not your fault. Listen to me… let me explain." It took all the willpower Caroline could summon to avoid breaking down as she told her friend that she alone had been responsible for her son's kidnapping because she had decided to become involved in something that put him at risk.

"It didn't matter where Nicolas was, they would have found him. I'm so sorry I had to involve you," Caroline said. "I and the people who took him are responsible for the entire situation, not you." She asked Debbie to note down anything she could remember about the kidnapping. Any clue, no matter how small, that could help her find him.

Chapter Sixty-Eight

After talking to her friend, Caroline felt her anger and frustration returning again. She knew she had to gain control of her thoughts if she was going to save her son. For now, saving him was her first priority. She wiped the tears away that were streaming down her cheeks, knowing only too well that the odds were stacked against her. Nevertheless, she would at least try to improve her chances of survival. Once again, she lifted herself from the sofa, but instead of returning to the kitchen, this time she went to her bedroom and flung open the doors to her closet. She pushed several boxes on the middle shelf to either side, to reveal a wall safe. Her hand trembled as she turned the dial through the combination.

She opened the door of the safe and took out a rectangular box constructed of highly polished mahogany. The box bore a brass plate that read: *Marksman of the Year, Caroline Gagnon, Presented by Jean-Claude Daneau, President, Paris Shooting Club.* She slowly ran the palm of her right hand across the top of the box, giving it a gentle caress. Then she reached into the safe a second time and withdrew a box of .22 caliber cartridges and set the box on the bed. She carefully opened it, revealing a polished, stainless steel .22 caliber Ruger MK II target pistol and scope. It had been more than five years since she had held the coveted prize in her hands. Holding it brought back a flood of memories; memories of her adolescence, the early days with François and the time she had spent with her father and how he had taught her everything she knew about shooting.

She studied the pistol for several minutes before inserting

cartridges into two magazines. After loading it, she returned the case to the safe and tucked the pistol, spare magazine, and box of cartridges under the pillow on the side of the bed where Francois used to sleep. Tomorrow at noon, she would go to her office, collect the memory sticks and the letter Mescheler had given her, go to the Brooklyn dockyard, and get her son back.

Chapter Sixty-Nine

The next morning, Caroline Dupré climbed out of bed at 7:00 a.m. sharp. The night she had just experienced was the worst since François' death. The thought of Nicolas being held somewhere by people who probably wouldn't hesitate to hurt him, had made sleeping almost impossible. During the night, she had dozed off only twice, each time for less than an hour. And each time she fell asleep, she could hear her son's cries for help and imagine the fear in his eyes.

For Caroline Dupré, this day would mark the end of the long-running, untidy saga. But Dick Marsden, who was on what was to be his last night of surveillance, felt confident for the first time that things would soon be wrapped up. Earlier in the evening, after he talked to her, Anderson had called him to tell him that Dr. Joseph Mescheler had been delivered to the TRG facility. Upon arrival, Mescheler had been taken by the manager of the facility and isolated in a room four floors below ground level, beneath the facility's research spaces, where the other scientists wouldn't be aware of his presence.

During Marsden's conversation with Anderson, Anderson had asked if he needed help rounding up the items from the Dupré woman. Marsden had explained that because he now had the boy, he had the upper hand and there was no reason for the Dupré woman not to co-operate. He explained that the boy would be brought to Brooklyn around noon on Saturday to make the swap later that afternoon and that Bearsden would provide back-up. He then suggested that Anderson remain at the TRG facility and he would meet him there sometime after midnight with the missing items, the woman, and the boy.

The fact that Caroline Dupré and her son were being brought to the facility pleased Anderson immensely. He was a man who didn't like to leave loose ends.

Getting up to an empty house was deeply depressing for Caroline. On several occasions, she caught herself about to knock on Nicolas' bedroom door, like she usually did when breakfast was ready. After a cup of tea and a quick glance at the Saturday paper, she tried to distract herself by watching the news. However, the stories of rising crime, corruption, poverty, and disease were too depressing.

The hours seemed to drag; after a light breakfast, she decided to take a shower and get dressed. At 10:30 a.m. she would go by car to her office and get everything ready. Unlike at home, in her office she would be able to steady her nerves and think. At home, there were too many reminders of her son's situation and his absence. Also, the guilt she felt seemed to increase as thoughts drifted into her head and layered her consciousness. When 10:30 a.m. finally came, she left the house and drove to Manhattan.

With the boy for insurance, there was no longer a reason to keep close tabs on her, so Marsden decided to let her go. After she left the house, he drove to Manhattan and collected the surveillance equipment from the room above the Vintage Bookstore. Afterwards, he drove back to Brooklyn where he would meet Bearsden at a small hotel off Atlantic Avenue. Bearsden had been instructed to take the boy there and wait for him.

During their conversation the evening before, Bearsden had commented how co-operative the boy was, but had laughingly stated that he had made it clear that if he didn't behave, his mother's head would be cut off and given to him in a box. Marsden had found Bearsden's tactics distasteful. But if it made controlling the boy easier, there would be less chance of him getting hurt trying to raise an alarm or trying to escape. The boy was, after all, very intelligent.

After collecting the surveillance equipment from the room on 5th Avenue, Marsden drove back to Brooklyn. He was still wearing the beard and moustache he had put on the day before. The temperature in the city was already rising and he longed for a shower and to jettison the disguise. For a brief moment, he had hoped that Bearsden, too, had recognized the importance of disguising himself before grabbing the boy. But after thinking about Bearsden's personality and the way the man always carried on about food, it wouldn't be difficult, even for a child, to single him out by his physique, his obsessive eating, and poor dietary habits. Bearsden resembled the first part of his last name; a big, clumsy, lumbering bear.

Chapter Seventy

At 11:15 a.m. Marsden's car rolled to a stop in front of the Moon Lite Hotel. He spotted Bearsden's car straight away and concluded that everything must have gone as planned. He entered the small hotel and approached the clerk on duty. A young man with tell-tale scars from a serious battle with teenage acne sat behind the front desk with his heels propped up, reading the *Daily News*. The front desk was four feet high and had one-inch thick plexiglass that extended from its top to the ceiling, an obvious sign that there were risks associated with running a business in that part of the city

Marsden asked the clerk which room the man and boy who had come in ahead of him had taken. Because the Moon Lite Hotel was a favorite with couples seeking a discreet romantic rendezvous, the clerk looked him up and down to satisfy himself that Marsden was not a cop then informed him that the man and boy were on the third floor, in room 313.

Marsden climbed the narrow staircase to the third floor. As he walked down the hallway, he could hear arguments coming from several of the rooms, as well as passionate lovemaking. The fact that acts of passion were on the minds of people on such a hot and miserable day seemed odd, especially since elsewhere, New Yorkers were avoiding situations that brought them in stifling proximity to others.

Marsden reached the room where Bearsden was holed up with the boy and knocked on the door.

"Who is it?" asked a voice from inside.

"It's me! Open up!"

The door swung open and a bald-headed, rotund figure of a man stood on the other side in front of him. "Glad to see you could make it!" said Dave Bearsden.

"Is everything alright?" Marsden asked.

Wiping the sweat from his brow, Bearsden replied, "As smooth as silk," then added, "It sure is hot, though! Next time, do you think you could manage to find a place with reliable air conditioning?"

As Marsden closed the door behind him, his eyes shifted toward the bed where the boy was sitting. "Is this the wonder boy?" he asked.

"Yep! Sure is!"

"Nicolas, right?" Marsden asked. The boy nodded. "You've no need to be afraid, son. In a few short hours, we're gonna deliver you to your mother."

"What have you done to her?" the boy snapped angrily.

"No one's done anything to your mother, son. She's fine."

"Then why am I here?" he demanded.

"Your mother has something that belongs to some very important people. She has no right to have it. So, they want it back."

"And that's why you grabbed me. To make sure she hands it over?"

"I can see there's no foolin' you, son! You've got it all figured out, haven't you?"

"Not really. But I know that kidnapping is a federal offense and you could go to jail for it."

"That's interesting!" Marsden chuckled. "You know, your mother said exactly the same thing. I have a suspicion that wittiness runs in your family. Nevertheless, I'm gonna tell you what I told her. The property she's holding is stolen and that makes what she's doing illegal as well. So I guess that makes us about even." He paused briefly before adding, "In a few hours, she'll get back what she wants and we'll get what we want and everybody'll be happy."

Marsden couldn't help but admire the boy's strength and courage. He had never made a noise and never tried to run away. He clearly understood the gravity of the situation. And after talking to him for several minutes, Marsden called Bearsden over and explained what he intended to do once he had the memory sticks and had verified their authenticity. While the two men were whispering, the boy called out to Marsden.

"Hey, mister! I don't know your name, but I'd like something cold to drink. Some juice, if you don't mind."

"No. I don't mind. And call me Bill."

"Is that really your name?"

"No. I didn't say it was my name. I said you could call me Bill. Is that good enough for you?"

"I suppose it'll have to do!" the boy replied.

Marsden finished his conversation with Bearsden and sent the heavily perspiring man downstairs to the vending machine just inside the hotel entrance, to get a couple of Cokes and a can of fruit drink. When Bearsden returned, his shirt was almost completely wet from his excessive sweating.

He handed Marsden the drinks. "Whew!" he said, fanning his dripping face with his hand. "It's like a sauna in here. I can't stand it any longer. Gimme a break, will you? Keep an eye on the boy while I go out for some fresh air."

He told Marsden there was a small park a block away and he wanted to sit on a bench under a tree and read the paper for a while.

"No problem," said Marsden, reminding him to take his cell phone and two-way radio.

For the next couple of hours, Marsden and the boy talked, mostly about the boy's mother, where he grew up, and the things he liked doing. Marsden was impressed by the boy's intelligence and his understanding of the world around him. At one point in their conversation, he even told the boy how intelligent and brave he thought his mother was and that he should be proud of his father because he had died for something he believed in.

The time was nearing 1:30 p.m. and Marsden wanted to take a shower, so he called Bearsden, who had been snoozing on the park bench, and asked him to come back and stay with the boy while he showered and changed clothes. When Bearsden returned, he was still complaining about the heat. Grumbling that he hadn't had a bite to eat since he left Virginia early that morning, he asked Marsden if there was some place nearby where he could find some food. Marsden told him he should go down and ask the hotel clerk if there was a pizza, hot dog stand or some other place nearby to buy sandwiches. *Fat bastard*, Marsden thought as Bearsden left. Missing a few meals wouldn't do him any harm.

Chapter Seventy-One

Sitting in her office, Caroline wrote two letters and left them on her assistant's desk. One was to her father and the other to her friend Debbie in Virginia Beach. Each letter contained a photocopy of the note Mescheler had given her the day before. She also left instructions with the letters, telling her assistant that she was working on something very important and that if she didn't hear from her by noon on Monday, she should mail the letters. Both letters contained a detailed explanation of what she was involved in. They described in detail the link between the TRG memory sticks, her husband's murder, the disappearance of Kristie Bremmer, the deaths of Patricia Maynard, Amanda Costanti, and Elizabeth O'Connell and the Kuala Lumpur massacre. She knew that if anything happened to her and Nicolas, her father and Debbie Creighton would do whatever it took to find those responsible.

At 1:45 p.m. she gathered the memory sticks and the note Mescheler had given her, and put them in her handbag where she had stashed her trophy target pistol. She also took two blank memory sticks and stuffed them in her trouser pocket. If the opportunity presented itself, she would switch the blank memory sticks with those containing the data and pass the blanks to Marsden. At 1:50 p.m. she left her office, went downstairs to her car and drove over to the dockyard in Brooklyn.

Chapter Seventy-Two

Caroline arrived at Pier 14 at 2:45 p.m. She pulled her car up close to the warehouse and turned it around to face the exit. She wanted to be able to get out of the place in a hurry if things went wrong. She had surveyed the area as she drove in and didn't see another car. The whole area was quiet. A kind of eeriness pervaded.

As she was sitting in her car waiting, the warehouse door slid open and a bearded man appeared in the opening. He signaled to her to get out of the car. Before doing so, she re-checked to make sure her pistol was fully loaded. As she stepped out of the car, the man smiled and shouted to her. "Glad you could join me."

"You can dispense with the humor, Mr. X, or whatever you call yourself."

"Call me Bill!" he replied, chuckling. "I believe you have something for me?"

"Not until I see that my son is safe and I have him. That was the deal!"

"You're right!" he said, raising a small two-way radio to his mouth. "Bring him in!" he instructed.

Shortly afterwards, a dark-colored sedan with Bearsden behind the wheel pulled up in front of the warehouse. When Caroline turned and looked in the direction of the car, she saw Nicolas' face through the windscreen.

"My baby! My baby!" she shouted, her heart racing and eyes welling up with tears.

"Not so fast!" Marsden reminded her, extending his right hand. "We still have some unfinished business here." With his other hand, he beckoned to Bearsden to bring the boy inside the warehouse. Bearsden climbed out of the car, entered the warehouse with the boy in tow, and stood next to Marsden.

"You've seen the boy. Now give me the memory sticks and the rest of the material. Come on! Be quick about it! This need not take all day!"

She slipped her hand inside her handbag and removed the case containing the two memory sticks. Holding the memory sticks in her left hand, she reached inside the bag again and withdrew an envelope containing the note from Dr. Joseph Mescheler. As she reached into the handbag the second time, she fought off the temptation to draw the pistol. Both men were standing about fifteen feet in front of her and neither of them had a weapon drawn. Nevertheless, she was sure that the round, sweaty one was packing underneath his long-tailed polo shirt. Although he was sweating profusely, it didn't make sense for him to wear the tail of his polo shirt outside, unless he was armed. She surmised that he was probably wearing a clip-on holster with a revolver tucked in it.

Even though she hadn't been on a firing range for a while, she knew she could hit both men before either of them knew what was happening. Her only problem was that with the caliber pistol she had, she would have to put at least two or three rounds into each of them in order to stop them. If she failed with either of them, her son's life probably would be terminated. Not wanting to take the gamble, she decided to play out the exchange.

Marsden walked over and she handed him the items. As he took them, he said, "This'll only take a moment," then turned and walked across the floor to a small table, on top of which was a laptop computer. He inserted one of the memory sticks into the computer, struck several keys and scrolled quickly through the contents of several files. He then repeated the same procedure with the second memory stick. When he had finished with both, he opened the envelope and skimmed the contents of the note Mescheler had written on both sides of the paper. Caroline was glad that she had not switched the memory sticks. When he had finished scrutinizing all the items, he looked at her with an expression of satisfaction on his face.

"This'll do nicely," he said. "However, I'm sorry to inform you that there's been a slight change in the plan. You see, the owner of this material wants to meet you personally. He has some notion that you'll run away and scream your head off to anyone who'll listen to you. I tried to convince him otherwise, but he says it's his property and he wants to debrief you to make sure his competitors don't profit from the knowledge you have of his investments and hard work."

"I should've known I couldn't trust you! Damn you!" she snapped. "I want my son!"

"Just take it easy! Everything will be alright. We're all gonna take a ride and when we get to where we are going, this'll all be sorted out."

Enraged, she reached into her purse. "Now, I'd really have to be crazy to fall for that crap a second time, wouldn't I?"

She drew the pistol from her handbag so quickly it took both men by surprise. Before Bearsden could get his hand on the grip of his pistol, she had her weapon trained directly on his chest. A look of astonishment registered on his face and his lower jaw dropped.

"Clear the holster with it and I'll put one right through your heart," she shouted. "Now, why don't you remove that thing, thumb and index finger only, and drop it on the floor in front of you."

Bearsden did as he was ordered. "Now put both hands on top of your bald head and kick the gun over here with your right foot!" she commanded.

Bearsden hesitated. "Do it, *now!*" she shouted, her voice stern and confident. For the first time in the whole sorry saga, she felt fully in control.

Next, she trained her weapon on Marsden. "OK, Bill, or whoever you are! Now you! I know you're too smart to have come here empty-handed. So why don't you lift up your right trouser leg. Slowly!" she instructed, with steely conviction. "And remove the ankle holster with the backup piece in it."

Marsden, too, was wearing a polo shirt, which was tucked into his trousers. She knew there was nowhere else to conceal a weapon. She had noticed when he turned and walked toward the laptop that he wasn't carrying one in the small of his back. Because he had shown that he was right-handed, he would have to wear the holster on the outside of his right ankle to be able to conceal and draw it with minimal effort.

As instructed, Marsden lifted his trouser leg, revealing a stainless steel, five-shot, Smith & Wesson .38 caliber revolver. With her weapon still trained on him, she ordered, "I want you to loosen the holster and let it fall to the floor. Then I want you to straighten up, put your hands on your head like your friend did and kick your pistol over here. Touch the grip while you're down there and I'll use the top of your head for a bull's-eye! And believe me I won't hesitate to put half the magazine dead center."

Like Bearsden, Marsden did exactly as he was told. When both men were disarmed, she called Nicolas over to her. He rushed to her side and put his arms around her waist, without saying a word. She kept her weapon trained in the direction of the two men, then barked, "Get on your knees, both of you!"

The two men hesitated, glancing at each other for inspiration. "Do it, *now!*" she yelled. Surprised by the sudden turn of events, they dropped to their knees with a look of bewilderment on their faces. She then told Nicolas to take the items from the table where Marsden had left them. But just as the boy started to move toward the table, a man's voice shouted from the loft behind her. "I wouldn't do that if I were you!" Then, after a beat, he shouted, "Surprised?" and broke into a bout of loud, staccato laugher.

"Young lady," the unseen speaker continued, "you wanna drop that pea-shooter before I cut you in half?"

Crestfallen and again fearing for her and Nicolas' lives, Caroline dropped the weapon and the voice behind her continued.

"Bravo! Bravo! Little lady, you're just full of surprises, aren't you? What aren't you capable of doing? Do you know you just disarmed one of the best in the business? But I guess you had an advantage! He underestimated your determination and obviously didn't know about your extraordinary skills with a pistol. I've gotta hand it to you! You're something else!"

Marsden knew from the voice and laughter, well before the man came into view, that it was Mack Anderson. When Anderson finally came into view, he was making his way across the catwalk in the loft of the warehouse. A few seconds later, he descended a small staircase to the warehouse floor. He stopped in front of the doorway and both men rose to their feet. Marsden looked particularly embarrassed.

"Don't worry about it, partner!" Anderson shouted. "This woman is a top notch marksman! Fellas, you're lookin' at a woman who loves pistols and rifles. She qualified for the French Olympic target pistol team when she was just sixteen. I'd say she had all of us fooled with her modesty. Lucky for you guys I did a bit more background work on her and found this hidden talent. I had a hunch this might happen. Good thing I decided to take the drive down to see what she was up to."

"How did you know where we'd be?" asked Marsden.

"I have my ways of finding out these kinds of things."

Chapter Seventy-Three

Mack Anderson was still gloating about his role as liberator. Meanwhile, a look of embarrassment was etched heavily into Marsden and Bearsden's faces as they retrieved their weapons. Marsden took the memory sticks and note from the table and put them into the laptop case. Caroline was still standing in the middle of the floor with Nicolas clinging to her. As Marsden walked past her, he grabbed her handbag, rifled through it in search of other weapons then tossed it on the floor. With Anderson's gun still trained on her, she picked up her handbag and turned and faced him. His ego still badly bruised, Marsden walked over to Anderson. "Let's take a ride upstate."

As Marsden was about walk away, Anderson put his hand in front of him and stopped him in his tracks. "I think you and I can handle this from here on," he said, just above a whisper. "No use Bearsden coming along. Anyway, don't you think it'd be better if he went back to the office and held things down there?"

"I suppose that makes sense," Marsden replied wearily. "I'll take the woman and the boy with me."

Anderson leaned toward Marsden again and suggested, in a slightly louder voice for the woman and the boy to hear. "It would be better if we split 'em up. You take the woman and the boy can ride with me. That is, if it's alright with you? She won't do anything stupid as long as I've got the boy."

"It makes no difference to me as long as we get this show on the road," Marsden replied.

When Nicolas heard that he was going to be separated from his mother, he panicked. "I wanna stay with my mom! Please! Let me stay with her!"

He was still clinging to Caroline's waist when Anderson walked over and pulled him away by his arm. As Nicolas was being hauled off, she grabbed him, kissed him on the forehead and told him she would be alright and that he needed to be brave.

Marsden opened the trunk of the car and placed the laptop case and her pistol in it with the surveillance equipment he had collected from the room above the Vintage Bookstore. He then ordered Caroline to get behind the wheel. Still holding the boy firmly by the arm, Anderson cautioned him to behave then pulled him over to the far side of the warehouse where he had hidden the van around the corner. He put the boy in the front seat and seconds later, the two vehicles sped away from the dockyard and across Manhattan before turning south on Interstate 95 and then onto Route 9 West toward upstate New York.

PART V

Chapter Seventy-Four

New Haven, Connecticut

Charles Rutherford Bingham sat behind a large, glass-topped, metal frame desk in a sparsely but tastefully decorated office that overlooked New Haven, Connecticut. In quiet contemplation, he was all but certain that the unfolding saga that had consumed his waking thoughts for over four months would soon be over and the risk to the Bingham name and reputation would have receded, back to the place where it belonged—untarnished and out in front, leading the way.

For more than a century, the name Bingham had epitomized success in the petroleum industry—success that started with his grandfather, Charles Alfred Bingham. Charles Alfred Bingham had been the sole heir to New Haven's largest newspaper, which he sold less than six months after his father's death to gamble the proceeds on the nascent petroleum industry. With money from the sale of the family paper and a few thousand dollars he borrowed from relatives, he had ventured west to Texas in search of black gold. Just over a year after he arrived in Texas, he struck pay dirt; during the next fifteen years he bought or wrangled his way to ownership of every Texas dirt farm he believed might be sitting on the precious black liquid. In the years following his catapult to successful oil man, Charles Alfred Bingham's shrewdness and eye for trends brought him a level of wealth which he freely admitted exceeded his wildest dreams.

When Charles Alfred Bingham died, his only son, Charles Carlisle Bingham, succeeded him as sole heir to the Bingham fortune and master of Alfred Bingham's creation, the Northeastern Petroleum Corporation (NEPCO). Like old man Alfred, Charles Carlisle Bingham proved to be as much of a visionary as he was an entrepreneur. An individual with insight into the future, he had taken advantage of the U.S. Communications Satellite Act of 1962 and began investing heavily in communications. As a result of his eye for things to come, he created Bingham Enterprises (BE), which brought the communications arm of Bingham's empire, Bingham Communications, under the Bingham umbrella.

By the early 1970s, the return on his initial investments in communications had enabled Bingham Communications to expand into research, development, design, and even building its own communications satellites. Old man Alfred Bingham's fascination with space and the beginning of the space age had left a technology legacy; his visionary pursuits had also become a source of inspiration, fascination, and passion for all the Bingham heirs who succeeded him. But under Charles Carlisle Bingham, space exploration received special attention; full support was thrown behind all space-related activities and politicians favoring them. Charles Carlisle Bingham became an ardent supporter of NASA and U.S. space exploration. He was also an early believer and proponent of manned missions to the moon, the Skylab project, and reusable space vehicles like the space shuttle. He believed that one day these programs would make significant contributions to manned interplanetary space travel.

By the time Charles Carlisle Bingham yielded control of the family empire to his son, Charles Rutherford Bingham, the latter was even more convinced that interplanetary space travel was possible. An ardent supporter and proponent of manned interplanetary space travel, Charles Rutherford Bingham was elated when a Texas billionaire helped bankroll Biosphere Two, the follow-on to the initial biosphere project which would help humans learn how to survive on a distant planet. Like the project's benefactors, he believed that Biosphere Two would serve as the first step toward colonizing Mars.

Charles Rutherford Bingham's fascination with outer and inner space prompted him to study, investigate, and even challenge several important assertions about space and the condition of the Earth. During the course of his own investigations and through the work of NEPCO oil exploration scientists, he had discovered something that no one else in the scientific world, or the public or private sector knew or suspected—that the world's petroleum reserves were being depleted far more rapidly than had been estimated. But much more to his astonishment was the fact that some reserves that were believed to exist, albeit in hard to reach areas, didn't exist at all.

Acting at first on intuition, Charles Rutherford Bingham began diverting billions of dollars from BE and some of his personal wealth to set up a high-powered scientific team to conduct research on the world's petroleum reserves, the melting of polar ice, the effects of man's use of carbon fuels on the earth's ozone layer, and on the development of a propulsion system for manned interplanetary spacecraft. By the time he took over as head of BE, the Transnational Research Group, or TRG, had become a laboratory which could boast that within the short span of five years it had employed the best scientific minds from the top universities, research institutions, and government agencies in the world. Each of the scientists recruited to work at TRG had been given a lucrative salary and provided with the best equipment and working conditions available.

Among those recruited to work in the sophisticated Adirondack mountain laboratory were several Nobel Prize-winning astrobiologists, geologists, astronomers, nuclear physicists, astrophysicists, marine biologists, biochemists,

chemists, and oceanographers. There were also engineers from several fields. TRG had been set up in such a way so as to avoid revealing direct ownership by BE; however, to a few in the world of politics Charles Rutherford Bingham was known as its main benefactor.

Bingham sat waiting anxiously for an important telephone call; as he waited, he turned around in his luxurious, swivel chair and fixed his gaze on the city of New Haven below. A few minutes later, the green light on the secure satellite phone in the open briefcase on his desk began flashing and the device began to buzz. It was the call he had been expecting—a call from Geoffrey Townsend, a long-time friend, Trinity College, University of Cambridge classmate, and current director of the International Space Agency. As the phone continued to buzz, Charles Rutherford Bingham pulled his thoughts back from the world below his window and lifted the handset with deliberate calmness.

"What's the situation?" Geoffrey Townsend queried. "I received your message a few minutes ago and it sounded urgent. Not bad news, I hope?"

"Quite the contrary, old friend," Bingham replied. "It's good news! Everything is under control. By tomorrow evening, all obstacles will have been removed and Noah's Ark II will be back on track."

"That's excellent news, Charles!" said Townsend excitedly. "It's precisely what I've been waiting to hear."

Chapter Seventy-Five

The sedan with Caroline Dupré behind the wheel and the van with Mack Anderson driving, turned north on Route 9 after leaving Route 9 West outside Troy, New York. Dick Marsden had not spoken since they left the dockyard, except to tell her where and when to turn. As the sedan sped along Route 9, she gripped the wheel with deliberate firmness.

Observing her from the corner of his eye, Marsden could see the look of disdain on her face. He knew the look was for him. He finally broke the silence.

"I would have preferred it if this had worked out differently," he declared sternly. "Believe me, I never had, nor do I have, any intention of hurting you or the boy. Things would've been different if you'd been more co-operative. As much as I wanted it to work out in a more civilized way, it soon became obvious that you weren't gonna let that happen. No… you just weren't gonna part with those memory sticks, especially after you found out what was on them and their connection to your husband's death."

When he finished his diatribe, she remained silent, staring straight ahead at the road. After several minutes, she turned her head toward him and gave him an icy look.

"What the hell was that supposed to be?" she snapped. "An attempt at remorse? Because if it was, it carries about as much weight with me as the lie you told about returning my son and leaving us alone. I should've known better than to believe anything a murderer and kidnapper had to say! People like you don't have consciences and you need a conscience to feel remorse."

"You're probably right!" he replied, sounding weary.

"What's in this for you, anyway? Money?" she shouted. "You and those thugs you call associates clearly aren't smart enough to be part of the bigger picture. The way I figure it, you're just hired help! You probably don't even have a clue what this is all about. And what's worse, you probably don't even give a shit! Do you?"

"No, and I'm not the least bit interested in finding out any more than I need to know."

"Why doesn't that surprise me? Do you even know where we're going?"

"As a matter of fact I do!" Marsden retorted. "So... now would you just shut up and drive!"

"No! I won't shut up!" Caroline said, scowling. "Do you really expect me to sit here and try to have a civilized conversation with you when I'm being taken somewhere against my will, and that thug of a friend of yours has my son and is more than eager to do God knows what to him?"

"Look! I've told you already, nobody is gonna hurt you or your son. And as far as where we're going is concerned, you're not stupid. You already know we're going to the TRG facility."

"And what do you think will happen when we get there? Do you think whoever sent you to track down Dr. Mescheler and get the memory sticks from me is gonna be waiting there to give me a medal for disrupting their plans? Can you guarantee nothing will happen to me and my son? Well... can you? Do you even care? Do you know who's behind all this and what it's all about? If you don't, then how the hell can you sit there and say what will or won't happen?"

She paused and took a deep, ragged breath. "Why do you think those memory sticks are so important?" she continued. "And why do these people want to silence Mescheler? If the man committed theft, even grand larceny, why didn't they just have the police or the FBI go after him? Can you answer any of these questions? No! You can't!" she barked. "Mister, my husband and a lot of other good people died because of what's on those memory sticks and that's not the end of it!" she added angrily. "Anyone who has come in contact with those memory sticks, or who has even been remotely involved with them, has met with an untimely demise."

"Are you finished?" Marsden shot back. "I surely hope so! Because you talk too damned much and you ask far too many fuckin' questions! But to answer your last question, no, I don't have answers to all your questions."

For a moment, the look of anger that had earlier consumed her face gave way to smugness when he conceded that he was ignorant of what was going on. She knew then that her surly attitude and her tenacious line of questioning had been thought-provoking.

"I have one more question," she said. "You examined the data on the memory sticks, but more importantly, you read the note Mescheler wrote. Didn't any of what he said trouble you? Did it at least arouse suspicion?"

"I'm not being paid to be concerned about what any of this means," Marsden said icily, knowing he needed to regain the high ground. "I accepted a contract and I'm fulfilling my part of the agreement."

"I'll bet that whoever is paying you for your services is pleased as punch that you're the kind of guy who just does what he's instructed to do and never thinks for himself or asks questions. Now, there's an interesting approach to life if ever I've seen one! The people at the top are always right and they always do what's best for everyone... themselves, their subordinates, and all the other poor, less fortunate bastards. That's why we owe them our unwavering loyalty, subservience, and unconditional obedience!" she added sarcastically.

Marsden didn't respond. Instead, he stared straight ahead at the road. She could see from the corner of her eye that he had emotionally retreated. His body language was signaling that the discussion was over. She returned her gaze to the road and resumed her tight grip on the wheel; the two vehicles, in tandem, continued their journey north on Route 9.

Chapter Seventy-Six

New York State
Adirondack Park, Adirondack Mountains

After a few hours, the two vehicles entered Adirondack Park. The evening sun was beginning to fall. As it descended, it illuminated the western sky with an unusual, almost fierce orange glow. Inside the van, Nicolas had long ago fallen asleep; Anderson was grateful he didn't have to deal with the boy.

As nightfall enveloped the Adirondack Forest, the two vehicles continued on Route 9 through the Park until they came to the junction for Route 28. It was around 9:30 p.m. when they saw the Route 28 signpost. When they reached the actual junction, Marsden instructed Caroline to turn west. They stayed on Route 28 until they reached the center of the Park then turned north onto Route 3. When they reached Tupper Lake, they turned and headed northwest, toward Potsdam. After driving northwest for about fifteen minutes, they left the main road and turned onto a private road, which seemed to double back to the southeast. As they drove along the road, Caroline noticed that it was ascending sharply.

Several miles later, they came upon a sign that read *Transnational Research Group*. Shortly after passing the sign, they reached a chain-link perimeter fence. There were signs on the fence that read, *WARNING: PRIVATE PROPERTY*; *NO TRESPASSING*; and *ARMED SECURITY GUARDS ON*

PATROL: USE OF DEADLY FORCE AUTHORIZED AGAINST TRESPASSERS.

Caroline immediately thought about Mescheler. He would have been familiar with the notices. *Was he still alive?* Somehow she doubted it.

As the car approached the fence, Caroline could see a barrier gate and a guard shack to the left of the entrance. As they drew closer, Marsden instructed her to turn off the headlights. As soon as she brought the car to a stop in front of the barrier, a guard, armed with an M4 carbine rifle and a 9mm Berretta pistol, approached the vehicle carrying a flashlight and asked for identification. He examined the photo on Caroline's driver's license, looked at her face and returned the license. He then took Marsden's driver's license and shone his flashlight into the car to compare Marsden's face with the photo on the license. Even though Marsden was wearing the fake beard and moustache, the guard didn't seem to view this as a discrepancy.

Upon seeing Marsden's name, he peered down at a small electronic clipboard he had removed from a case on his belt and said, "Yes… Mr. Marsden. You're expected." Then the guard removed what appeared to be a small digital camera from another pocket and took a photo of Caroline and Marsden. He asked Marsden who was in the van behind his car. Marsden told him his associate was driving the vehicle and that there was a young boy with him.

Not leaving anything to chance, the guard strolled back to the van with Anderson behind the wheel, shined his flashlight inside and asked Anderson for his ID. Anderson gave the guard his driver's license and told him there was no identification card for the boy. Anderson's fake moustache also raised no concern for the guard. Once more, the guard took out his digital camera and photographed Anderson and the boy. After checking the trunk of the car and the inside of the van, he turned and started to walk back toward the barrier then signaled the other guard at the barrier to let the two vehicles pass.

The guard standing at the gatehouse was also heavily armed and holding a short leash with a panting German shepherd at the end of it. When the barrier went up, Caroline drove forward slowly and entered the perimeter gate. As she entered, she could see a second inner perimeter fence that stood about fifty yards behind the outer fence. Both fences were crowned with concertina wire and there were several armed guards with dogs patrolling between them. She could also make out in the darkness a trail or service road that probably ran along the whole area.

After the car entered the area, Marsden reminded her to turn the headlights back on. The road they were on had a fine, smooth surface and was slightly wider than the two-lane secondary road they had taken when they left the main highway. As they drove along, it ascended and wound its way through the forest. There were speed limit signs about every two hundred yards to remind drivers not to exceed 30 miles per hour. Unusually high speed bumps, located roughly every fifty yards, guaranteed compliance.

As the car wove its way up the hill through the forest, Caroline turned toward her unwelcome passenger and announced mockingly, "Marsden! So that's your name! Is that all there is, just Marsden?"

Marsden returned her piercing gaze. "What difference does it make? Just drive!"

"Touchy, aren't we?" Caroline replied, returning her attention to the road.

After about a mile, the car rounded a long bend in the road and a large, white, well-lit building on top of a hill came into view. As they approached the building, they came upon another barrier and gatehouse. Recalling the routine from the main entrance, she turned off the headlights and brought the car to a stop in front of the barrier. Again, an armed guard approached the car, took out an electronic clipboard that displayed all four of their photos and shined his flashlight inside both vehicles.

She noticed that the guards at this gate wore black paramilitary type uniforms, similar to the ones worn by police S.W.A.T. teams. They also carried Heckler & Koch MP-5K submachine guns and 9mm Sigsauer pistols, instead of the M4 assault rifles and Beretta pistols carried by the guards manning the outer perimeter fence. After identifying the occupants of both vehicles, the guard signaled to another guard at the barrier to let them through.

Both vehicles passed through the gate towards another chain link fence erected about one hundred and fifty yards from the building. Caroline turned on the headlights and followed the road up to the building and around to its east side, as directed by signs for visitor parking. The van with Anderson at the wheel followed closely. When the two vehicles pulled into a small parking lot facing the east side of the building, she could see a man standing at the bottom of the stairway that led up to an entrance door.

Chapter Seventy-Seven

As the occupants of both vehicles got out, the man at the bottom of the stairway beckoned them toward the building. Caroline got out of the car first and Marsden followed her. Anderson followed the two of them, pulling Nicolas, who was barely awake, by his arm. As they approached the building, the man waiting near the stairway intuitively extended his hand toward Marsden. "You must be Mr. Marsden!"

"I am."

"I'm Dr. Joshua Benton. I'm the manager and Chief Scientist here at TRG. I trust that you had an uneventful journey?"

Marsden eyed Caroline before replying. "Not too bad, but I've had better."

"Tomorrow morning we'll be receiving a special visitor," Dr. Benton declared. "In the meantime, come inside and have some refreshments and I'll show you around the place and then to your quarters."

Quarters? Caroline thought it sounded civilized. She was expecting something more akin to a prison cell than a four-star hotel.

They entered the building and stepped into a long, white-walled corridor with several doors on both sides. Shortly after entering the corridor, they came upon a guard station manned by two more guards in black paramilitary uniforms with Sigsauer pistols. The guards informed them that if they were carrying weapons, they would have to surrender them before proceeding farther into the building. One of the guards then added that they could collect their weapons when they left the facility.

At first, Anderson made a fuss about giving up his weapon, but the man escorting them assured him it was a routine security matter. Anderson was still hesitant to give up his weapon, especially since he hadn't been asked to surrender it when he had dropped off Mescheler earlier that evening. His anxiety about relinquishing his weapon had caused him to overlook the important fact that when he delivered Mescheler, he had only entered the reception area; this time he would be entering TRG's most sensitive work spaces.

After surrendering their weapons and passing through a metal detector, they walked down the immaculate, well-lit corridor until they reached a four-way intersection about half way down its length. Their escort pointed out that the building's main entrance was just to their left, but its use was restricted to VIPs. In the entrance area there were several large portraits, presumably of the facility's benefactors. The man leading them then pointed out that the floor contained a large conference room, several executive-size offices and six VIP suites, each equipped with a generous bedroom and lounge area. Turning right at the main intersection of the corridor, they walked a few feet and entered an elevator that descended four floors below.

Their escort explained that the floor was a dormitory where the research scientists lived while working at the facility. As he led them down the hallway and through a set of locked glass doors, he told Caroline and Nicolas that they would be housed in rooms in that area and the men who accompanied them would stay on the other side of the glass doors with the researchers. Caroline realized that she had been right; it was an up-market prison, but a prison nonetheless.

As the man took Caroline and Nicolas to their rooms, he told everyone they could order whatever refreshments or food they desired from the menu in their rooms. They only needed to press the button on the internal communications unit and inform the kitchen staff of what they wanted. Caroline asked if she and her son could be together. She glanced towards Nicolas as she said it, and noted his hopeful smile.

The escort told her he saw no reason why they couldn't. He then informed all of them that because of the need for strict security, the entire floor they were staying on would be locked down for the evening and they wouldn't have access to any of the other floors until the special visitor arrived the next morning. After explaining security policy and showing them to their rooms, the chief scientist went about his business. Caroline was worried and frightened, but for the first time in four days she was alone with her son.

Chapter Seventy-Eight

Once inside her room, Caroline sat on the sofa with Nicolas and held him in her arms. "I'm so sorry for what I've put you through. It's all my fault!" she declared. "You've been a very brave boy."

She didn't want to frighten him, but she had to tell him some of the background to what was happening. It would help him understand why the people they were dealing with were so dangerous and that they needed to find a way to get away because they wouldn't honor the promise they made to let them go. She tried to maintain a positive attitude for his sake, but she knew their situation was almost hopeless because being locked away inside the TRG facility was like being inside a maximum security prison.

The sense of danger that she had felt after she received the call notifying her that he had been abducted had returned, except this time it was much stronger. After their walk through the facility, she sensed that danger was imminent. Her adrenalin level was elevated, but she was fraught with anxiety. No one outside the people she had just seen knew where she was and it was at once clear that they'd been taken to a place of no return. She struggled to purge the thoughts from her head, because she needed to comfort her son and assuage his fears. To do this and find a way out of the situation they were in, she would have to draw on what remained of her inner strength. The anger that had prompted her to avenge her husband's death and the reckless intrusions into her and her son's lives was still strong and she would use it to strengthen her resolve.

Much to Caroline's surprise, the night at TRG passed uneventfully. Although she and Nicolas were hungry, they elected not to eat anything provided by the facility for fear that it might not be safe. But through the glass doors and a few doors down the corridor from them, Dick Marsden and Mack Anderson indulged in TRG's hospitality and waited eagerly to collect the remainder of their fee for fulfilling the contract with Mr. Smith. But by now, the ideas sown in Marsden's head by Caroline during the drive to the facility had begun to germinate. And although both men were elated about closing the case, neither of them was comfortable with being locked down inside the facility.

Chapter Seventy-Nine

The next morning at 9:00 a.m. sharp, an executive helicopter arrived at the facility and landed on the helipad on the roof of the building. Immediately after it touched down, Dr. Joshua Benton, facility manager, chief scientist, and head apparatchik scurried onto the roof to greet its VIP passenger. The VIP who clambered from the helicopter had two bulky bodyguards with him. He was Charles Rutherford Bingham, President and Chief Executive Officer of Bingham Enterprises (BE) and master of the Bingham empire.

Although just in his mid-forties, Bingham's face was youthful and his eyes radiated a dazzling intellect that immediately explained why his position at BE had been an act of pragmatism, instead of an ascribed birthright. A tall, slender, striking figure of a man with a head of thick, dark hair, he wore a classic cut charcoal grey suit, one of many made for him by the best tailor of London's Savile Row, and a crisp white shirt, open at the collar. Each bodyguard carried a carry-on size silver, metallic suitcase.

"It's good to see you again, Mr. Bingham!" Benton shouted above the noise of the helicopter's whining engine and spinning rotors.

"It's good to see you again too, Joshua! Is everything in place?"

"Yes, sir!" Benton replied, handing Bingham an envelope containing the memory sticks and the note written by Joseph Mescheler to Caroline Dupré. "Richard Marsden, his colleague, a Mr. Marcus Anderson, and the Dupré woman and her son arrived late last night. They're all on level four. Mescheler is also on level four, but they're not aware of his exact whereabouts in the building."

"Good!" Bingham replied gleefully. "I'll deal with Mescheler later, but first things first. I want to see the Dupré woman."

"Shall I bring her up straight away?"

"That would be splendid!" Bingham said as they walked toward the building's entrance. As they entered the building, Bingham was struck by a playful but sardonic idea. "Oh, Joshua!" he shouted, revealing a look of satisfaction that quickly gave way to smugness. "Leave the boy with Mr. Anderson when you bring her up. She'll be more likely to co-operate if she knows he's in good hands."

"Yes, sir!"

As the men descended the staircase that led from the roof to the main floor, the whining rotors of the helicopter slowed and stopped. When they reached the main floor, Bingham and his two bodyguards turned down the main corridor and headed for the executive office at the west end of the building, while Benton continued down to level four. When Bingham entered the office, the guards deposited the two cases inside the door and took up positions outside.

Excited by the presence of his generous benefactor, Benton ignored the elevator. He raced down four flights of stairs and made his way to the dormitory suite where Caroline Dupré and Nicolas were being detained. He opened the door to the suite and stepped inside.

"Have you ever heard of knocking before entering a room when it's occupied?" Caroline snapped.

"At TRG, we've dispensed with such formalities. We're all one big happy family," Benton replied sarcastically. "Besides, I've come to take you to meet our special visitor."

"Who? The President of the United States?"

"That's a good one!" Benton replied, laughing. "I'll have to remember that one! But as we're not doing a search for comedy talent, I'm afraid you'll have to cut your performance short and come with me. Now, if you please!" he commanded, sternly.

Caroline shot a quick glance at Nicolas, who was sitting at the table watching and listening to the exchange.

"The boy will have to stay behind. But I can assure you he'll be in good hands. Mr. Anderson will look after him until you return."

Right on cue, Anderson appeared in the doorway. Upon seeing Anderson, she turned to Nicolas. "Don't worry, honey. I'll be back in a few minutes."

As she brushed past Benton, she cursed him through clenched teeth. "Bastard!" As she moved past Anderson, who was still standing in the open doorway, she warned, "If you disturb a single hair on his head... I swear on my mother's grave I'll kill you!"

"Promises, promises..." Anderson retorted wryly.

Followed closely by Joshua Benton, Caroline Dupré made her way to the elevator and the two of them ascended to the main floor. When they arrived, Benton directed her to the office at the west end of the building. One of the bodyguards opened the door for her to enter, but told Benton he had to remain outside. Caroline's heart pounded and her pulse raced. She swallowed hard and walked in.

Chapter Eighty

When Caroline stepped inside the office, she was amazed at how spacious it was. On one wall there was a bookcase filled with hundreds of rare science books. Bookshelves ran the entire length of the wall. The remaining three walls were adorned with at least a dozen paintings by famous American mid-west artists, including Charles M. Russell, Grant Wood, and Charles Ephraim Burchfield. The wall opposite the bookcase boasted a magnificent stone fireplace with a wide mantelpiece, ornamented with several rare pottery vases from the American southwest. Two comfortable high, wing-back leather chairs for reading were positioned in front of the bookcase and two large leather sofas stood on either side of a coffee table that occupied the space in front of the fire place. The coffee table and sofas rested on a large antique Mayan Indian rug. Directly in front of her was a massive mahogany desk with an intricately carved Native American scene on its front panel. The desk stood in front of a large window that overlooked the Adirondack Forest below. Behind the desk was a large, leather high-back, executive-style chair with its back toward her.

As she stood in silent awe, the chair swung around to reveal a man seated comfortably in it. She recognized him immediately.

"Mrs. Dupré!" the man announced. "So… What do you think of our little facility? Pretty cozy, isn't it?"

Caroline responded with shock and surprise. "I know you!" she said. "You're Charles Rutherford Bingham!"

"That's right! I am," he declared.

"So that explains it," she said bitterly.

He gave her a quizzical look. "I'm afraid you'll have to enlighten me," he said.

"A portrait of you was in the main entrance of the building," she barked. "I knew there had to be something unusual going on here when I saw it! Now it all makes sense—a portrait of you on the wall, the memory sticks, panic about a missing research scientist, and me and my son being dragged here. It all makes sense!" She could feel anger rising and fought the impulse to clench her fists.

"Does it now? Tell me, Mrs. Dupré," said Bingham, "what's wrong with a facility like this having a portrait of one of its major benefactors on a wall?"

"There's nothing wrong with it, provided it's a true representation of the relationship between the two. But it's a known fact that you don't share control of anything with anyone. It's not in your nature. If you ask me, I'd say you're the owner of TRG!"

"Excellent deduction! Now what?"

"During the past ten years, I've seen you no less than a dozen times on television, trumpeting your unwavering support for space exploration, especially manned interplanetary space travel. A few years ago, it was rumored that you managed to gain a lot of clout with all the right people at NASA and the ESA. There was even talk of you having directly influenced NASA and the ESA's decision to step up research and development on larger artificial habitats, to facilitate and even extend the duration of future research missions to Mars."

"You know… your captors were right! You're an extremely clever woman. Did you make all of these deductions on your own? Or did you get a little help from Dr. Mescheler?" He paused then added, "Now, as I was about to say…"

But before he could continue, she interrupted him again. "Let me see if I understand this correctly! You threatened my life, kidnapped my son and brought us here against our will just so you could personally administer me an IQ test?"

As she spoke, Bingham was quietly sizing her up. "Did anyone ever tell you that it's rude to interrupt someone when they are speaking? I'll forgive you this time, but as I was about to say, did you know that because of my tireless efforts and encouragement, NASA has all but succeeded in developing an advanced propulsion system that uses the reaction between matter and anti-matter to reduce the time it takes to fly to Mars to just over six weeks? Did you also know that my personal funding of several biosphere projects provided NASA and the ESA with the technology to enable them to construct artificial habitats on the Martian surface, each of which can sustain life for up to twelve hundred occupants by producing its own oxygen and food? Bingham Enterprises also developed a method of deep drilling that will enable geologists on Mars to reach frozen water thousands of feet beneath the planet's surface? Did you know these things?"

"No! But what does any of it have to do with the fact that the TRG, your personal laboratory, has uncovered corroborative evidence that shows that rising ocean and sea levels, deforestation, global warming, ozone depletion, grossly overestimated petroleum reserves, deteriorating weather conditions, increasing seismic activity, rising ocean temperatures and a host of other problems, have brought the planet to the brink of doom?"

"You clearly have a good grasp of all the problems and have covered them pretty well in your summation, so I won't bother repeating them. But what you've just said is precisely the connection." The smugness of his smile made her cringe. For all his charm, she knew that the glossy exterior masked a man capable of extreme cunning and manipulation—a man who could sacrifice the rest of humanity for his own glory and personal benefit.

Pointing to the memory sticks on his desk, Bingham pressed on with his patronizing speech. "You see, you yourself, albeit with some help from Mescheler, have already deduced from this data that the earth is dying. The terrible thing is, due to a steadily increasing global population and the rush for global industrialization, demands on the planet and the environmentally destructive measures being taken by most countries are all increasing these problems exponentially and they will all reach their limits in the not too distant future."

"So, by not disclosing TRG's findings, you've single-handedly decided to allow this crisis to continue to develop without trying to stop it?"

"In a word... yes! You see, no matter how you look at it, it's a nasty situation. But I at least have a solution—a costly one, but a solution nonetheless. I've always had my suspicions about something like this happening. So, when the opportunity availed itself to do something about it, I leapt at it. I knew manned travel to Mars was inevitable. I just had to find a way to convince the morons in Washington and a few other pinheads at NASA and the ESA that it would one day prove a worthwhile undertaking."

Bingham rose from his chair and walked slowly over to the window. Gazing out over the Adirondack Forest below, he continued his self-congratulatory oration.

"Yes, I curried favor, made some powerful friends and a few powerful enemies. I also had to buy or coerce a few people along the way. But most of them were too hungry for power, wealth or prestige to see the big picture. You would be amazed if you knew who money could and did buy! Cabinet officials in the U.S., Canada, Europe, and Asia, U.S. Senators and Congressmen, governors, mayors, senior law enforcement agency officials and even a few prime ministers and presidents. The list goes on."

He turned suddenly and faced her. "Do you want to know something funny?"

"Yeah, don't keep me waiting. The suspense is killing me and I could use some laughter right about now!" she scoffed, her dislike for him growing by the second.

He raised his brows and a look of condescension consumed his face. "You see, most of them didn't even want to know why they were doing what they were being told to do. They just voted this way or that way, or pushed this issue or policy like I told them to, and the money, or whatever they asked for in return was given to them."

Bingham droned on, carried away by his own diatribe which boasted his unique insight into the preservation of human existence and the greed of politicians, bureaucrats and other petty men. As he spoke, she glanced down at the memory sticks on his desk and remembered she still had the blank ones she had taken from her office the day before. She knew she could switch them if he turned his back to her again. Then, as luck would have it, to add emphasis to the point he was making about changing climate conditions, Bingham turned and pointed to the forest outside the window and began explaining the effects of decades of acid rain on the region's flora.

As soon as he turned away, she removed the case containing the blank memory sticks from her pocket, slid it onto the desk, grabbed the case that held the memory sticks containing the data and quickly slipped it into her pocket. After making the switch, she interrupted Bingham.

"And you're doing all this for what? To show how powerful you are? You're no different from them!" she shouted scornfully.

"No! That's not true, Mrs. Dupré! Power has very little to do with it. You see, about five years ago, I designed, urged, and pursued the creation of a very special program with NASA and the ESA until it became a reality. Oh! They were reluctant at first, but they eventually signed on to the project. The arrangement was actually quite straightforward. In fact, it was quite a bargain for them. I agreed to provide the brains, financing, technology, and materials for developing larger artificial habitats suitable for Mars and they, at least initially, agreed to provide the transport. Later on, the whole thing would become a private affair. Once started, in a five year period, as many as three hundred pre-fabricated artificial habitats could be transported to Mars and assembled. After ten years, the project, which I call Noah's Ark II, will have artificial habitats on Mars capable of sustaining life for some three hundred and sixty thousand people. But, like everything else, the project required an extraordinary amount of capital to keep it going. And because most of my wealth has come from petroleum, and continues to do so, it would have been nothing short of suicidal to disclose the TRG findings. Under pressure from the rank-and-file, politicians in capitals around the world would have begun putting the brakes on fossil fuel exploration and, more importantly, consumption. Shit! Even my competitors were willing to pay to keep this kind of information buried. And they did!"

"I'm curious!" Caroline said. "Just who would be among this three hundred and sixty thousand or so people to colonize Mars?"

"Interesting you should ask… Myself and anyone dear to me, of course… I suppose the rest would consist of some of the great minds from science, medicine, philosophy, and other social sciences, together with artists, great politicians and anyone with enough money to secure transport and a place in the colony. It may seem cruel to you, Mrs. Dupré, but when conditions on Earth begin to deteriorate more rapidly, the ensuing situation won't be conducive to an orderly departure. It'll be pandemonium and no one will be able to guarantee that the people with the knowledge to ensure mankind's continued existence will survive. But at the rate Noah's Ark II is progressing, in another ten years or so, everything will be in place. So you can see how you and your friend Dr. Mescheler caused me a great deal of inconvenience. Because of these memory sticks, I've had to halt activities in a number of areas to prevent having to explain them if this data was disclosed."

"You're not going to get away with this! Someone will stop

you!"

"I already have gotten away with it, Mrs. Dupré! And there's no one to stop me because no one will know."

"I will!"

"Precisely… which brings me to the reason why you were brought here. Mrs. Dupré, I've actually come to respect and admire your courage, tenacity, and intelligence. You really impress me, which is precisely why I can't allow you to leave." Bingham then reached into the top right-hand desk drawer and pressed a buzzer to summon the chief scientist. As he pulled out the drawer, he added, "I believe it's time to end our little discussion, Mrs. Dupré. Dr. Benton will see you to your room. It was a pleasure meeting you."

"Damn you!" she shouted, as Benton entered the room and grabbed her by the arm.

Chapter Eighty-One

After Caroline was taken away, Bingham lifted the handset for the facility's internal communication system and called the room where she and Nicolas were being held.

Anderson rushed over to the table and answered it. "Anderson here!"

"Mr. Anderson. This is Mr. Smith. Please listen carefully. The Dupré woman is on her way back to her room. She and the boy must not leave this facility. Is that clear?"

"Crystal clear, sir!"

"Good! You must also see that our friend Dr. Mescheler is also taken care of. This is a very delicate and important task and you must not allow anything or anyone to interfere with its completion. I'm leaving the balance of the agreed fee for you and your colleague with Dr. Benton. I've included a five hundred thousand dollar bonus in anticipation that you will carry out my next set of instructions. However, if you feel that you're not up to the task, you are free to decline."

"I believe we can do business," Anderson interjected anxiously.

"Good then! When you have taken care of Mescheler, the Dupré woman, and the boy, I need you to close down the shop here. You must be thorough. There must be nothing left but ashes. Do you understand?"

"Perfectly!" Anderson replied.

"I've instructed Benton to provide you with whatever you need. However, he's unaware of my precise plans. In addition to returning your weapons, he'll give you a crate of incendiary and smoke grenades. There are a number of highly flammable and explosive chemicals in this facility. But to make them work for you, you must disable the alarm and fire suppression systems. You'll be able to do this from the panel located below you in the building's engineering and service control room on level five. I suggest you do this straight away. Incidentally, once the destruction begins, you must make your way to a secondary control panel in the guard house near the perimeter fence. Once there, you'll be able to perform a complete lock-down of the facility, but you must move quickly to prevent others from evacuating the building.

"I've told Benton that effective immediately, you and your colleague are to have unfettered access to any and all areas of the facility. Let me make myself clear, Mr. Anderson. No one, I repeat no one other than you and your colleague is to leave this facility. You need not worry about the security guards. The ones working in and around the facility are my personal employees. They will be extracted from the compound when they're convinced that everything is going according to plan. You and your colleague's departure is a matter of concern for yourselves. Tell me now, Mr. Anderson. Are you the man for the job or aren't you?"

"I'm your man!" Anderson replied.

"Good! Then I suggest you get started immediately. Good luck, Mr. Anderson, but somehow I don't think you'll need it."

As soon as he hung up, Bingham took the memory sticks and the note written by Mescheler, went to the roof of the facility and boarded his helicopter. He was confident that all evidence of his plan would be destroyed and he could now resume the activities he had been forced to suspend.

Chapter Eighty-Two

As Bingham's helicopter headed southwest over the Adirondack Forest, Anderson began carrying out his instructions. First, he went to Marsden's suite and told him they could now move about freely and that Benton would be returning their weapons to them shortly. He then told Marsden that he had been instructed by Smith to round up Mescheler, the Dupré woman, and the boy. He didn't tell Marsden, however, that they were to be killed, nor did he tell him about the instructions he had received to destroy the facility. His doubts about Marsden's ability to carry out this kind of mission had been growing since the start of the operation and he knew there was no room for hesitation in what had to be done.

Marsden was surprised to learn about Smith's sudden hasty visit. But more important, he was surprised that Smith had contacted Anderson and not him. He attempted to ask Anderson what had happened, but Anderson was in too much of a hurry to explain. Anderson's only words to him were that he would fill him in later and that he needed to get Mescheler and bring him to the Dupré woman's suite. Puzzled as to why things were suddenly moving so quickly, Marsden collected the scientist and took him to the woman's suite, while Anderson went off to level five to disable the alarm and fire suppression systems.

When Marsden and Mescheler reached Caroline Dupré's room, she was inside with Benton, the boy, and one of the facility's security guards. The guard had just put a small wooden crate on the floor near the door. He also brought along the weapons Marsden and Anderson had surrendered when they entered the building. Marsden reached for his pistol and shoulder holster from the guard and strapped it on. "Will someone tell me what the hell is going on here?" he demanded.

"You have a few things to take care of," replied Benton. "But you must ask your colleague to explain the details to you."

"What about Smith?"

"What about him?" Benton snapped.

"Where is he?"

"Are you disappointed you didn't get the chance to meet him? If you are, let me put your mind at ease. He rarely meets with anyone. But Mrs. Dupré here did have the honor of sharing a few precious and memorable moments with him. However, to answer your last question, I suspect he has already left. His visits to the facility are usually about as long as they are frequent. If there's nothing else, Mr. Marsden, I'll leave you to your work."

After Anderson had left, Marsden looked around the room, disoriented and seemingly confused by the changing scenario. He ordered Mescheler, Caroline, and the boy to move to the couch and took a seat on a chair opposite them. They sat in silence for several minutes. Caroline instinctively pulled Nicolas closer to her. She put her arm around his shoulder and began caressing his back.

"When can we leave?" Nicolas asked. "Did you give the people what they wanted?"

"Yes I did, honey."

"That means we can go home now, right?"

Shaking her head she said, "No, baby. Remember what I said last night about their dishonesty? Well it looks as if they have a few more plans for us. You've been a brave young man so far. I need you to continue to be that way. Can you do that for Mommy?"

"Yes, but does that mean I have to stay hungry?"

311

Just as Caroline was about to respond, Mescheler interrupted. "The fruit on the table is safe. It's OK. The boy can eat it."

"Thank you," she said to Mescheler, fixing a harsh gaze on Marsden. "Mr. Smith! Is that all you know about your employer? Because if it is, then you're even dumber than I thought you were!"

"When I want your comments on something, I'll ask for them!" Marsden barked.

"You may not have asked, but you sure as hell need them because you haven't a clue about what's going on, do you? You didn't earlier and you still don't! I believe you're the only one here who's still in the dark. Even your thug of a colleague knows more than you, which raises the question, who's in charge, anyway?"

"Will you shut up?" Marsden shouted.

"Or you'll do what to me? Something your Mr. Smith hasn't already planned to do? You know, you're a pretty dim light bulb!"

"I told you, you and your son could go as soon as Smith got what he wanted and spoke to you."

"Well, he's done both and you still think he's the kind of person who leaves loose ends around? Your Mr. Smith and the distinguished Mr. Charles Rutherford Bingham are one and the same. And Dr. Mescheler's suspicion about the whole existence of this facility was right on target. Over the past ten years, this place has provided 'Mr. Smith' with all the scientific evidence he needed to validate the environmental theory about global warming. Bingham is no idiot. He's eccentric, but he's nobody's fool. He has spent billions of his family's fortune to push space exploration and interplanetary space travel. He has continued to pump billions of dollars' worth of petroleum out of the ground, knowing full well that global petroleum reserves have been grossly overestimated. He also knows that global population growth, ozone layer destruction, rising sea levels, shifts in climatic conditions, and increases in crop failure are expediting the Earth's end. The man has been obsessed with space travel and space exploration for years and he's the only person greedy, selfish, and farsighted enough to come up with a plan to escape the impending doom. What's worse is that he was able to buy off or coerce every politician or government official whose help he needed to pursue his diabolical plan. What he is planning to do is quite possibly the darkest deception ever carried out by mankind."

"My God!" Mescheler exclaimed. "I never knew what we were doing had such profound implications."

"That's not all!" Caroline said. "In about ten years, give or take a few, he'll have operational artificial habitats on Mars capable of accommodating up to three hundred and sixty thousand selected individuals. Unfortunately for the rest of us, the fare for his Noah's Ark to Mars will likely exceed what we have in our bank accounts. So you can see, public disclosure of the TRG data would have threatened his plans, because if governments, and more importantly the public, found out about the data, the first thing they would do is halt the use of fossil fuels and look for ways to begin reversing the effects of global warming.

"Bingham needed the uninterrupted cash flow from oil profits and conspiring associates in the business to sustain funding for his plan. Selling off existing stock from BE corporations or other BE assets would have raised too much suspicion, so it was easier to skim funds from oil profits for the last ten years and then cook the books."

Satisfied by his stunned silence, she then asked Marsden, "What do you think of your business deal now? People have already died and many more are going to be sacrificed because of you and your damned contract. You're just as guilty as Bingham. But you still can't see that he's using you! I wonder which one of you—you or your friend—is going to take care of us? Or did you think we'd just waltz out of here the way we came in? Wake up, damn you!"

Mescheler added gloomily, "You're wasting your time on these people. You can't tell them anything! They're going to have to see for themselves the magnitude of the tragedy caused by their greed and selfishness."

Just as Mescheler was finishing his comments, the door flung open and Anderson burst in. He picked up his pistol from the table near the door and immediately began taunting Mescheler.

"You still peddlin' advice and spinnin' yarns, Doc?" Turning to Marsden, he said, "It's time to wrap things up and get out of here."

He attached the silencer to his pistol. "Smith doesn't want any loose ends." He then leveled the pistol and waved it back and forth between Mescheler, Caroline, and the boy. "Who wants to be first?"

"What are you doing?" Marsden shouted.

"I have orders to clean things up here. Besides, they know who we are. You know we can't risk that!"

"This wasn't part of the deal!" shouted Marsden, "especially not the boy! He's just a kid! And since when did you start taking orders from Smith?"

"Look! I've got the rest of our money plus a bonus sitting in my suite," said Anderson. "Benton left it there a little while ago. As soon as we take care of matters here, we're done!"

Anderson trained his pistol on Mescheler. "OK, Doc, it's checkout time!"

Anderson was about to squeeze the trigger when Marsden grabbed a small vase from the table. With a shout of, "*No!*" he hurled it at Anderson. The vase struck Anderson on his forearm, causing him to turn away from his target. As his body twisted, his finger pulled the trigger, sending the bullet slamming into the carpeted floor and ricocheting into the bedroom door.

Marsden leapt on Anderson and smashed his elbow into his jaw. As the two men struggled, Mescheler, Caroline, and Nicolas took cover behind the couch. Anderson maintained his grip on his pistol, squeezing off several stray rounds. He was clearly the stronger of the two, but Marsden managed to throw him off balance and they fell to the floor. Marsden tried to remove his pistol from his shoulder holster, but Anderson knocked it from his hand.

When the two men rolled over, Caroline grabbed Marsden's pistol, took Nicolas by the arm and signaled Mescheler with her head to go into the bedroom. As they scurried across the floor, Anderson caught their movement out of the corner of his eye. He summoned all his strength and threw Marsden off him to get a bead on them. He managed to get off two shots before Marsden leapt back on him.

Chapter Eighty-Three

Caroline, Nicolas, and Mescheler made it safely into the bedroom and closed the door. Anderson's last two shots had missed their target. By now, both men were up on their feet, locked in mortal combat. Enraged by their attempt to escape, Anderson struggled harder. Marsden grabbed the wrist of Anderson's trigger hand to stop him from getting off more shots, but he was weakened by a barrage of punches and head-butts from Anderson. As Marsden's grip loosened, Anderson began forcing the weapon downward; as he lowered it, he pulled the trigger, sending a bullet through Marsden's right side. The impact knocked Marsden backward and onto the floor. Marsden instinctively grabbed his side with his left hand and began applying pressure on the wound, but his effort was of little use because he was bleeding profusely from the large exit wound.

As Anderson moved past Marsden toward the bedroom, Marsden tried to grab his leg and trip him, but Anderson reacted quickly and struck him across the base of the skull with the butt of the pistol. He then fired several shots through the door. Completely enraged now, he began kicking the door.

"If you know what's good for you, you'll open this door!" Anderson shouted through the door. "If I have to break it down, I'm really gonna' be pissed off! You'll pay for it. I'll make you suffer! I'll do the boy first and you'll be forced to watch!"

After a few minutes, Anderson's kicking and shouting subsided. Inside the bedroom, Mescheler stood on one side of the door with his back pressed against the wall and Caroline and Nicolas stood on the other to avoid being hit by shots fired through the door. Suddenly, the banging resumed, except this time with greater ferocity. Moments later, the blade of a fire axe penetrated the door and it became clear to Caroline and Mescheler that the door wouldn't hold much longer. Within minutes, Anderson had smashed his way through and began firing left and right. Caroline dropped to the floor, throwing herself on top of Nicolas. Slow to react, Mescheler was hit in the shoulder.

Anderson opened the door and stepped slowly through, being careful to locate Caroline, whom he knew had Marsden's pistol. She and Nicolas had slid along the floor to the side of the bed. She had initially thought about going into the closet, but realized that it would be a straight -on shot if Anderson fired through the door. As Anderson entered, his peripheral vision enabled him to see Mescheler, who was bent over from the waist, holding his shoulder. He reached over and grabbed the man and put his pistol to his head.

"Come out or I'll put a bullet in his brain! Do you hear me? I'll kill him right where he stands!"

Shielding Nicolas behind her, Caroline got up slowly. She still had the pistol in her right hand.

"Drop it!" Anderson shouted. "Drop it or he's a dead man!"

Caroline brought the pistol around in front of her and lowered her hand to drop it on the floor. As she did so, Anderson trained his pistol on her and shouted, "I should've done this a few weeks ago. It would've saved me a lot of trouble!"

Just as he was about to pull the trigger, Dick Marsden appeared behind him and brought a chair down across his shoulders. Although weakened by his wound, the blow was still powerful enough to send Anderson staggering forward. Anderson hunkered and fell toward the foot of the bed; as he did, he pulled the trigger. The stray bullet from his Mark 23 struck the bed in front of him and kicked up fibers as it seared its way into the mattress.

Anderson recovered quickly from the blow, turned and fired at Marsden. The bullet struck Marsden in the center of his chest. He was dead before his body hit the floor.

He then spun around to get Caroline in his sights. But before he could train his pistol on her, she fired and the bullet struck him in the wrist of his shooting arm. Having no time to take aim, she squeezed off another round, but Anderson had turned his body sideways to make himself a smaller target. The bullet only grazed his left shoulder.

Anderson fired three rounds in her direction, but luckily they all missed their target. Still, the stray shots bought him enough time to retreat. On his way out, Anderson grabbed the small crate containing the incendiary and smoke grenades and headed for level three, stopping only to tie the two suitcases containing the money together with his belt in order to drag them from his suite and load them onto the elevator. After sending the suitcases to the main floor, he used the card key he had been given by Benton to open the first three doors on level three. As soon as the doors opened, he fired on the people working inside to prevent them from rushing toward the door, and threw in smoke and incendiary grenades.

When he opened the fourth door, a startled and near-paralyzed Benton turned and stared into his eyes. Anderson raised the pistol with his uninjured left arm and fired three shots. The first shot missed the chief scientist, but the second one struck him in the throat. The man let out a gurgling noise and grabbed his throat before the third bullet struck him in the middle of his forehead. Anderson then tossed in grenades. Only seconds after he started, most of the rooms on level three were filled with smoke, fire, and deadly fumes.

Anderson repeated the same thing on level two until he ran out of grenades, then he made his way up to the main floor. He dragged the suitcases from the elevator and then to the van. He tossed them onto the passenger seat and headed toward the gatehouse. He was ready to complete Bingham's last instruction —lock-down of the building and its total devastation.

Chapter Eighty-Four

Caroline, Nicolas, and Mescheler were still on level four when the fires started. After checking the corridor to make sure it was clear, they headed for the stairway. When they reached level three, smoke and toxic fumes had already penetrated the stairwell. It was then that they realized that Anderson had set fire to the building before making his escape. Coughing and with eyes stinging, they struggled up to the main floor only to find that the fire had already engulfed the west end and part of the east side of the building. The entire corridor on the main floor was filled with dense smoke and toxic fumes.

Desperately, Caroline looked around for a means of escape. It seemed crazy to have come so far and endured so much to save her son, only to die with him. A vision of François' face flashed into her mind. It was almost as if he were urging her on.

First, they attempted to exit from the main VIP entrance, but the door was locked. Nearly overcome by smoke and fumes, they got on their hands and knees and crawled below the smoke toward the east exit. It was unlocked. *Thank you*, she muttered under her breath.

As they emerged from the burning building, they saw the van speeding down toward the gate with Anderson behind the wheel. After gulping much-needed fresh air into their lungs, Caroline suggested that they make a dash for the gate behind Anderson. When they reached her car, the key was still in the ignition. Anderson hadn't bothered to remove it, probably because he didn't expect anyone to escape the burning building.

Remembering that Marsden had placed several weapons in the trunk of the car before they left the dockyard, Caroline went to the rear of the vehicle, opened the trunk and removed her .22 caliber target pistol and a duffel bag containing a M4 carbine, a MP-5K submachine gun, and a Glock 32 .380 pistol.

As Caroline and Nicolas climbed into the car, Mescheler looked back at the building, which already had flames leaping from its windows. "Wait!" he shouted. "We can't just drive off and leave all those people to perish in there! Some of them are my friends!" He bolted toward the burning building.

"You can't go back in there!" Caroline yelled. "It's too late! By now, they'll all be dead from the smoke and fumes or the fire. The only thing we can do is get the hell out of here!"

Mescheler stopped a few feet from the car and lapsed into a trance-like state. When he finally turned and faced her, she could see tears streaming from his eyes.

"We don't have time to be sentimental or to feel pity!" she shouted, knowing that if the scientist delayed much longer, she and Nicolas would have to leave without him. "We've got to get out of here while we still can. This is our one chance to save ourselves! Do you hear me, Dr. Mescheler?"

Her sharp words seemed to snap him back into reality. He slowly returned to the car, flopped onto the seat and pulled himself inside with his uninjured arm. Before he could close the door, Caroline had started the engine and sped off.

The car rounded the driveway from the east toward the front of the building then turned and headed down the drive toward the gatehouse. As Caroline drove away, she could hear explosions coming from behind her. She peered briefly into the rearview mirror and saw a large plume of dense black smoke climbing into the air above the building. With a leaden feeling in her gut, she knew nobody would have survived the carnage and that she, her son, and Mescheler were intended to have been among the victims.

As she sped toward the barrier and gatehouse, she could see

Anderson's van ahead of her. Although the barrier was raised and the gate was open, he had stopped inside the fence near the gatehouse. She knew he would see her coming, but she had no alternative but to drive straight toward him.

As Caroline's car raced toward the gate, the sound of helicopter rotors began to fill the air. She instinctively looked over to her right and saw at least two dozen security guards, dressed in black paramilitary uniforms, racing toward two helicopters which were descending on a hill west of the burning building. The helicopters were similar to those used by the military, except they were painted black and unmarked. They had arrived to evacuate Bingham's private security force. Gripped by fear, Caroline's fingers tightened around the steering wheel.

Chapter Eighty-Five

When Anderson reached the gatehouse, he found that the security personnel had abandoned it and their other posts and had headed for the extraction area on the hill. He was ready to complete the final part of his instructions. First he would have to restore power to the security system and activate the emergency lock-down mechanisms he had disabled earlier from level five. But to prevent anyone from escaping, he left the security alarm and fire suppression system disabled so the fire would continue its destructive sweep through the building.

When Anderson stepped out of the guard house, he was surprised to see the car with Caroline behind the wheel speeding toward him.

"Damn it!" he swore aloud as his left hand went for the pistol, tucked inside the waistband of his trousers. "You've got more fuckin' lives than a cat, but this one is your fuckin' last!"

He took quick aim and squeezed the trigger, but the recoil from the pistol was far too much for him to find the target using only his non-shooting arm. He raced around to the driver's side of the van, paused and fired two more shots at her car before tossing the pistol on the passenger seat and speeding away. One of the bullets he fired struck the car just above the windscreen and was deflected upward. All of the other shots missed completely.

As the two vehicles raced down the winding road toward the outer perimeter fence, their occupants were tossed about each time they flew over one of the high speed bumps. The rough ride was especially bad for Mescheler, and he groaned from the pain in his shoulder each time the vehicle pitched. Between speed bumps, Caroline was able to cut the lead Anderson had on her.

Her car gradually began to close on the van, but Anderson started to swerve from side to side. After a few more speed bumps, she drew to within a few yards of his rear bumper, but Anderson accelerated and pulled away until they reached the next curve. When they entered the curve, Caroline accelerated and pulled her car up nearly alongside the van, but Anderson again reacted quickly and began ramming her car from the side in an attempt to force it off the road. She heard Nicolas give a terrified scream, but this was no time for soothing words, as she had to give driving all her concentration to prevent Anderson from getting a chance to force them off the road.

When the two vehicles came out of the curve, Anderson accelerated and again increased the distance between them. Once more she closed on him at the next curve. As the two vehicles dueled out of the curve, Anderson braked sharply and turned the wheel of his van to the right. The move caught Caroline off guard and she ran off the road and crashed sideways into a tree near the shoulder of the road.

"Damn it!" she shouted then turned to Nicolas, who was on the back seat. "Is everyone alright?"

Nicolas managed to produce a nervous "Yes," and Mescheler gave a nod, his lips pursed in pain.

"Good then!" she snapped. She jumped out of the car and grabbed the Glock 32 .380. Anderson's car was nearing the speed bump before the last curve. She knew that if he rounded the curve and accelerated, he would be gone. She took careful aim with the .380 and squeezed off two rounds as Anderson's car entered the curve. Her shots failed to find their mark. Suddenly, she realized that after the last two shots there wasn't enough time to make the necessary adjustments in her aim to compensate for the balance and recoil of the weapon.

As she was about to take aim for another shot, she stopped and yelled, "Shit!" then tossed the Glock onto the seat and grabbed her Ruger MK II .22 caliber target pistol. The pistol didn't have a scope, so she knew the sights would have to do.

Anderson was just coming out of the curve when she raised the pistol and took aim. As she was aiming, Anderson saw the straight road unfolding in front of him. He knew that he was nearly home free. As the van started to come out of the curve, Anderson pushed the accelerator toward the floorboard and the tires squealed and smoke spewed from the rear wheel wells. He continued to accelerate and within seconds, the van was approaching sixty-five miles per hour.

As Caroline aimed, she could see that the vehicle was descending as it moved to her right. By now, the van was more than seventy-five yards away. She knew she would only get one shot. But what was worse, the target was farther away than normal and moving. She had never hit a moving target with a pistol, at any distance.

As she leveled the sights to her right eye, she inhaled, held her breath, steadied her aim and allowed her upper body to track the target. She released half the air in her lungs then, just as the van was about to find cover behind the trees, she squeezed the trigger. The .22 caliber long round burst from the barrel and found its target, the right front tire of the van. When the bullet struck the tire as the vehicle was traveling at nearly seventy miles per hour. Anderson had been steering with only his uninjured arm and lost control. As Caroline lowered the pistol, she saw the van leave the road without braking and flip over onto its right side. Although she couldn't see through the thicket of trees below, it sounded as if it had slid several yards after it flipped and slammed into a tree. Seconds later, there was a loud explosion.

Running down the road, she rounded the curve and sprinted to the place where the vehicle had disappeared. By now, Nicolas and Mescheler were out of the car and running behind her. She looked back over her shoulder. "Stay back!" she yelled. "Don't come any closer!"

As she drew nearer to the vehicle, she readied her pistol but soon saw that Anderson was unconscious and trapped inside the burning van. Suddenly, there was a second explosion and the van was engulfed in flames. She knew there was no hope for Anderson now and stood still for a moment, filled by a euphoric sense of relief.

Now Nicolas and Mescheler came up behind her. Suddenly, Nicolas shouted, "Mama! Mama! Look!"

Caroline followed his pointing finger and saw two silver metal suitcases. One was on the shoulder of the road and the other was just over the edge of the embankment. They were still intact.

"Stay where you are!" Caroline told Nicolas. Certain of their contents, she made her way over to the shoulder of the road, collected the first suitcase and looked down the embankment to where the second case lay. She sat on the ground and, using her heels to dig into the side of the steep hill, she skidded on her butt to where it rested. As soon as she grabbed the handle, Mescheler knelt over and helped her back up with his good arm. She put the two suitcases down and opened one of them. Inside were stacks of crisp new five hundred dollar bills, neatly packaged in plastic. She had found the contract settlement and bonus money Bingham had paid Marsden and Anderson. It had been thrown from the van when it flipped; she knew all too well that it was blood money.

"Wow!" Nicolas exclaimed.

The three of them stood staring into the open case for several minutes, then looked at each other. Caroline asked, "Are you guys thinking what I'm thinking?" They all nodded yes. She then winked and declared, "You know, there must be dozens and dozens of worthwhile causes and projects that could make use of this kind of money. Don't you think?"

They returned to the car with the cases. Caroline inspected the damage to the vehicle and took a look at Mescheler's shoulder. The bullet was still inside, but his application of steady pressure on the wound early on with his uninjured hand had all but stopped the bleeding. But from the way he was holding his shoulder, she figured the bullet must have shattered at least part of the bone and that he was in a lot of pain. She helped him remove his shirt and made a sling from it to immobilize his shoulder. She knew he needed medical treatment as soon as possible.

Although the lab was located in the middle of nowhere, it would only be a matter of time before local law enforcement and emergency services arrived. They all agreed they didn't want to be around when they did.

After Caroline had determined that the car was still drivable, they got back in and headed for the main road. There were no signs of security personnel anywhere between the place where the van had gone off the road and the outer perimeter fence. The whereabouts of the guards didn't concern her, as long as they weren't at the gate to stop them from leaving.

Chapter Eighty-Six

As the Honda approached the barrier, Caroline could see that it had been raised. She looked on both sides of the road near the checkpoint and didn't see any guards. Just to make sure that they cleared the gate quickly, she floored the accelerator and the car sped through. They were out of danger. When they were several hundred yards clear of the outer perimeter gate, Mescheler turned his head and looked out of the rear window. "Please tell me this was a bad dream and that I'm gonna wake up and it'll all be over."

Caroline looked at Mescheler and smiled. "I'm sorry, but it wasn't a dream and in a manner of speaking, we're not out of the woods yet."

Grimacing from the pain in his shoulder, Mescheler replied, "But I think we'll be alright." Shaking his head, he added, "It pains me though that Bingham got away clean... memory sticks and all! All this death and destruction and we didn't stop him. None of this can ever be linked to him."

The mention of Bingham's name jogged Caroline's memory. She leaned slightly to one side and withdrew the small, thin case containing the two memory sticks from her rear trouser pocket and, with an ear-to-ear grin, declared, "Maybe not that clean!"

"Are those the real memory sticks?" asked Mescheler. "How did you get them? When did you get them?" he added excitedly. "Didn't Marsden turn them over to Bingham?"

"I pulled a switch on Bingham when he had his back

turned," Caroline reported proudly. "The memory sticks he has are blank. It was actually kind of easy. The man is an egomaniac. He loves to hear to himself talk. So I played along and waited for my chance."

Mescheler laughed heartily and slapped his thigh. "I'd give anything to see the look on his face when he discovers he's got nothing!"

Caroline glanced at Mescheler. "I think we'd better get that looked after. It's starting to bleed again. We'd better head for Syracuse. We'll get you to a hospital and Nicolas and I will take a flight on to New York."

Nicolas had been quiet nearly the entire time, but he suddenly sprang to life. "You mean we're going home now?"

"Yes, baby. We're going home!"

Once on the main road, she used the cell phone Marsden had left in the car and called 911 emergency services. She told the police what had happened and that she was on her way to the hospital with a gunshot victim. Some fifteen minutes later, her car was joined on the road by several State Troopers, a Deputy Sheriff's patrol car, and an ambulance, all with their emergency lights flashing. They stopped long enough to transfer Mescheler to the ambulance then continued to the airport with their police escort.

Next, she called her father in Paris and her grandparents in Virginia Beach to tell them what had happened and that she and Nicolas were safe. Her last call was to the CNN's New York bureau. She told the CNN producer she spoke to about Dr. Mescheler and the TRG facility and that she had information that would expose a conspiracy involving high-level politicians and government officials from the U.S. and several other countries.

By the time she and Nicolas reached the airport, there were reporters and cameras from all the major news networks and several local stations. After being interviewed for over two hours by the police and the FBI, she found the CNN reporter among the media horde, handed him the memory sticks and password Dr. Mischeler had given her husband. As soon as she finished speaking with the CNN reporter he made a phone call and dispatched a cameraman, sound technician, and a nearby reporter to the hospital in Syracuse to conduct an exclusive interview with Dr. Joseph Mescheler. When the CNN crew arrived, Mescheler was on his way to surgery, but he insisted on confirming Caroline's story first.

By the time Caroline and Nicolas' plane landed at New York's LaGuardia Airport, CNN had already scheduled a special report for live airing at 6:00 p.m. The network had assembled a panel of experts linked up from CNN studios around the country and the world to explain and comment on the startling discovery of Charles Rutherford Bingham's elaborate plan.

The CNN report lasted well over two hours; when it ended, the President of the United States held a nationally and internationally televised press conference to tell Americans and the rest of the world about the outrage he and his administration felt about the discovery of the sinister plot. A number of high level officials in his administration, including his Energy Secretary, the director and several senior officials from NASA, the directors of the National Oceanic and Atmospheric Administration and the Environmental Protection Agency and several senior Justice Department and FBI officials had already admitted their involvement in the deception. Their resignations had been offered and accepted and they had all been arrested.

The president closed his speech by reminding listeners that the task ahead was not a task for the U.S. alone, but one for people around the world. To emphasize this, he said that within the next few days, he would address the United Nations General Assembly and the United Nations Security Council on the matter and ask all member states to commit themselves with expediency to the environmental recovery of the Earth.

When the CNN anchor returned to recap the story and the president's speech, he told the viewers that: "Earlier today, CNN attempted to reach Charles Rutherford Bingham to get his comments on his alleged involvement in the conspiracy, but was told by a BE spokeswoman that Mr. Bingham was not available. The spokeswoman did, however, read a statement that had been prepared by Mr. Bingham himself. The statement said, and I quote, 'Those responsible for these allegations should refrain from doing so without substantive evidence to prove them. I can assure all of you that I am innocent of these charges and in due course, I will be vindicated,' end quote."

The news anchor ended the bulletin by adding that: "Not long after the statement was delivered to this network, we learned from a source close to the Bingham family that at around noon today, Charles Rutherford Bingham boarded his largest private jet and left the country for an undisclosed destination. His whereabouts and when or whether he will resurface to defend himself against these allegations are unknown."

Chapter Eighty-Seven

Nearly three weeks had passed since the exposure of Charles Rutherford Bingham's sinister plan. Since then, Caroline and Nicolas had been making the best of the peace and quiet they were finally beginning to have together. For much of the first two weeks she had been hounded relentlessly by the media. Although she was disappointed that Bingham had managed to escape into hiding, she was pleased that many of those responsible for the death of her husband and the other innocent victims would be punished and that none of their victims had died in vain. In a strange way, the end of the deadly saga was helping to bring closure for her.

With the summer holiday already started, she and Nicolas decided to spend the remainder of it with her father at his holiday home on the French Riviera. Less than a week later they boarded an Air France flight for Paris. As the plane climbed and headed out over the Atlantic Ocean, Caroline began to wonder if all that had happened was predestined; only now did she allow herself to begin to think about the possibility of finding someone else to share her and Nicolas' life. She settled back in her seat; as she drifted off to sleep, she told herself that if the right man came along, she wouldn't allow thoughts of François to get in the way or overshadow a future with him.

The flight was nearly over when she began to stir. Just as she was shifting in search of a more comfortable position, Nicholas announced that he had to go to the toilet. Wearily, she shifted to let him out. As she watched him move down the aisle, a tall, thin, silver-haired man with a moustache and an immaculately trimmed beard appeared in the aisle beside her seat. She didn't look up, but she could sense him staring down at her.

Finally, she turned and faced him. "Can I help you?" she asked.

"I hope so!" the man replied, smiling. "May I sit for a moment?"

Caroline reluctantly moved into Nicolas' seat.

"Mrs. Dupré, isn't it?"

"Yes," she replied cautiously. "And who might you be?"

"Your son will be back soon, so I'll take only a minute or two of your time," the man said, as he reached into his jacket pocket, pulled out a business card, and handed it to her. Only a name was printed on the card, but a handwritten telephone number had been added. The name on the card was Niles Peter Thornton and the telephone number was in London.

"Mr. Thornton, I presume."

"That'll be me," he replied.

"Why have you sought me out among all the people on this flight, Mr. Thornton?"

"Now, you've asked a very important question! You see, I work for a well-organized, well-funded, and not to mention ultra-professional and very secretive organization. I know what you're thinking…'and which organization might that be'?"

He paused momentarily. "The thing is… I can't tell you until you've made a commitment to join. A bit of a 'Catch 22', isn't it? But I can tell you this much, we have nothing but the best of retired and ex-intelligence officers and specialists: MI6, CIA, MI5, FBI, BND, MOSSAD, ASIS, etc. Of course all of these are no more than alphabet soup to you, but their business is putting out nasty fires like the one you recently helped extinguish."

The elderly gentleman paused for a beat. "Let me put it to you straight, Mrs. Dupré. After very careful consideration, I and several of my colleagues have concluded that you are a natural and you would be a tremendous asset to us. You handle yourself well in dodgy situations. In fact, I would venture to say much better than some I've seen with training and many years of experience. But that's beside the point." The man paused again. "Are you interested?"

Shocked and surprised, Caroline replied. "I think you've confused me with someone else! Wonder Woman or GI-Jane I am not!" Leaning closer to him, she asked, "And what do you mean by 'after careful consideration?'"

"I'm glad you asked that question. You see, we're practically everywhere we need to be! We had been on to, or at least suspected, Bingham for several years, but we weren't able to do anything until he collected all the data and we could confirm precisely what he intended to do with it. Some months ago, our inside man at TRG was on the verge of getting everything we needed, but we think his cover was blown and he had to make a quick exit. But if he hadn't taken what he did when he left, and you hadn't helped him, there would have been nothing on Bingham and his twisted plan would have remained a dark secret."

"Do you mean Dr. Mescheler?"

The man replied smugly. "That'll be him! That is, as he was known to you and others at the time." He then boasted, "Do you see now the sort of things we do? We're the good guys!"

"You took a lot of risks with that man's life!" she said admonishingly.

"I know. But they were risks he accepted. Besides, it worked out in the end. Didn't it?"

"Look, Mr. Thornton, I'm flattered that you think I have what it takes to do whatever it is your organization does, but I won't kid myself. I don't have what it takes to do that type of thing again. Maybe you and Dr. Mescheler do, but not me. Thanks for the invitation, but I'm afraid I'm going to have to decline."

"What a pity," Thornton said, turning her answer over in his head. "I'll tell you what, Mrs. Dupré, don't say no just yet. Keep the card and give the whole thing a bit more thought. Take as much time as you need. But my gut instinct tells me that after your recent experience, returning to your old job will be anti-climactic. You don't know it yet, but you're already one of us. You'll see!"

Fantastic Books
Great Authors

Meet our authors and discover our exciting range:

- Gripping Thrillers
- Cosy Mysteries
- Romantic Chick-Lit
- Fascinating Historicals
- Exciting Fantasy
- Young Adult and Children's Adventures

Visit us at:
www.crookedcatbooks.com

Join us on facebook:
www.facebook.com/crookedcatpublishing

1	2	3	4	5	6	7	8	9	10
11	12	13	14	15	16	17	18	19	20
21	22	23	24	25	26	27	28	29	30
31	32	33	34	35	36	37	38	39	40
41	42	43	44	45	46	47	48	49	50
51	52	53	54	55	56	57	58	59	60
61	62	63	64	65	66	67	68	69	70
71	72	73	74	75	76	77	78	79	80
81	82	83	84	85	86	87	88	89	90
91	92	93	94	95	96	97	98	99	100
101	102	103	104	105	106	107	108	109	110
111	112	113	114	115	116	117	118	119	120
121	122	123	124	125	126	127	128	129	130
131	132	133	134	135	136	137	138	139	140
141	142	143	144	145	146	147	148	149	150
151	152	153	154	155	156	157	158	159	160
161	162	163	164	165	166	167	168	169	170
171	172	173	174	175	176	177	178	179	180
181	182	183	184	185	186	187	188	189	190
191	192	193	194	195	196	197	198	199	200
201	202	203	204	205	206	207	208	209	210
211	212	213	214	215	216	217	218	219	220
221	222	223	224	225	226	227	228	229	230
231	232	233	234	235	236	237	238	239	240
241	242	243	244	245	246	247	248	249	250
251	252	253	254	255	256	257	258	259	260
261	262	263	264	265	266	267	268	269	270
271	272	273	274	275	276	277	278	279	280
281	282	283	284	285	286	287	288	289	290
291	292	293	294	295	296	297	298	299	300
301	302	303	304	305	306	307	308	309	310
311	312	313	314	315	316	317	318	319	320
321	322	323	324	325	326	327	328	329	330
331	332	333	334	335	336	337	338	339	340
341	342	343	344	345	346	347	348	349	350
351	352	353	354	355	356	357	358	359	360
361	362	363	364	365	366	367	368	369	370
371	372	373	374	375	376	377	378	379	380
381	382	383	384	385	386	387	388	389	390
391	392	393	394	395	396	397	398	399	400

Lightning Source UK Ltd.
Milton Keynes UK
UKOW04f1856230115

245029UK00001B/4/P